C000079009

"The years that had pas
only their spri

Only the
Springtime

by
Terry Reeve

Based on a true story from the late 18th and
early 19th century set in a Suffolk town

environmentally friendly book printed and bound in England by
www.printondemand-worldwide.com

Mixed Sources
Product group from well-managed
forests, and other controlled sources
www.fsc.org Cert no. TT-COC-002641
© 1996 Forest Stewardship Council
FSC

PEFC
PEFC/16-33-415

PEFC Certified
This product is
from sustainably
managed forests
and controlled
sources
www.pefc.org

book is made entirely of chain-of-custody materials

30127 05758586 6

www.fast-print.net/store.php
Fastprint Publishing
www.fast-print.net/store.php

Only the Springtime
Copyright © Terry Reeve, 2011

Cover design by Terry and Penny Reeve

First published 2011 by
FASTPRINT PUBLISHING
Peterborough, England

By the same author

Fiction:
Spirit of the Fen (Diggory Press, 2008)
The Last Thing on My Mind (Terry Reeve, 2010)

Non-Fiction:
Wheel 'em in, Bungay! (Terry Reeve, 1986, revised 2000)
The Day Bungay Burned (Morrow and Co, 1988)
A Common Privilege (Morrow and Co, 1996)
A Childhood Like Ours... (Fastprint Silver Publishing, 2009)

This book is dedicated to my daughter, Charlotte, who shares her name with its main character

The image of the young woman on the front cover of this book is not Charlotte Ives, but is believed to bear a close similarity to her. The image of the man is from a portrait, oil on canvass, of Francois-Rene de Chateaubriand painted by neo-classic portrait painter Anne-Louis Girodet de Roussy-Trioson (1767-1824) in 1808. It is currently housed in the museum at St Malo, France, Chateaubriand's birthplace.

1

"Mama! I'm home! Where's Papa?" Charlotte Ives was removing her bonnet as she entered the parsonage, up the two steps past the stout pillars of the portal and through the front door into the hall. It was 7.30 in the evening, and outside that late autumn day in 1795 it was pitch dark. She removed her ankle length green coat, and her mother, coming in from the withdrawing room, took the garments from the slim, 15-year-old girl as she shook and fluffed her long black hair which had been confined in her bonnet.

"Papa has not arrived back from Beccles. He was hoping to catch the Yarmouth mail coach, so he should be home soon," her mother replied.

Standing side by side, it was easy to see they were of the same kin. Both had long, oval faces, and their hair had the same texture, though Sarah Ives, not quite as dark as Charlotte's, was showing signs of grey through the bun she wore. And while her daughter's eyes seemed almost jet black, and sharply bright, her's were softer and azure blue.

The two women moved into the drawing room and sat down. Sarah Ives resumed the sewing she had been doing, and asked:

"Did you find Bible study stimulating this evening?"

Charlotte went regularly each week to Bible study in the vestry of St Mary's Church, the square-towered Norman building which stood at the top of the hill in the centre of Bungay, opposite the old building which was once a Guildhall. Truth to tell she did not need to go. After all her father, the Rev John Ives, was the curate at St Margaret's Church in the parish of Ilketshall St Margaret, about three miles to the south of Bungay, a market town standing just on the Suffolk side of the River Waveney which formed the border between that county and Norfolk; so she was well versed in the Bible and religion, and went regularly to church with him and her mother, though on occasions the two women would attend the services at St Mary's. She was a shy girl, an only child largely content with her own company and that of her family, but she had dutifully taken her parents' advice that attending the Bible classes would enable her to meet more people, particularly of her own age, socially, in contrast to the house parties her father would host periodically at the parsonage, standing not 100 yards from the River Waveney.

But it was the Bible study she enjoyed rather than those she met there, though there were a dozen or so from her own social class, among families living at St Peter's Hall, and Upland Hall, and the large house at Stow Park for example – both young men and young ladies, but also others of all ages. She enjoyed formal conversation with them, and readily took part in the Bible discussions. But mostly she enjoyed the beautiful phraseology of the Bible, and the sometimes flowing and descriptive prose, particularly in the New Testament. She was deeply and dutifully religious – she had been from a young age, as soon as she had been old enough to sit at her mother's knee by the fire on a Sunday evening, when the shadows from the lamp were long and creating gently dancing patterns on the high ceiling, and listen to her reading passages from the Bible, her voice gentle and expressive. She came to love Christ's teaching, His gentleness and compassion, His miracles, and marvelled at His ultimate sacrifice for the world.

At an early age she resolved to herself to follow His teaching as closely as she could, and her parents were proud of her humility and selflessness which became apparent as she grew up in that Suffolk town made prosperous by the river trade. Charlotte would enjoy sitting by the river on summer days, watching the boats plying to The Staithe to unload their cargo, and would wave cheerily to those on board; see the comings and going from the busy tanneries which lined the banks there – tanning was an industry created by the river's access to the port of Yarmouth and beyond, from where coal, timber and grain were also transported. Stout and strong Suffolk horses would haul carts to the Staithe, to be loaded with those commodities for carriage to other parts of the town, and to outlying villages.

From that vantage point, Charlotte could look back at the Parsonage, a large, attractive house, once thatched, but now neatly tiled, and with climbing roses weaving their way around the ground floor windows and door, and first floor windows, that presented themselves to her from that perspective. It was topped with tall chimneys, and on its river side stood tall poplar and yew trees, some standing almost on the bank of the Waveney. To the west it was bordered by a palisade fence, with conifers standing behind it, protectively, and on the horizon behind the house more trees, so that it seemed to Charlotte a secluded, cosy and secure home, a beautiful picture in its landscape, somewhere comfortable, relaxing and homely for her and her family.

She was a promising artist, and on occasions she would set her easel beside the river, well back from the house, to try to capture it in its setting on paper and canvas, especially in the summer, with the trees abundantly in leaf and the roses in full bloom around the windows. Sometimes she was satisfied with the result, but was always keen to try to improve on her work – she was a conscientious and diligent girl, patient and content.

John Ives, though a parson of many years standing, and well respected by his congregation, was a man of the world too, well versed in secular as well as religious life, and an avid reader of the newspapers, particularly The Times and the Norwich Mercury, which regularly brought news from other parts of the country and sometimes abroad. Reports of parliamentary debate and decision in its pages would often exasperate him, and on occasions he was moved to write letters to the editor's column outlining his forthright views on the issues of the day.

He was an intellectual, and a much travelled man, having spent time in America – as well as one who also enjoyed a glass of ale, wine or port with the best of them. A regular member of the gentlemen's club in the town, he would entertain others there with stories of his travels, and was not averse to a modicum of exaggeration, in order to retain their interest.

At Beccles, six miles away along the valley road, he had a circle of associates too, and would travel there often for meetings and a tankard or two. It was where he was that evening.

In the drawing room at Bungay, after a mild day, it was not cold enough to light the fire in the inglenook, and Charlotte and her mother chattered while the latter sewed.

"And who was at Bible study this evening?" Sarah inquired.

"The usual group – no new members: Joshua, Elizabeth, Ruth, Lydia of course, another girl I haven't got to know yet. Oh yes, there was another person there who I do not recall seeing before, older than most of us. His name was Samuel – Samuel Sutton, I think he said."

"Probably one of the Suttons from Ditchingham. They have a son, who I believe is in the Navy, and doing well."

"Yes. I would venture to say he was over 30, and he mentioned the Navy during discussions. I was not bold enough to speak to him directly, though he appeared to me to be affable, and good humoured."

"The Suttons are a well respected family," Sarah said, with conviction. "Perhaps Samuel's vessel is in port at Yarmouth, or he is home on leave from the Navy, and he has taken the opportunity to visit his parents."

Charlotte did not confide it to her mother, but she had thought Samuel a handsome man, and now imagined him in full naval uniform, on board one of the monarch's fighting ships. He had an open face, with a square chin, and earnest, thoughtful blues eyes beneath his often tousled brown hair. He was tall, and strong looking, and had seemed attentive and helpful to everyone around him. She was at a time in her burgeoning womanhood in which she was beginning to take more notice of male company, and though this man was probably twice her age he had immediately interested her, in his bearing. There was a certain confidence, yet modesty, about him, and even in the short time she had sat in the same circle as he and discussed the Bible, she sensed a decisiveness there. And he had smiled at her twice, and picked up points she had made in discussions and elaborated on them in an encouraging and supportive way.

"He must be away a lot, at sea I mean. When one reads the newspapers there seems to be a battle taking place or the threat of one, regularly – with the Spanish, or French, or

Dutch – and ships being sunk. It must be awful for his wife and family."

"As far as I know he isn't married, though my knowledge of the Suttons is limited, I must confess."

Sarah paused and looked at the ticking clock on the tall, somewhat cluttered, mantle above the inglenook, where it vied for space with the candlesticks, a statue of the Virgin Mary, two small paintings Charlotte had done, a vase of bronze chrysanthemums, and pewter containers secreting crochet hooks, pins and other small items discarded into them over the course of weeks and months. It chimed quarter past the hour of eight as she did so.

"Your father IS late," she observed, and sighed resignedly as she spoke. "I expect they are having their usual generous portions of ale or porter again. For a clergyman he does not always set his flock a good example of moderation, I must say."

Charlotte looked at her mother, who had always tacitly disapproved of her husband's socialising and over-generosity. Sarah was a thrifty woman, not given to excess, but generous, nevertheless, in her own discerning way, and an attentive hostess when her husband entertained. Her daughter provided gentle support for her father.

"Mama, he has never been in an alcoholic stupor, like some of his friends from the club. He is a fine host, and always maintains control."

"There are times, my dear, when he seems to take delight in seeing his guests totally inebriated while he, having imbibed the same amount of ale, remains completely normal. He sees it as a game, I think! Perhaps he feels he is entertaining his guests, and they are too polite to chide him."

And she tutted her disapproval, and concentrated on her sewing.

A few minutes later the two women heard the big front door opening, and voices in the hall. Sarah sighed.

"It sounds as if your Papa has brought one of his friends home again – that means he will be up well after midnight, when he really ought to retire by half-past 10 o'clock, for the sake of his health," she said in a vexed tone.

Shortly afterwards, the Rev John Ives entered the room, followed by a man neither his wife nor daughter recognised. He was not one of his familiar friends from the town, or from the gentlemen's club – and furthermore, he had one arm well bandaged up to the top of the arm, and resting in a sling secured around his left shoulder. He limped heavily, and there was a scar and bruising to the right side of his face, and the brow above his deep brown eye on that side was swollen and purple, and partly closed.

The two women stood up, startled at the sight.

"Sarah – Charlotte, forgive me," said the parson, standing several inches taller, and somewhat more portly, than the slightly built man, with pointed features on his long face beneath dark, unruly hair.

"This is Francois-Rene de Combourg, the Frenchman who I spoke of a few days ago, when I met him at Beccles. He has had a fall from his horse, and received serious injuries as you can see. The bandages cover a broken arm, and broken collar-bone, and he suffered severe concussion when his head hit the ground."

Sarah immediately went to the stranger, took his good arm, and guided him to a chair by the inglenook.

"Sir, you must sit down and rest. Your injuries appear most alarming – you must be in great pain." The visitor bowed his head in acknowledgement, and sat down on the settee with some difficulty.

"Merci, Madame – thank you, I am moved by your concern. The pain now is not so bad, and my head has cleared now. It must be made of hard material – wood, I think!"

But he winced as he smiled at his attempt at humour. Charlotte, now seated opposite him in the homely and comfortable drawing room, looked up, and caught his eye, and returned his smile shyly. Her father spoke then:

"Sarah, forgive me for bringing Monsieur Comburg here without forewarning. But at this moment, he has nowhere to stay, and we are a Christian family. He did not ask if he could stay with us until other accommodation could be found for him, but I felt we should give him refuge until he has somewhere else to go. "

His wife's response was instinctively Christian – those who knew her well remarked privately that it often seemed she carried out her duties as a parson's wife with greater religious fervour than her husband did as the parson.

"M Combourg – you must stay with us, of course. This is a big parsonage, with several spare bedchambers, and you will be comfortable here while you recover. You are most welcome."

"Madame, you are most gracious, most charitable. I would not have come but M Ives insisted…"

"….And I insist – we all insist. We offer you our hospitality and help in your recovery for as long as you need it," Sarah interrupted him.

"Just a few days, Madame, while I make arrangements for other accommodation. I do not wish to outstay this most generous welcome."

Maria, the housemaid at the parsonage, had gone home for the evening, so Sarah and Charlotte prepared a simple supper in the kitchen while the two men remained talking in the withdrawing room. When the women returned they found them with a glass of port in their hands, discussing the latest news on the revolution that was tearing France apart.

M Combourg moved his position in his seat frequently to gain comfort, wincing at the pain as he did so. Charlotte watched this mysterious stranger from a foreign land with some fascination as he spoke, in reasonable English, with some candour, of how his unfortunate accident had occurred, and how he came to be in England.

The family learned that he was from an aristocratic family and, soon after the outbreak of the revolution, had left France and travelled to America, where he spent some months in both populated and remote areas, staying with American Indians for some time.

He returned to France, but only briefly. In his absence the oppression and pursuit of the aristocracy by the revolutionaries had intensified, and with many other members of his class he left his native shores again, arrived in England via Jersey, and made his way to London. There he had the friendship and support of other émigrés who settled there but, with few belongings and even less money, they found life hard, and had to get used to a life of poverty, in great contrast to the affluent life they had enjoyed at home before the Revolution, which had brought the monarchy into disarray and left the charismatic republican Napoleon's confident of taking charge. But with the large royalist following not content with the situation, executions and bloodshed continued and attempts to return the King to the throne of France were regularly plotted.

"There have been times, my good friends, when I have lived in an empty garret room, and have had to fight for food. I have been in England for two years now and for much of that time have lived the life of a beggar, destitute. But I have had good friends there, two particularly, called

15

Peltier, and Hignant, who have established associations with well placed people, and we have managed to survive."

He paused, and took a draught of porter, before continuing.

"It was one of these who read in a newspaper, I believe the Yarmouth newspaper, that there was an association of antiquaries seeking someone to translate ancient documents that had been discovered, written in Latin. That is how I came to be in Beccles. I have a good understanding of Latin, and have been able to be of much service to them, and they to me in the payment I have received. That is, until I discovered that I was not as good a horseman as I had previously supposed."

And he winced again, and moved carefully in his chair.

"Monsieur, what hard times have befallen you, someone who had grown used to a much different life in France. And what of your family – do you have family, Monsieur? Did they follow you to England?" Sarah inquired.

M Combourg's expression gave the impression that, had he been able to shrug his shoulders, he would have done so. But he had to content himself with a reply in a tone half of regret, half of resignation:

"Madame, I confess they decided to remain in France, near Paris, at the time I decided to leave. I fear for them – my mother, sisters, aunts, uncles, cousins. It is difficult to discover news of them, though my fellow emigres have managed to learn some information."

He paused, and a sad and distant look clouded his face.

"You had mentioned a brother to me previously – have to had news of him?" John Ives question carried concern. "I was the youngest of ten children, some of whom did not survive. Two sisters and a brother did, until this dreadful Revolution – now it has taken my last surviving brother. Those evil republicans who believe they can make France a better place think nothing of executing people without proper trial. Many lives have been taken that way – including my brother's, and other close relations. They were all put to the guillotine on the same day."

Charlotte's heart went out to Francois as he uttered those words, forcing them through his lips with controlled anger and emotion. As she fixed her gaze steadfastly on his solemn face, he seemed a man lost to his fate at that moment, desolate, despairing, at pain from his injuries, adrift in a foreign country, like a boat without a rudder on a stormy sea.

"Et maintenant – now, now I fear for the rest of my family. I have learned that they have been thrown into prison too, arrested without good reason, with little hope of a fair trial if they are tried at all. You may ask why I do not go back to them, to help? That would be putting my head through the rope – the noose I think you say - as I entered the country. These people, these revolutionaries, watch every port in France, every vessel, for returning émigrés, ready to arrest them and almost certainly execute them. I have made my journey here – I cannot go back. It would do my family no good to learn that I have been executed for trying to reach them. But one day, one day monsieur et mesdammes, I will return to my country, when the monarchy has been established again, to play my part in her recovery."

The last sentences Francois had uttered were driven with sudden energy, a mixture of anger and determination, though perhaps in hope rather than conviction. Then he slumped back into his chair. Sarah intervened.

"Monsieur, you are exhausted. Please forgive us – we should not put you to this inquisition when you are in pain and discomfort, and burdened by misfortune. You must need to sleep. John, be so good as to help M Combourg up the stairs and to his room, where his bed is waiting."

Her husband helped their guest to his feet. He seemed more unsteady than when he had arrived, and welcomed his host's supportive arm.

"Thank you, madame – thank you for your kindness and compassion, and your generous hospitality, of which I am not deserving. I hope to feel better in the morning. Goodnight, madame – goodnight, Miss Ives."

He caught Charlotte's concerned look as he turned to go out of the room, and managed a tired smile in return as he met her eyes.

2

N ext morning, the Ives family were having breakfast, prepared by Mrs Honeywood, the cook, and served by Maria, when M Combourg appeared. He had slept long, and appeared refreshed. Having been helped down the stairs by John Ives, he took his place at the table with apologies for his lateness.

"Please Monsieur, do not apologise," said John. "Rest is the best medicine you can have and you must rest as much as possible."

"You are most understanding, Sir. But I do not intend to spend all my time in idleness."

The Frenchman took the cup of tea offered by Mrs Ives, and then continued:

"When we spoke during our meetings at Beccles, where I had also been giving some French lessons to students, you mentioned that your daughter would also like to learn my native language. I would be delighted to teach her – it would be in some small way recompense for the hospitality you are showing me. And I would continue it once I have found accommodation in the vicinity."

He looked at Charlotte, who raised her head and returned his inquiring smile with a shy smile of her own, accentuating her dark, almost black eyes which momentarily met the dark brown eyes of Francois-Rene, before she lowered them.

"Thank you, Monsieur. I would be most grateful," she said self-consciously. The Frenchman nodded a silent response as Mrs Ives added:

"That is a most generous gesture. Charlotte is an eager student and keen to learn. You may use the music room or Mr Ives' study, when he is out, as a classroom. But do not feel you must start immediately – only when you feel well enough recovered."

"That is quite right – only when you are ready," her husband emphasised. "But when that time comes, I see no reason why you should not use our home as a base for other students to call at for lessons. There are others, I'm sure, in Bungay, young people and adults, keen to learn and improve their culture. This area of England is somewhat impoverished as far as cultural learning is concerned, and if we can help to put that right it will be a great service to our town."

"Again, thank you. My lack of finance is an embarrassment to me, and if I can earn something by passing on my language to others I can begin to feel worth something again," said Francois, as he began the breakfast put before him. "Being active will help me regain my strength, and my hope is to walk in Bungay for exercise before too long."

~~

Charlotte sat at the piano in the music room, guiding her slim white fingers nimbly, gently over the keys, coaxing out the expressiveness and emotion of one of Beethoven's more relaxed, quieter pieces, one which allowed time for its thoughtful mood to dwell with the pianist through the keys, and to read those thoughts. In the morning, after breakfast, was Charlotte's favourite time for practising her music in the large, high-ceilinged room, with its bay window looking out on the garden which ran down to the River Waveney. It was close to the end of October, but still the air was mild, and the sun was shining from a blue sky, making the bronzed leaves on the trees and the garden shrubs glisten with their dampness. On such days, Charlotte thought, as she played, you could almost smell the rich dampness of the earth and grass and leaves as they mingled and merged and waited to form part of the shroud that winter would cast over the garden in a few short weeks, as nature prepared to sleep.

There was something exciting about that aroma. Nature might be ready to sleep, but though she loved the warmth of the summer best of all, there was an expectancy in approaching winter too – the beauty of snow, the joy of the Christmas season and the celebration of Christ's birth. And presents – she was still not too old to be eager and excited about the gifts to be exchanged in front of a glowing fire in the withdrawing room, the singing of carols (which she would play for), the festive conversation around the Christmas dinner table…

But that was still weeks away – today there was something new to look forward to, she told herself, as she left the piano stool and went and stood by the window to fully enjoy that autumn view, and watch the river flow gently on its inexorable journey through its flood plain from Bungay, to Beccles, past small villages on its north and south banks, and to Breydon Water, and out to the great North Sea at Yarmouth.

Yes – today, she reminded herself with nervous excitement, she was to have her first lesson in French from M Combourg, who had arrived so unexpectedly four days earlier, injured and weak, but who had already made a pleasing impression on the Ives household. Despite his condition his flamboyance, his colourful conversation, were already proving delightfully stimulating, and his knowledge of the world, particularly its music and literature, were broadening Charlotte's learning. Her father had observed the previous evening that M Combourg, despite being a penniless French refugee in England, had that distinctive aristocratic air about him.

He was attentive and friendly towards Charlotte too, and she enjoyed that. Her innate shyness, born of her sheltered life in the parsonage and her activities dominated by the church, meant she was unsure how to respond. Her self-consciousness annoyed her. Francois would on occasions try to hold her gaze with his, but she quickly dropped her head and looked away in confusion.

His glances and his handsome smile seemed to be stirring in her feelings that she had not known before, and a quickening of her heartbeat.

But somehow she felt they were wrong, and tried to put them aside.

Charlotte left the window and went back to the piano, taking up the piece she had been playing earlier. It helped her to concentrate and relax.

She became so absorbed in it for a few minutes that she did not hear the door open quietly, nor the footsteps over the floorboards and the deep rug that covered part of it, until she was suddenly aware of someone leaning on the side of the piano, watching her and listening intently.

It startled her and her hands fled from keys to her breast as she let out a muted cry.

"M Combourg! I did not hear you come in!"

"My apologies Miss Ives. But I did not want to interrupt your beautiful playing. There is such maturity in your touch. I was enjoying listening."

Charlotte blushed, but this time held his eyes – those piercing brown eyes which this time came with a gentleness and a smile.

"I enjoy playing, and practising. Mama says practice makes perfect, but I'm far from that. Your comments are most kind."

"They are not spoken lightly, Mademoiselle. I have heard many pianists who are well known in France, and many harpists, and you have their style and – how do you say? – expressiveness."

Francois-Rene paused for a moment, and then turned and took a few steps towards the window.

"Ah, quel beau jour, n'est-ce pas? Les vetements d'autome, les coleurs – ne sont-ils les plus meilleur de l'an?"

"Monsieur?" Charlotte left the piano stool and went towards him with a puzzled expression on her face. He smiled, and stretched out his free hand and took her arm lightly.

"Miss Ives, I speak in my native tongue. I believe you would like to learn to speak it too, to speak French. I was saying that it is a beautiful day outside, and that the colours of the cloak of autumn are the prettiest of any time of the year. I will teach you how to say that, but to learn a language you must start at the beginning. You must first learn some basic words, know how sentences are constructed in France, know the tenses and declensions of our verbs – it will give you a start to understanding how beautiful our language is."

"It sounds most complicated, Monsieur. But yes, I would love to learn, and to be able to read French literature, and learn of your authors. Papa said you might be able to start today? Can we?"

Charlotte's eyes were bright with expectation and eagerness – keen for knowledge and to broaden her education in every way she could, and it was an excitement which attracted the Frenchman.

"I will make you a pact. Miss Ives. No, a bargain I think you call it – I will make a bargain with you: for one hour's tuition in French each day, while I am here, you will let me listen to you playing the piano for one hour. Do you agree to that?"

"Monsieur I do agree!" Charlotte bobbed slightly in a mock curtsy. "But I believe I will have the best of the bargain. Can we start now? Do say we can!"

Her enthusiasm was infectious. Francois gazed at her oval face, with its healthy pink glow, her dark eyes shining and her small, well shaped mouth slightly open as if waiting to take in his answer, and felt a nascent affinity with this pretty English girl whose family had welcomed him so readily into their midst. How could he refuse her? His smile became a gentle, accommodating laugh.

"Mademoiselle, if you can find some paper on which we can write, and a pen, then yes – we will start now."

"Thank you! Thank you, Monsieur. And you must tell me which composers you like, so I can practice their pieces, to play to you."

"I will, Miss Ives."

That morning in Bungay, far from his native Brittany, the autumn sun streaming through the window, lifted the heart of Francois and brought him a feeling of contentment – something he had rarely felt since he arrived in England as a penniless immigrant, unsure of his future, unsure where to go, unsure what to do with his life. Now here he was, in a comfortable, welcoming home, discussing French language and French literature with an attractive, intelligent young woman who was bright and keen to learn, inquisitive of France and its people, its history – his home country, from which he had deserted his family and fled abroad. How long ago was it? Two years? Three, four? It was now towards the end of 1795, but he was losing track of time, drifting from one place to another, not in control of his fate. Yet fate was beginning to smile on him again, he felt, as he sat there, at that oak table in the withdrawing room beside Charlotte. She and the rays of sun, still warm as they shafted in, seemed to lift him out of the waves of depression that had frequently overcome him over the past months. And the physical pain of his injuries seemed to ease, too.

That same sun warmed Charlotte, effused the feeling of excitement within her breast which at the same time confused her. Here she was, with a man from a foreign country who must be at least 10 years older than her, a stranger just a few days ago, yet already a bond of friendship, of common interest, was forming – an affinity she had not felt with anyone else. She was at a time in her life when feelings raced, and because they were new she was not yet ready to interpret in her mind what they meant, even why she felt them. Only recently, at Bible study, Samuel Sutton had caught her attention – there had been an indefinable attraction there. But now, that seemed a distant memory. Now, here she was beside this man from another country, injured, perhaps vulnerable, who wanted to teach her, and who she wanted to entertain with her piano playing.

Outside the unhurried river, maturing and growing as it flowed past the town, with another 20 miles to go to its estuary at the North Sea, reflected the contentment of those two souls.

Charlotte already knew some very basic French – her parents had resolved when she was still very young that she should have regular learning in English language, and Latin, as well as mathematics, history, and geography, and into her language tuition had inevitably come references to French words. She liked the sound of them, the accents. As well as being eager to learn, she was also a quick learner, and by the end of the morning she could put some basic sentences together.

When Sarah Ives came into the room towards midday, her daughter greeted her eagerly:

"Mama – comment va-tu?"

"Bien, Charlotte, merci – et tu?"

"Bien, Mama!"

And she laughed at the brief conversation she had managed, and looked at Francois-Rene for praise.

"Et tu, monsieur?"

"Tres bien, madmoiselle – very good. Your daughter learns quickly, Madame."

Sarah smiled, and he caught a glimpse of how alike mother and daughter were in their facial features. He estimated that she was between 35 and 40 years old, but young looking and slim, and everything about her movement and demeanour was welcoming.

"She enjoys learning, and we enjoy teaching her. My husband, though a clergyman, is also a learned mathematician, an expert on Greek history, and enjoys geography too. And I encourage Charlotte to read, and sew, and appreciate art. She enjoys painting."

She paused, then added: "I can see you are getting along well. I just came to say that cook is preparing luncheon, which we take in the dining-room at 12.30 – but I expect Charlotte has told you that, Monsieur."

"Merci, Madame. The Greek race and it's history interests me considerably – your husband and I have discussed it during our meetings at Beccles, and I look forward to conversations on it. Greece had such great writers at the height of its empire, and I'm keen to study their work."

"Yes, my husband is well versed in them, and I know he has enjoyed your talks – he enjoys all conversations, though

I fear sometimes his tongue is loosened by too much ale and porter, and he talks too much."

Francois-Rene noticed that a cloud seemed to come over Sarah's face as she spoke – clearly she disapproved of her husband's drinking habits, though in his meetings at Beccles he had never noticed it affected him greatly, unlike some others present at the same time.

He remained silent, but the brief hiatus was broken by Charlotte, eager to enjoy a little more learning before luncheon.

"Monsieur, do teach me some more phrases – I want to be able to speak French fluently within one year. And I want you to tell me more about France, too. What is it like? Where have you been in France? What is happening there at present? There is a lot of talk about a revolution!"

Mrs Ives looked on with approval for a moment as the two went into an animated conversation, eyes bright and attentive to what each other was saying, and then withdrew.

3

few days later, the sound of piano playing could be heard through the Ives household. Charlotte was at the piano, playing with feeling and expression. Francois was leaning on the instrument, gazing at her intently in silence, watching her play, watching her face concentrating on each note, feeling the gentleness of the piece.

Outside, early winter seemed to be setting in – there was a cold east wind chasing the bronzed leaves around the garden, and ruffling the surface of the Waveney out of its calm progress; every so often it would rain and the wind would batter it against the window panes and rattle the casement, as if drawing attention to itself, and warning those inside that autumn was over, and they should expect no kindnesses from the weather from now on.

But inside that room the log fire was blazing, warming the air and the polished oak of the furniture, drawing out the aromas from the depths of the dense wood to mingle with the scents of the fire itself, and relax the inhabitants.

As Francois watched Charlotte as she played, that feeling of enormous contentment surged through him again. He told himself how fortunate he was to be there. Though far from his family, he was also far from the troubles that were engulfing France, far from the privation he had experienced in America among the Iroquois Indians, far from the days in London when he had no money and virtually no food. Now he had money, though a modest amount, from his work translating documents for the antiquarian society in Beccles.

"Yes," he told himself as he leant there, "my life has changed for the better. Even the misfortune of the fall from my horse and my injury has proved provident in that it has brought me here to this house, at this time, and provided me with the company of this charming, beautiful girl. Look at her features, listen to her music! And while I am teaching her my native language she is attentive, conscientious, and we are natural in our relationship together. I yearn for my country, I yearn for my family, but great is the consolation of Miss Ives' company. I feel sometimes that if fate were to dictate that I should stay here forever, I would feel that fate was smiling on me, that it had rewarded me in a way I perhaps do not deserve. How beautifully, tenderly she plays – it is as if she loves the very instrument, as well as the music she draws from it. It seems she makes the very act of turning the page part of the performance.

"Francois, beware of your feelings – you are being drawn to Miss Ives as much as to her skill as a musician and her keenness to learn. Those feelings have got you into trouble before. Be mindful of their power!"

The Frenchman sighed. As his gaze still fixed on Charlotte's face, she glanced up as her fingers continued to move slowly across the keyboard, and smiled as she saw him watching her.

It was a smile he would never forget, wherever he was in the ensuing years. It not only lit her face naturally and without a hint of duty, it seemed to light the very clothes she wore, her whole personality, coming from the very depth of her soul and exposing her whole self with a trusting openness.

Francois marvelled inwardly at the vision in front of him, the effect she had on him.

"Was Eve before her fall as beautiful as this?" he mused to himself, as he returned her gaze.

"I cannot conceive that she was."

"Monsieur, what are you thinking?"

Charlotte's gentle inquiry broke his reverie.

"Mademoiselle, pardon. I...I was just thinking...just wondering...the piece you are playing? I don't recognise the composer."

"This is by Bach – Johann Sebastian Bach. It is one of his early cantatas, and one of my favourites. Do you like it? This section is called, Just as the Rain and Snow Falls from the Sky. It is a pastoral work, very peaceful, and at one with the countryside I feel. Sometimes when I walk to Papa's church, or go with him in the trap, I have this piece in my head, and I look around at the land, and see the sower sowing, or the crops growing, the flowers in the hedgerows, hear the bird song; and I think that this is the rural countryside Bach had in mind when he was composing this cantata. It makes me feel...feel enfolded by nature, I suppose. That is the purpose of music is it not? To make you feel involved in what the composer is trying to convey?"

"Oui, mademoiselle, vraiment. That is exactly my sentiment. I was watching you play, so beautifully, and in my mind was the paysage, the country areas, around Brittany, where the beauty of nature is abundant. It is very green in springtime and golden in the autumn. There is a feeling...a presence, do you say?...about it. These memories are very warm for me."

And a wistfulness passed over his face.

"Monsieur, you miss your homeland, do you not? I can tell it from how you are."

"Oui...yes, I do, very much de temps en temps – ah, pardon, sometimes, I should say. But you and your parents have made me feel so at home here, that sometimes I feel I am in my own land. And I thank you for that."

And Francois-Rene took her hand, interrupting her playing, and still holding her gaze, lifted it to his lips and kissed it, tenderly.

For a moment, Charlotte felt her dark eyes melt into his brown pupils, as if trying to pierce the thoughts and feelings inside. Then she pulled her hand away suddenly, lowered her eyes, and swallowed hard.

"Monsieur, I…I am flattered that you enjoy my playing," she said, embarrassed suddenly, and trying to regain her composure. "This music…this piece…Bach is trying to…I think he is trying to paint a picture of the countryside and God's hand on it. I have learnt the words that have been written with the music, to tell the listener, or the one who is playing. I will recount them to you. She cleared her throat:

'Just as the showers and snow from heaven fall and return again not thither, rather give the earth moisture and make it fertile and fruitful, so it gives seed for the sowing and bread for eating: Just so shall the word which from mine own mouth proceedeth, be too; it shall not come again to me empty, but shall do what I have purposed and shall that accomplish for which I send it.'

"That is what the music is saying to me too."

"And it says it to me too, mademoiselle Charlotte. Words can speak music without an instrument, and music can speak words without a script; words can evoke music and also music can speak words that cannot be written in any other way, just as a beautiful painting speaks from its frame. But, my apologies – I interrupted your playing. You must resume, s'il tu plais."

"Oh, I had almost finished, Monsieur – I have played enough for today. I…I think I must go to do some preparation for my Bible study class. Thank you…thank you for listening, monsieur."

Francois inclined his head in acceptance as Charlotte opened the door, and glanced back at him for a long moment, before closing it behind her.

In fact, though Charlotte went to her room, she found it impossible to concentrate on her Bible work. The image of Francois kept interrupting her thoughts, her mind was confused. He had kissed her hand! She knew that was not unusual – it was a formal greeting favoured by the French, and it was by way of thanking her for her playing. But it was the look in his eyes as he held her gaze that was filling her mind, and the effect it had on her. What was this feeling in her breast? Her heart had tugged as she dwelt on those deep brown eyes, and now there were these sensations she had never felt before. The other night, thinking of Samuel, and his attentiveness to her, had made her feel she meant something to him, and that was pleasing. But this new feeling was completely different, and much stronger, and something she was finding difficult with which to contend. What did it mean? What did she really feel? What did he feel? She only knew that already she could not wait for the time to come when she would play for him again, and he would continue to help her with her French, and with classic literature, and they would share conversations. He was handsome in a way, and there was a mystery about him – he exuded an air of knowledge, and yet of...she couldn't quite define it…of regret, perhaps, something from his past that troubled him. Perhaps it was guilt that he had left his country in its time of need. He would have a moody, faraway look on his face sometimes. But Charlotte put that down to the fact that he was far away from his home.

The other night, she had looked forward to seeing Samuel again at Bible study – now that had dimmed, and time with Francois seemed so important. He would only be here a short while, until he was fit enough to move on, and then she would not see him again.

And suddenly she found that prospect unbearable – she wanted him to stay always, so he was there to share her thoughts and interests, to share her feelings, good and bad, to support him when he needed support, and to feel his care around her when she needed it.

Those feelings engulfed her with a glow of warmth that she did not quite understand, and was ignorant about how to handle.

"What are these feelings, what do they mean?" she asked herself again.

And try as she might, she could not concentrate on her Bible work.

Dinner that evening was a relaxed and hearty affair. Mrs Honeywood, the cook, large and well proportioned, with a rosy face and an apron that wrapped right around her, prepared it to her usual good standard, and it was served by

Maria the maid – a somewhat quiet girl of 18 who gave the impression that she was unaware of what was going on around her, but seemed to know most of what was, just the same.

Mr Ives and Combourg got into animated conversation about America – both men had been there, at different times, though in different areas, and they exchanged stories and anecdotes about their travels with great eagerness. For the most part Charlotte and her mother listened attentively, and contributed where they could. Charlotte loved to hear her father when he was in full flow, and now Francois too, in his remarkably good English. He also talked, with some sadness, about his time in Paris, where he went after the revolution broke out in 1789, and the effect the revolt had had on life in France.

"Its affect was not so apparent in Brittany and the rural areas of France, but in the capital life was very difficult – and still is I believe," he said. "Fighting, mutiny, fear, death. It is not the Paris I first knew. I can only hope that whatever the outcome it will be better for France in the long run."

"But you were not born in Paris, Monsieur?" Sarah inquired.

"Non, Madame. I was born in St Malo, but I spent most of my childhood in Combourg, about 50 miles from there."

"Combourg – the same as your name? How strange!" Sarah said.

"Ah, Madame…" Francois looked a little embarrassed at the comment. He looked round the table at each of the diners, before continuing, hesitantly at first.

"I have to confess – I have to make a confession, I think you say. My real name is not Combourg – I changed my name after coming to England."

"Why was that – in case you were followed by revolutionaries?" Mr Ives asked.

"No no monsieur – nothing so sinister. The reason is that I found people could not pronounce my real name properly."

"So what is your real name, Monsieur?" said Charlotte, fascinated.

"My real name is Chateaubriand – so you see what I mean," replied the Frenchman, ruefully.

"People called me all sorts of things, including Shatterbrain, which I believe in your country is a name given to someone without any brain, or who is thoughtless or cannot remember things. So to make it easy for myself I changed my name to Combourg. It was the first name I thought of, and most people can say it easily."

Charlotte let out a girlish giggle at the sound of Shatterbrain, and the Frenchman glanced a piercing smile towards her, as her mother remarked, with a smile on her face:

"Scatterbrain – we do call people scatterbrained sometimes if they cannot understand simple things. So now your secret is revealed, shall we continue to call you M Combourg, or your real name, Chateaubriand?"

"Madame, my full name is Vicomte Francois-Rene de Chateaubriand – but please call me simply Francois."

"Vicomte? You mentioned that you were from the aristocracy, but the title? That suggests you are one of the elite class in France," Mr Ives observed.

"Oui, yes," he said, almost apologetically. "And that is why our family and many like ours have been the target of the revolutionaries, who want to eradicate our class, to chase us out as you would chase out vermin. Our home was the Chateau de Combourg – it has been in the family for hundreds of years, but I fear the revolution has already claimed it from us. Now, in England, people know me simply as Combourg, and here I enjoy being treated as an ordinary person. It is much easier for me."

"We shall call you Francois, if that is your wish," said Sarah, decisively. And as the maid appeared, hoveringly, she added: "Maria, Charlotte and I will retire to the drawing room, and you will clear the table, though I'm sure the men will remain for a while, with their drink and conversation."

And she left, with a reproachful glance at her husband.

"Now, tell me more of your time among the American Indians, Francois – I did not travel to that part of the continent," said John Ives after they had left. "The impression, from what one hears, is that they can be savage and dangerous – were you ever fearful while among them?"

"Oh, non, monsieur, no. They are a peaceful people at heart. Certainly, among the Iroquois, the tribe I spent most time with, I discovered that their philosophy was to be at peace with the land on which they lived and drew sustenance from – land that belonged to them as they saw it. But yes, if they felt threatened, or were attacked, they would strike back with great force and determination, and could be very fierce. They would call on their gods – their spirits, I think – to help them protect themselves. I felt no threat against myself while I was among them. I confess I felt more threat in my own country, before I left."

"Hmmm – some say there is a danger of us feeling such a threat here in England. They talk of the mood of republicanism not remaining on mainland Europe, but finding its way here, before long. There is much concern at that prospect."

"Peut etre – perhaps that might happen, though I think not. There would be nowhere safe if that were to be so," observed the Frenchman.

"Many people would not agree. In this very town the leading inhabitants have got together to form the Bungay Loyal and Constitutional Society, ready to protect us from any republican insurgence. That has happened in the last few months. There are plans to form volunteer militia corps – perhaps two or three, ready to fight if called upon. Word is that that is happening in many towns up and down the country. They see the republican threat as very real. I myself have become a member of the society, though mainly to help calm any feelings of panic that may occur. You don't feel Napoleon has his eyes on England, Monsieur?"

"Bonaparte has his eyes on anywhere he thinks he can conquer, that is true. But let us see what happens in France – success in his campaign there is by no means certain, though," Francois paused and sighed deeply, "the present news from my poor country is not good. He is beginning to dominate the people, who seem to want to change."

He fell silent, concern in his eyes as grim thoughts passed through his head. Then he seemed to brighten up, as if throwing off the images there.

"No matter. This is good port, monsieur!"

John Ives took the cue to fill the Frenchman's glass again.

"I'm pleased you approve. This is the best port I can find anywhere – I have it brought up from London. I drink much of it."

"Not too much at one time, I hope!"

The clergyman glanced at him with an expression of contented mischievousness.

"My wife does not approve, monsieur – Francois. But I find that drink does not have the effect on me it seems to have on many others. We have dinner parties here at regular intervals, as you would expect in my position, and the gentlemen enjoy port after the ladies have retired, as we're doing now. I don't want to boast about it, but usually by the time the guests have drunk themselves to sleep, I am still fully alert.

"There was one occasion last year," he continued, leaning forward on the table towards Francois, as if confiding in him, and laughing as he did so, "one occasion when the Duke and Duchess of Norfolk were here. We were drinking this same brand of port after dinner, at this very table. The conversation was good and prolonged, and our drinking was good and prolonged, and I tell you, sir, that between us we emptied four bottles of this vintage – four bottles! In the end His Grace the Duke fell asleep in his chair! I remained awake of course, relaxing with my glass. Eventually he woke up, and was most apologetic at falling asleep in front of his host, but I told him I quite understood. And I also told him that while he had slept I had emptied a further bottle myself!"

And the clergyman put his head back and laughed, and acknowledged the more discreet laughter from his guest.

"Physicians may caution against it, but for people like me a glass of port can be medicinal. That is my belief."

"Quite so. I enjoyed more than a glass of wine from my home region when I was back at home," Francois observed diplomatically. "I can see that your hospitality is most generous, and I thank you again for the way you have received me."

"You are most welcome, monsieur – It is an advantage to have another man in the house for a while, when normally I have two ladies for company."

"Two most attractive ladies, monsieur, who are nursing me most attentively." He put his hand to his injured shoulder. "My injuries are already feeling much better. Charlotte is a most intelligent young lady, and I marvel at her command of the piano."

"She is a good and dutiful daughter, who is very much enjoying your tuition in French, and in French and Italian literature. She speaks often about how she enjoys learning with you, and playing for you, and my wife and I note the effect it is having on her. She is, as we say in England, coming out of herself. It tells us that her confidence is growing – she is beginning to throw off a little of her reserve, her shyness."

"Her company alone is improving my health – her very presence has a healing influence on me. I will always remember her with great affection."

John Ives studied Francois for a few moments, before replying. There seemed to be a tacit question in the remark. But he said only:

"I'm pleased your recovery is progressing well. But I feel it will be some time before you are able to ride again, or to make a long journey. There is still a frailness about you. Your stay here is not close to an end yet, and I know your other students are keen for you to continue your work with them. Do not feel you have to be in any hurry to leave."

4

"Charlotte, I do believe you are much taken by this Frenchman, and more than you are keen to admit. You haven't stopped talking about him this evening!"

Charlotte was walking home from Bible study with her friend Lydia Manning, who lived the other side of the bridge over the River Waveney, in Ditchingham. They were of similar age and had known each other since they were small children, visiting each other's home and playing together, and now maturing together. Now as they walked, Lydia was teasing her about Francois, and trying to coax more from her.

Charlotte, felt herself blush.

"Only while we have been walking home," she said, defensively.

"And during the break in study. And you have described him in great detail, and with such excitement. I do believe you are falling for him!"

"Do you mean...?"

Charlotte did not finish the sentence, not quite sure what she intended to say. Instead she continued:

"Oh, Lydia, he is quite handsome, and it is the way he looks at me, the way he listens to me, the interest in his eyes and in his way of speaking to me...he makes me feel...I don't know how to describe it. I have not experienced these feelings before. My heart seems to beat faster, and I find myself looking forward to each new day because I know he is there, and I will see him, and he will praise my playing, and we will discuss literature, and history, and Italy, and..."

"You see – you are falling for him!" said Lydia, triumphantly. "Look how your eyes are sparkling when you speak of him. I can tell, Charlotte!"

"Do you think so? How can you tell? I've known him for less than a month. He has made me feel different, made me want to know more about him, everything about him."

"You are different, I have noticed that, and it is because of him, isn't it? You must introduce me to this man who has captured your heart!"

"Lydia, it is not like that! We just get on well together," Charlotte retorted indignantly.

They had reached the entrance to the parsonage. Looking up, she noticed the glow of a lamp coming from the window of Francois' room.

"I would invite you in to meet him now, but he will not be down again this evening," she said, with more composure. "But I will arrange for you to meet Francois, so you can tell me what you think of him."

The two friends kissed each other on the cheek, and said farewell.

That evening, as she lay in bed waiting for sleep to envelop her in its caress, Lydia's words glided in and out of her mind..."this man who has captured your heart."

"Is that what is happening – has happened? Is that why I feel as I do, so looking forward to playing for him and learning from him? These feeling are so new to me. I must be careful to control them perhaps. Yet they are becoming so strong."

In the ensuing days and weeks, Charlotte found herself looking forward more and more to the times of day she spend with Francois, and more envious of the time he spent with his students, who came from the town, and from Beccles, to learn the French language under his guidance in the upstairs room her father had set aside for that purpose. She became restless between times, calming herself only when she was studying work on her own that Francois had set her – Italian writers such as Tasso and Dante, and some of the work of France's Moliere, and Jean Racine. She worked hard at it in order to please him, and read the notes he had written for him, sometimes in margins of pages relating to the works, with special care. Sometimes she would take her pen, and guide it over the words he had written, as if he were holding the pen himself and her hand was on his, gently, feeling its warmth, feeling his soft, smooth olive skin. She had felt his hand on her own just once, when he had taken it as she played for him on the piano. Now, playing for him had become a special part of her daily routine, as if it was a homage to this man, who had come suddenly one evening, without warning, into her life.

For his part, Francois did his best with his other students. But they were not as attentive as Charlotte, nor as conscientious, nor did they concentrate in the same way. They were there, he decided, because their parents wanted them to be, rather than for themselves – Charlotte, on the other hand, wanted to learn and absorb as much knowledge as she could, and he valued his time with this girl, no, this young woman, who he had come upon, and whose infectious nature had given his life a focus, filling a void that had been there for so long before.

One morning, after Charlotte had attended to his injury, gently rubbing a balsam prepared by the town physician into his shoulder, and bandaged again one of the wounds to his arm which was slow to heal, and after she had played for him as he rested again, they sat at the table to resume studies. Maria brought them a drink, delivered as always with a nervous half-smile but without a word – though she understood now when Francois said, "Merci."

The day after he had revealed his real name to the family she had teased him about Shatterbrain, and they had laughed together about it. And she said:

"And now I know you have the title of Viscount I shall call you My Lord, as becomes a Viscount. How wonderful to be a member of the French aristocracy!"

Francois had protested, but from then on she would often address him as 'My Lord' and somehow, far from putting a barrier of formality between them, she felt an added friendship, an intimacy almost.

"Today we will talk more about two Italian writers with very different backgrounds, and styles, and with an entirely contrasting focus in their works," Francois began on this occasion. "Torquato Tasso and Dante Alighieri. I gave you some notes on them, and pieces of their work to read…"

"I have read the notes my Lord, and studied the pieces. I have tried to understand what they are trying to say, and what their mood conveys, but I am having difficulty with it."

""Bien, mademoiselle – I did too when I first read Tasso. He was born in the 16th century and had a troubled life. Sometimes in that situation a writer produces his best work because there is a depth of feeling in it. Eventually he went mad, and died at quite a young age.

"Now, the work he is remembered for most is a religious drama about the Crusades, *La Gerusalemme Liberata,* which he was commissioned to write, but I believe it was influenced by the women in his life. He fell in love with a woman in Padua, but he left her there when he travelled away, and later fell in love with the daughter of a nobleman, Lucrezia Bendidio, who was a singer. He was so…so infatuated, I think you say, with Lucrezia that he dedicated more than 40 poems to her. But her feelings were not the same for him. She later married a widower, and I believe he was so saddened by that that it became the beginning of his madness.

"The two pieces I have asked you to study were two of those poems. They are full of emotion, his deep feelings for Lucrezia. There is a certain sensuousness about them I think, and…"

"My Lord, what does sensuousness mean?" Charlotte interrupted him.

Francois, taken aback slightly, thought for a moment, considering his answer carefully. It was not a question he had expected. At last he said:

"It is a…a physical feeling between a man and a woman. It can be seen by the movements of a body, or a face, which gives out signals, one to the other. It can also be manifested by the way they touch each other. I think you would say it is a physical intimacy going beyond the feelings of close friendship – it…it makes two people attracted to each other in a more physical way. I find it difficult to define it in words that truly convey its meaning."

Francois was clearly uncomfortable in his struggle to give a discreet answer to the question posed by this young woman, who lowered her eyes, and blushed as he spoke. He had seen up to this point a purity, a chasteness, in Charlotte, but in trying to describe this English word to her, he suddenly admitted to himself the realisation, which he had tried to put behind him, that he wanted to embrace this person to whom he was so drawn.

"Mademoiselle, give me you hand," he said. And as Charlotte tentatively moved her hand across the polished oak tabletop towards his, he laid his own hand gently on it, enfolding her slim fingers in his palm. She lifted her eyes to his, and he saw in them a look of...of what?

A hint of fearfulness and uncertainly, yes, but were they also appealing, conveying an unspoken understanding of the moment, wanting re-assurance of it in her young mind? She did not pull her hand away immediately.

"This touch, mademoiselle, between a man and a woman, hand on hand, would be an intimate touch, showing a closeness beyond day to day friendship. A sensual touch would go beyond that meaning into something more...an attraction more physical than spiritual."

The two held each other's gaze, their hands remained where they were, one on the other, for a few seconds. Later, when Charlotte looked back, it seemed a beautiful eternity.

Suddenly, there was a knock on the door, and Maria came in. Charlotte snatched her hand back to her side of the table, and felt her face burning. Francois looked down at his notes in a more controlled way.

"Beg pardon, Miss – I've just come to clear the cups."

"Yes, yes, thank you, Maria."

When she had left the room with her laden tray and a fleeting backward glance, there was an awkward silence. Charlotte felt her face still red, and she was afraid to look up at Francois, even when he said:

"I hope, mademoiselle, that that explanation of the word was sufficient to make clearer what I was saying. But to return to Tasso himself, his life was an unhappy and disturbed one, made tolerable for him only when he was writing – he was due to be named Italy's greatest poet of his time, at the time of his death."

He coughed nervously, before going on: "But let us turn to Dante for comparison. He was a much more stable character, though a wanderer, and undoubtedly the greatest poet Italy has seen."

He told Charlotte of Dante's best known work, an epic poem of the 14th century called The Divine Comedy, written on his travels in real provinces and countries but also focussing on imaginary worlds created by his restless mind.

He said he was born into Florence, into a noble family, and lived there for 38 years, that his mother died when he was seven years old, that his father, Alighiero II, made his living by money-lending and renting of property, and died in the late 13th century, while Dante was still a boy.

Francois, it seemed to Charlotte, felt more comfortable talking about Dante than Tasso, but she resolved to understand more about the life and work of both.

"In their time they were incomparable writers," Francois said. "I enjoy writing – did enjoy writing before I left France, and I still write from time to time – but I could not aspire to the phrases and imagery of those two, or indeed of our great French writers, or your Shakespeare."

"My Lord, you must write – you mustn't keep inside you what you feel, the ideas that are in your head. I can tell you have the skills in you. Promise me you will set aside more time to write while you remain her with us."

She had regained her composure as she got up from her chair and collected the notes Francois had left her. He looked at her as he left the room, and said:

"There are many thoughts and feelings in my head, mademoiselle."

Then with a slight bow of his head, added: "I apologise if I embarrassed you during our discussions."

The following day, two weeks before Christmas, in the early evening, Sarah was sitting sewing in front of the fire in the withdrawing room. Charlotte was busy at the table making decorations in the candlelight, and Francois was in his room, when the doorbell clanged loudly in the hall. A few moments later Maria knocked at the door and entered.

"Beg pardon, ma'am – Captain Sutton is asking to see Miss Ives."

"Oh, show him in Maria, please."

Charlotte looked up, startled, from her work.

"I wonder what he can want," she said, a slightly puzzled expression on her face.

"Captain Sutton, ma'am."

The tall, upright figure of the Naval man stepped into the room, dressed not in uniform but in a smart frockcoat and breaches to below his knees. A scarf was round his neck.

"Good evening Mrs Ives, Miss Ives. My apologies for calling without forewarning, but, Miss Ives, it would be a privilege if I could walk you to Bible class this evening. I believe I mentioned it last time I was there, some weeks ago. I have just returned to Ditchingham for shore leave for the Yuletide period."

Charlotte, looking embarrassed and taken aback, stood up, recalling the attraction she had felt for this man at their first meeting. But much had happened in her mind, and her outlook, since then.

"Oh, Captain Sutton – please forgive me – it is most discourteous of me to have forgotten that. You see, I....I haven't been regularly to Bible class in recent weeks. We have an unexpected house guest, who is injured, and I have been caring for him, and he has been helping me with tuition. I had not planned to go this evening."

The Captain looked crestfallen, but he quickly hid is disappointment.

"I do understand Miss Ives. Forgive me again for calling unexpectedly. My parents had heard that there was a Frenchman staying in Bungay following an injury, but they were not aware that it was here. I will make my way to church now. Good evening Mrs Ives, Miss Ives."

He turned to the door, but as he was leaving he turned back, and said, a little hesitantly:

"I shall be here until the first week of the New Year. Perhaps...could I accompany you to Bible class that week, before I return to my ship?"

"I...I'm not sure...I don't...."

Charlotte glanced at her mother, as if for help. Sarah responded.

"Captain Sutton, Charlotte is most grateful for your interest, but she feels committed to our injured guest, and we are not certain how long he will be staying with us. But we will send a note in good time to let you know if she will be resuming Bible study. We both apologise that you have made a wasted call."

"Not at all, Mrs Ives – I do understand, and thank you."

He smiled at both women, his gaze catching Charlotte's confused expression.

When he had left, her mother picked up her sewing again, and said:

"My dear, you could have gone with Captain Sutton. The Viscount is in his room and will need no more attention this evening. The captain clearly would have enjoyed your company."

"I know, Mama, I know. I feel awful at declining his invitation but..."

"But, my dear…?" Sarah coaxed gently.

"Oh, I don't know…I feel…I don't know how I feel! This is all new to me!"

She got up, and walked towards the window, heavily cloaked in velvet curtains, and then back to the table again. Mrs Ives sighed a mother's sigh, and went to her daughter's side.

"Captain Sutton, I think, is keen to be your first suitor – and he would be eminently respectable. He is from a noted family. But I can tell from your demeanour over the past few weeks that you have feelings for the viscount beyond your commitment to nurse him, beyond your gratitude for his help for your studies."

Charlotte's head was down, her hands toying with the decoration she had been assembling.

"How can you tell, Mama? I haven't said anything. Has…has Francois said anything to you?"

"There is no need for either of you to say anything, my dear. The signs are there for a mother to observe clearly. Even Papa has made comment, and he is not one to quickly pick up on such things."

She motioned her daughter to sit down, and sat down beside her, and took her hand in hers.

"My dear, you are still young, but nevertheless of an age when suitors will begin to come calling. Captain Sutton is a handsome man, with, I would surmise, a good career in the English navy ahead of him. The viscount has delighted us all with his stories, and his presence, his help with your studies; he has become part of our household. I can well understand you feel attracted to him. I believe he has feelings for you, too, though – no, he has said nothing to me or Papa.

"But once he is well, he will be leaving, he will return to France, and that will be that. We will all miss him, but that will pass. Captain Sutton, on the other hand, though he will be away for long periods, will still have his home here to return to. Do you see what I am saying?"

Charlotte felt her mother's hand in hers. They were very close, and shared most thoughts and feelings with each other. Her hand felt comforting, caring, soothing, a maternal bond that would never be broken.

But she thought too of the moment Francois had taken her hand, gently, and the feelings that had risen in her breast at that moment. But there was more, that only the hand of a man, and a man outside the family, could convey, and she wanted to feel that again.

"Yes – yes, I do understand, Mama. I know you are right. When I met Captain Sutton at Bible study I hoped he might accompany me there again – I wanted him to ask. But since Francois has been here, my feeling towards him have been…different…stronger…It is difficult to explain."

"You don't need to explain. I do understand, Charlotte. You are coming towards womanhood. They are feelings I remember myself, when I first met your father…"

"So, they are right then? It's not wrong to feel them?"

"Oh, my dear!" Sarah put her arms around her daughter and hugged her close, in the subdued candlelight. "My dear, there is no right or wrong about these feelings. They are perfectly natural. It is how you deal with them, that is important – and sometimes you have to try to curb them, to put them in perspective, before they take over. And at your age, that is not easy."

Charlotte put her head on her mother's breast.

"They are strong, Mama. Each day, each hour I spend with him, they seem more powerful."

5

C hristmas came in the Ives household, and with it the snow. On Christmas Eve Charlotte went out into the garden and picked some sprigs of holly from the tree which that year was full of bright red buries, and ivy to go with it, and arranged it in wreaths in the diningroom, withdrawing room and the music room. In the last, she also wove it around a painting she had created of the Nativity, and placed it on the grand piano.

Francois complemented her on it warmly, but later in the day, as evening draw near, he became quiet and melancholy, almost morose. Before Maria closed the curtains on the darkening day and the snow-covered garden scene, he stood for some time gazing out on it, saying nothing. Eventually Charlotte, still working on some of the Christmas decorations, ventured:

"My Lord, you seem sad...pre-occupied? Are you still troubled by your injuries?"

Francois half-turned towards her, and said, almost inaudibly: "Non, non mademoiselle. Je va bien."

Charlotte was quiet for a while before trying again:

"Are you thinking of your home, your family, and Christmas in Brittany?"

Francois was silent again, for what seemed some minutes, and then turned slowly towards her. She stopped what she was doing.

""L'observation – c'est vrai...pardon: you are right mademoiselle. There are troubles in my country, in Paris, and my family are there, at risk perhaps, in danger. The latest news from France is not good – there are many being put in prison for opposing the revolution, there are people being beaten, even executed at the gallows.

"Yet here am I, chez Ives – a comfortable, safe home, with good attentive people, caring for me – nothing is too much trouble for you and your parents. You make me feel part of your family. I am without money, yes, but I feel surrounded by...je ne sais quoi. Yes, I feel surrounded by love. But I should be with my family."

Charlotte felt a tug at her heart. She felt moved to go to him, to put her arms around him, to comfort him in his sadness. But she said:

"My Lord, you can do nothing at the moment, only put your trust in God. And when your injuries are fully healed, then you can travel to France. In a few months."

Suddenly the Frenchman raised his voice, which till then had been almost monotone, to a level which seemed like anger.

"A few months? A few months you say? What might have happened to my country, my family in a few months? And I can do nothing – I am of no use either to my family or my country like this! I am failing them!"

He thumped his fist heavily on the table, and his head went down, and he breathed heavily, before raising his face to look at Charlotte again, and said, in a loud undertone: "Besides, mademoiselle, I am selfish. I don't want to leave here. Yet I don't deserve this cocoon I am in."

He held Charlotte's startled gaze, brown meeting dark grey, flashing unspoken messages between them. Then he looked away.

"Excusez-moi, mademoiselle," he said abruptly, and left the room. Charlotte sank her face into her hands.

Despite the manifestation of Francois' mood the previous day, Christmas Day itself was a joyous, bounteous occasion. John Ives had many duties to perform, and services to attend, both on Christmas Eve and Christmas Day, celebrating the birth of Jesus, and on the following Sunday, when he had been invited to preach the sermon at Holy Trinity Church, one of two parish churches in Bungay. Mrs Ives, Charlotte and Francois, walked up the hill on the cold frosty morning together, through the snow, between the high pitched roofs of the shops and homes on either side, their breath as they chatted vaporising in the cold air. The ladies were snug in their long skirts and capes and bonnets, with fur muffs covering their hands. Francois had borrowed an overcoat from Mr Ives, somewhat ill-fitting, but warm. It was only the second time he had been out of the house since he had arrived, and Charlotte was concerned that he would slip on the snow-covered street and injure himself further. But it gave her the excuse to slip her hand through his arm, to give him support.

Standing there beside him, in the packed congregation, singing the celebratory hymns of Jesus' birth, as a pale winter sun heightened the colours and the images in the stain-glassed windows, she felt a contentment she had never felt before, an inner contentment she dared not, then, put into words to anyone. Spending so much time with him, playing for him, learning from him, attending to his injuries, conversing with him, she felt so close to him – and hoped in the depth of her heart that he felt the same, that he was drawing on the close friendship – was it no more than that? – in the same way.

 She was beginning to learn much from him about France and its political history, as well as its art and literature, and passed on what she new about English history. He was fascinated that the church they were now in, worshipping and praising together, had its origins before his country, through the Normans, conquered England in 1066. Now, as they sang, she noticed him looking around, and taking it all in.

And he sensed her watching him, and glanced at her, and smiled; she felt his smile warm her down to her toes in her thick leather boots.

The festive meal on Christmas Day was bounteous. Mrs Honeywood, with a little help from Mrs Ives, had excelled herself, and after Mr Ives had offered thankful grace before the four dined on five courses, an offering of fish being followed by two roast pheasants, with boiled parsnips, cabbage and turnips, washed down with mulled wine. Then followed sweetmeats, and finally Christmas pudding, topped by a sprig of holly, the brandy alight as Mrs Honeywood carried it proudly into the room. A bowl of a variety of fruit – apples, grapes, oranges and bananas – decorated the centre of the festive table, and the diners helped themselves. The men also enjoyed a tankard of ale acquired from the King's Arms almost next door – an alehouse with which the parson was not unfamiliar; and afterwards Mr Ives brought out a bottle of his best port.

The conversation was lively. Francois, having thrown off his melancholy of the previous evening, was in fine form, regaling the party with stories of his time in France, and later in Jersey, and America, and Mr Ives brought stories of his travels – mainly for the benefit of Francois, his wife and daughter having heard most of them several times previously.

It was late in the afternoon before Charlotte and her mother retired, leaving the two men to their port and conversation. The warmth from the yule logs glowing in the inglenook, the subdued light of the flickering candles, the effect of the prolonged feast and the attendant alcohol had left a drowsily relaxed atmosphere to the room. It hung in the folds of the blue velvet curtains which muffled the sound of a biting east wind, in the colourful wall hangings and portraits of ancestors, in Charlotte's Christmas decorations, in the comfortable armchairs of the two men as they settled into them with their glasses in hand.

The Frenchman looked at his host, and raised his glass to him.

"Monsieur, I thank you again for your hospitality – I make no apology for repeating it. I have been here nearly three months now, and not once have you or your wife asked how long I am likely to be staying. I am greatly in your debt, yet I have little opportunity to repay your kindness."

John Ives returned his toast.

"Think nothing of it. You will stay until you are fully recovered from your injuries and have plans as to where you will go when you do leave. We are in no hurry to see you out of the door – your company is pleasing to us, particularly to Charlotte, who we can clearly see is benefitting from your tuition and your company. We are happy to accept that as your payment of debt, though we ask and expect none.

"Clearly you are still suffering pain in your shoulder," he added, as he saw the Frenchman wince as he adjusted his position in his chair, and the strapping holding his arm, which he had replaced after taking it off to dine.

"There is still pain – usually bearable, but sometimes less so. The physician has said lately that it is likely to be six months before it is back to full health and strength, and my damaged ribs trouble me still. But Miss Ives is an excellent nurse, and listening to her playing the piano, and having her company during tuition, is the very elixir I need to aid my recovery."

"She is indeed a beautiful and dutiful daughter – God has blessed us well," her father observed, nodding approvingly to himself. "Monsieur, if it takes six months for you to return to full health, then you will remain here till then."

"Thank you, monsieur." Then a mournfulness clouded his face as he looked into his glass.

"Monsieur, the latest news from France is not good. From the newspapers I have read and the mail that has reached me, my family are in desperate danger. My mother and sisters are currently under arrest by the new regime - some of my relatives have been executed without fair trial. Indeed it seems they were not given full reason for their arrest. My country is in chaos, and it brings great sadness to me. I am moved to return there as soon as possible."

"But what could you do if you did, monsieur? I understand the feelings you have, and your anxiety to protect your family, but in your current state it would be futile for you to return, even if you could. Would you not immediately be arrested and thrown into prison, or worse, yourself, as soon as you were identified? The risk to you would be far greater than the worth of your help to your family.

"My counsel to you would be to remain in this country until some order is arrived at from the chaos. Make your plans in England in preparation for your return, armed with renewed strength and knowledge of the situation to which you will return. We have a saying in this country – 'Discretion is the better part of valour.' It means that often, holding back and weighing up a situation carefully is wiser than charging in when not fully acquainted with the circumstances."

"I thank you for your wise counsel – I know it is well founded. But when my heart is with my oppressed family, and I learn of the brutality in Paris, and my injuries here render me helpless, it beats away in my brain – it is always in my mind. It is difficult to sleep at night."

Francois moved his free hand across his brow and down his face in a gesture of despair. His host left his seat and went to him, put his hand on his shoulder.

"I understand monsieur – it is difficult to be patient in such circumstances, and await the right time. As for sleeping – another glass of this excellent port might help that, for tonight at least."

A flicker of a smile crossed Francois' face.

"Ah, monsieur – now you will try to…how do you say it…drink me sous la table?"

6

T he passing of the old year into the new one, 1796, was marked quietly in the Ives household. A toast was offered for a healthy and fruitful year on the land, and Francois offered his own, for his family in France, and for France herself – that this should be the year in which her troubles and differences were ended and the country should move forward peaceably, in what ever form of regime. Mr Ives said brief prayers along the same lines, both for the year that had gone, and the one which had now arrived.

Francois was in one of his melancholy moods, contributing little to the conversation. Charlotte sensed his mind was on his family, and when they were alone in the withdrawing room she ventured:

"My Lord, I wish that I could somehow lift your spirits, that I could say something to encourage you, to re-assure you. But I am not fully acquainted with the ways of the Revolution, and how life is in Paris, though I know what you have told me. I grieve when you grieve."

"Well you shouldn't," Francois said sullenly but sharply, not lifting his head from its downward position, his eyes dull. And he continued, almost in a monotone: "There is nothing you can do, nothing I can do. Even if I was there, what could I do? I would be in prison myself, or executed.

Perhaps that would be the best thing. The executioner would do me a service by ending my miserable life – my eyes would close for the last time, I would be no more. These feelings of depression I get would be no more. Oui, that would be the best thing for me and everyone else. I am no good to anybody! No one would miss me, and I would be better buried in a wilderness somewhere, covered by nettles and brambles."

His eyes remained fixed on his lap, his head supported by his good arm. Charlotte looked at him, her heart saddened by the words she was hearing. Gently, she stretched her hand across the table, and tenderly caressed the hand beneath his chin. It was something she had not dared to do before.

"I would miss you, my Lord. I would grieve for you most desperately. Don't say these things. Your family needs you, and one day, perhaps this year, you will see them again; and your country – perhaps one day you will find a way of serving the France you love; though when you go from here, I think I will feel the overwhelming sadness that seems to be filling your mind now."

Her hand remained on his, against his face. As she looked at him she caught the reflection of the flickering fire in his eyes. But he remained unmoved for a while, until finally he lifted his head slowly. Moved his arm so that her hand was now in his, and looked into her eyes, though still with no expression on his face.

"Miss Ives... if there was one thing, one person, who could keep me here, keep me sane, lift my mind from the abyss it would be you, my dear Charlotte. You are the...the sparkle on the rippling Seine in springtime, the beauty of the rose window in Notre Dame. Your attention, your care, your music – your presence, nourish me, most of the time. They stay in my mind and help me fight my daemons. But I do not deserve those gifts, or your interest, because in time my melancholy would bring you down too, and that I could not bear."

Charlotte felt her heart beat faster as she heard his words and looked into his eyes, which had quickly resumed their staring, unseeing dullness.

He who had come to mean so much to her, so filled her mind, over the past few weeks, had said that he had similar thoughts of her too! She felt so flattered, so elated at those beautiful words – if only she could find similar phrases to lift the clouds from his mind too. Oh, if they could rise through the air together, like two birds, through the clouds and into the blue sunlit sky above...

But after a while Francois parted their hands, and stood up, stiffly.

"Mademoiselle, I am tired – I must retire, though my thoughts will not allow me much sleep. Goodnight."

Charlotte suddenly felt desolate, and she too stood up.

"Goodnight, my Lord."

And then, with another surge or courage, she added, brightly:

"Tomorrow is the first day of the year, and I have noticed that you are beginning to walk a little easier. I will take you for a walk outside – not too far, just to the Staithe and back?"

Francois looked back, non-committally.

"Peut-etre," he murmured.

The next day they did go for a walk, slowly, along the river bank, and down to the Staithe just beyond the end of the garden and the long carriage path through it which was the entrance to the property. It was cold and crisp, with a winter sun, and the river had its dark winter aura too, running high and fast on its journey. At the Staithe, Bungay's terminus for the sailing wherries plying their trade to and from the port of Yarmouth 20 miles away, they watched the vessels unloading their cargoes of grain or hemp or coal, or taking on hides from the tanneries which lined the river in parts of the town. The river trade had brought Bungay prosperity ands led to businesses being set up to offer work and wages to inhabitants. That day, many men were busy going about the many tasks associated with the shipping.

"Do you not think there is a beauty about the wherries, with their tall sails and smooth, sultry movements over the water?" asked Charlotte as they watched the activity.

"Mmm, not only the wherries mademoiselle, but the entire tableau – the sails, the river, the fields beside, the sounds and the smell of the water, the trees touching the banks. It reminds me of the Seine and Paris - though of course there are many more buildings along the banks, and you have Notre Dame Cathedral overlooking it. Yes, but here St Mary's Church is not so different!"

"Not so widely known my, Lord, but perhaps it is our Notre Dame – it dominates our town and can be clearly seen when travellers approach from any direction."

"Mademoiselle – do you think we should climb on to one of those wherries and ask the captain to sail us to France, and down the Seine to Paris? He would be able to sell his cargo there. It would be a great adventure, and I would take you to all the best parts of that beautiful city! And I will become emperor of France and call an end to the Revolution with one sweep of my arm!"

Charlotte laughed a gay laugh which Francois took up, and they bantered about what else they would do on such an adventure. Francois was a different man that morning, and Charlotte was so happy to see it – gone was the morose dullness of old year's night, and in its place the dashing, flamboyant Frenchman she had come to know and love...

"...Love?"

She was almost startled by her own idle thought. What did it mean? In her naïve adolescent innocence it had meant a word which described the bond between mother and

71

daughter, father and son – perhaps even the friendship between close friends of the same gender.

Now had that natural attraction she had sensed when he came into their autumn home, and passed through the phases of friendship and closeness and compassion, passed the final thresh-hold and become...love?

The word struck at her heart. But had he not the night before held her hand, not for the first time – and for the first time also called her "my dear?"

And suddenly, standing there beside the complex and mysterious man in the exhilaration of a bright Suffolk winter's day, came the realisation that the growing feelings within her of emotion and desire amounted to the love of a woman for a man.

In her intimate moments as she lay in bed she convinced herself that Francois had the same feelings as her – that the magnet between them was now more than the close friendship that came through her playing for him, tending to his injuries, and he tutoring her in French and Italian literature, and Latin. She could not sleep for thinking about the things he had said, the way he had been, analysing them closely and concluding that, taken together, they did convey, tacitly, his love for her. She clasped her arms around herself and imagined it was his arms who were around her, holding her closely, whispering his ardent messages to her.

"He cannot at the moment…, no, because of his injuries. But when he has fully recovered he will, I know he will, and I will tell him I love him! Oh, beautiful man."

And she prayed again, earnestly, as she had done each night for a long while, that his injuries would heal quickly, and that the troubles in his mind would disappear so that never again would he be plunged into the depths of despair which engulfed him from time to time, and made him seem a different person.

When Samuel called a week later, as he had promised, to escort her to Bible study class, Charlotte's instinctive feeling was one of annoyance, and a two-fold guilt – on the one hand that she did not want to go despite his attentiveness, and on the other that to walk out with another man would be betraying the feelings she felt for Francois, and that she was sure he reciprocated. But she knew she had a duty to go with him.

"Good evening, Samuel. Thank you for calling – it is pleasing to have someone to walk to class with rather than going on my own. And we can discuss tonight's topic on the way there and on the way back."

The naval man beamed a smile at her which showed his pleasure in accompanying such a beautiful young woman. His time away from home in exclusively male company gave him little opportunity to mix socially with the opposite sex, and here was someone he had felt an immediate rapport with when he first met her. She returned his gaze in welcome.

Bible study proved as stimulating for her as it always was – she enjoyed the debate on the wider messages contained in the Books of the old Testament, or the psalms, or the gospels of the New Testament, and that evening the class concentrated on Luke's version of the birth of Jesus.

On the walk back to the parsonage she and Samuel continued the discussion animatedly for a while, finding that their views largely concurred. Then Charlotte fell silent for a while, fighting her innate shyness to ask him something that had been in her mind for some days, and which she felt he might be able to advise her on. Finally, she found the courage to ask tentatively:

"Samuel, forgive me for asking…I would welcome your advice on a matter which…it is to do with age…I hope you won't mind me asking but…is it proper for someone to have feelings for someone who is much older than they are – ten or fifteen years older – just for example of course."

The last phrases came out in a hurry, and Charlotte was grateful that the cold night air had already coloured her cheeks as she felt herself blush deeply.

Samuel looked at her, slightly startled at the sudden question. He was thoughtful for a moment, composing his answer, and then replied:

"There are those who would say that the closer the ages of two people, the better it is for a relationship. But I feel what is more important than age is how well the two people in question relate to each other – how they see each other as a friend, or a...well, as a person they might be looking to spend their whole life with. Having the same outlook on subjects such as...religion, or...or learning, or...entertaining house guests."

Charlotte stopped, and turned towards Samuel, at the top of the hill leading down to her home.

"So...if those feelings...real feelings, I mean to say, are the same for both people, they can make up the gap there would be in life's experiences, which the younger of the two would not have had?"

"Yes. The older of the two, if he has the right feelings of caring, would help in the bridging of the gap. Besides," Samuel added, "an age difference of ten years between two people aged, for example, 15 and 25, would not seem nearly so great as they moved to later life. I think there is a phrase I have heard cook, at the Lodge, say, 'They'll grow together.'"

"So you don't think it would be wrong for two people of those different ages to have those feelings?"

"No, I don't think so Charlotte. I'm sure in particular cases...say if it was two people we knew, that...well..."

But his faltering finish enabled Charlotte to say, buoyantly: "Thank you Samuel, thank you – I knew you would advise me well."

Samuel waited for a few moments, hoping Charlotte would say more. But instead she resumed the walk down the hill, between the tall houses and inns on either side, and as he followed eventually he said:

"Charlotte, you only have to ask my advice on anything – I will always be eager to help. Now may I ask you something?"

"Of course, Samuel."

It had been in his mind all evening, and the turn of the conversation gave him the courage to put the invitation to her. As they approached the parsonage doorstep, he asked:

"Charlotte, I have very much enjoyed your company this evening. I…in two days time I have to return to my ship, and I expect to be away for six months. I wonder if – would you do me the great honour of accompanying me to the summer ball to which my parents and I have been invited at Ditchingham Hall. I have been given the opportunity to be accompanied and I would be so grateful if you would be my consort."

Charlotte, her face still glowing from the conversation, had not expected the sudden proposition. Three months ago she would have glowed with excitement at such an invitation, which would have set her heart fluttering and left her counting the days until Samuel's return, and planning, with the help of her Mama, what she should wear for such an occasion. But in the intervening time Francois had come into her life, courted her (at least in her own mind), and won her heart.

Thoughts flew through her mind: she could not betray Francois' feelings for her by accepting the invitation, for surely it would not be long before the Frenchman openly declared his affection for her, and she, her's for him. But Samuel had been kind and attentive to her, and it was clear from his manner that he would be greatly disappointed if she declined. Oh, why did fate put such a decision in front of her? Why could it not have been Francois who had asked her to the ball? She could think of nothing more heavenly than dancing in his arms all through the night.

Her upbringing had taught her tact and politeness, and after a brief pause she replied.

"Thank you Samuel – that is an offer I could not lightly decline. But the summer is some time ahead, and I feel I have a duty to continue to care for our French guest, who is recovering only slowly from his injuries. How long he will continue to need my attention I don't know – but, do you need an answer immediately? Could I let you know nearer the time whether I am able to accept the invitation? I could send a note to your parents."

"Yes, of course. I can wait as long as you like. I have no plans to ask anyone else, and I pray that you will be able to accept. Thank you for your company this evening. Good night, Charlotte."

And he smiled his affectionate smile at her as she said, "Goodnight, Samuel," and watched him leave through the gate.

Samuel's elation at the way the conversation had gone put a spring in his stride as he made his way over the hump-backed bridge into Ditchingham, convinced that Charlotte's feelings for him matched the fondness he had for her.

Charlotte went indoors, also elated at the outcome of her question to Samuel.

Winter in Suffolk that year was long and cold, with little opportunity for Charlotte to encourage Francois to walk out with her as part of his convalescence. Snow covered the garden for several weeks, and ice formed even at the sides of the gently flowing Waveney. The birds which frequented the garden fluffed their feathers for warmth and were grateful for the scraps which Mrs Honeywood put out on the lawn for them each day. The English maiden and the Frenchman would stand at the window now and then and watch them gather in great numbers to take advantage of the treats.

In the music room, the blazing logs in the inglenook provided a cosy contrast as, under the patient tuition of Francois, Charlotte made good progress on her French, and practised new pieces on the piano to play for him – more Bach, Beethoven and Mozart. The two spent much of the time together – time treasured by Charlotte who, admitting her love to Francois to herself, constantly sought signs that it was reciprocated. In his cheerful moments there were many – it became a habit for him, each time she had finished playing for him, to take her hand and kiss it tenderly, and praise her skill, and she would curtsey and say, "Thank you, my Lord."

Francois found the title quaint, and he smiled at it as they held each others eyes, and read the messages in them. That he was growing ever more fond of her there was no doubt – in his room on his own he would muse that he was back in his beloved Brittany, walking with her there, giving her a conducted tour of the castle at Combourg, taking her to St Malo, the town of his birth, with Charlotte speaking French fluently. He thought of what it would be like introducing her to the French aristocracy, and taking her to the grand social gatherings and sumptuous banquets.

But in his heart, he knew none of those things were possible. All he could do, as part of his French lessons for her, was describe French life, French customs, French geography to her, and enjoy her eager re-action to it.

He told her, too of the tumult and upheaval in his country the revolution had brought – the ousting of the royal regime and the efforts to introduce a republican establishment; of the terror of the situation, particularly in Paris, of the executions and imprisonments. The newspapers brought reports of the frequently changing situation, and the atrocities – of the imprisonment of his own family, including his mother, the execution of his brother for no good reason, it seemed to him. On his own, he would weep for his family and his country, and when his daemons of depression came, he would curse his life, and the way he had fled France, and convince himself that execution would be a deserving punishment for him. On one occasion he wound a shirt into a short rope, and put it round his neck, imagining himself on the gallows as the tricoteuses worked away as they watched.

But in the morning he would go down to breakfast, and see Charlotte in her burgeoning beauty, and his spirits would be lifted.

The pupils who came to the house for tuition in the upstairs room Mr Ives has set aside for Francois were, on the whole, less committed to learning than Charlotte, but he tried to convey to them, too, a feeling of the divisions in France and descriptions of the way it had affected normal life.

It was often a topic of conversation during the evening meal. Mr Ives would have forthright views on what should be done to bring peace in France and Francois would temper them with his assessment and the practicalities. Charlotte and her mother would join in too, before withdrawing at the end of the meal to leave the gentlemen to continue their discussions over porter.

Over the course of the weeks and months, the observations of Mr and Mrs Ives made it clear to them that the Frenchman's presence had a greatly beneficial effect on their daughter – her confidence had grown, she was far less shy than she was, she was learning the art of good conversation along with her academic learning, and from her rapport and animated demeanour in his company made them feel sure there was a mutual attraction between them.

"My dear, Charlotte's social progress since our guest arrived has been remarkable, and I would venture to say, not co-incidental," Mr Ives said one evening, when Francois was in his room and Charlotte at Bible study. "He has had the most beneficial effect on her."

"That is my intuition as a mother, John. They get on so well, and are so attentive to each other, and she does seem to be the one who can coax him out of his frequent depressions."

"Ah, those – every time there is bad news from France he becomes melancholy and morbid. It is a worrying trait, I have to say. But that is something he can only sort out for himself – he needs to get back home to his family, and to where he may be able to have some influence. After all he is a member of their aristocracy – if that still survives over there after all that has gone on."

Mrs Ives sighed. "It seems as if he has lost much of his family in the uprising – and if the way of life he knew there has gone too, there seems little point in his returning…"

"A man has got to do what he can for his country – if he wants to make a difference he needs to be there," her husband interrupted.

"Let me finish John, please...What I was going to say is that it is clear Charlotte will miss him terribly when he has gone – she will be beside herself. She has developed a great feeling for him – you may not observe it, but a mother can tell. Not to put too fine a point on it, I believe she is falling in love with him, and there is no doubt he has feelings for her too."

"Love? Would you got that far, my dear? Yes, they do get on very well together and she has responded well to his tuition but...the time will come when he must depart, and that will be that."

"Yes, the time will come, though the physician has been concerned about infection in his wound, and the break has not healed as quickly as hoped, I understand. But I also observe that it is now improving to his satisfaction. But does he need to return to France – what is there to go back to?"

Mr Ives looked as his wife, with her eyes bright and face earnest in the candlelight.

"My feeling is that he will want to return when he is well enough. Besides, he has been a good house guest and little trouble, but nevertheless feels he is outstaying his welcome. What are you suggesting – that we ask him to stay indefinitely?"

Mrs Ives lowered her gaze. "Would that be such an impossibility? He has become almost part of the family over the past....how long is it?... It must be five months."

"My dear, it has not escaped my notice that you too have developed an affection for Francois – perhaps as the son we never had."

Both fell silent and thoughtful at the remark. They had wanted a son, and brother for Charlotte, but that situation had not materialised and Mrs Ives' physician had told her that it was now unlikely, and probably inadvisable, and they shared a mutual sadness at that. It reflected in Mrs Ives face when she looked up.

"Do you not feel it too, John? That when he goes it will leave a void for all of us, not just Charlotte? He could never be the son we wanted so much...but perhaps...a son-in-law?"

"You're suggesting we offer him Charlotte's hand in marriage? There is quite a gap in age is there not? And from what Francois has told me of his earlier life, he is very much a man of the world, if I can put it that way."

"I've said I believe they are falling in love. Age need not be a barrier."

"I'm not sure about marriage. Even if there was not an age difference, and despite the clear affection there is between them, I'm not sure I would be happy with him as Charlotte's husband. I have misgivings. Anyway, any approach would have to come from him – he would have to make his views known to me."

"Could you not speak to him John, to get an indication of his feelings?"

"No, Sarah, no. That is not the way it should be done. Besides, we are only guessing at Charlotte's feelings – we don't know them for certain. Has she spoken to you about this?"

"John, I'm her mother. I'm concerned about the affect it will have on her when he leaves. But you are her father – I must leave it to you."

7

I t was April. Winter had melted away, March had passed relatively calmly, save for some chill winds from the east which had brought back memories, passed down from grandparents and great-grandparents, of the great fire which had devastated the town of Bungay a little over 100 years before, in 1688. That had been a cold March day, with a bitter east wind, the sages of the town would say, which burned all but a handful of homes and factories and shops and pubs in Bungay and left hundreds of people homeless. Many had departed to Norwich or Yarmouth, to find accommodation, never to return. But with the help of a petition to the King and diligence on the part of the church, and the Town Reeve and the Town Trust, Bungay had recovered and been rebuilt, with substantial houses replacing those, mainly of timber and thatch and wattle and daub, that had been destroyed, and made it a more affluent town than it had been before the fire, boosted by the growing river trade and the tanneries along the river frontage. Many of those running the town acknowledged that the great fire had been a blessing in disguise, ridding Bungay of many poor tenements and ill-kept homes and leading to many improvements in the re-building process.

But this spring the breeze was mild and gentle, the air unusually warm for April, as Charlotte and Francois stepped outside the front door of the parsonage. Apart from the slow walk through the front garden to the Staithe earlier in the year Francois has barely been outside. But the lotions and balms the physician had treated his infected leg wound with had finally done their work, the inflammation had cooled and subsided, and that morning, he had had the sling removed from his injured arm and shoulder. There was great stiffness in it, but the physician was satisfied that the break had healed and he could begin to use the limb with care. Now, by way of celebrating that significant progress, Charlotte had suggested they go out for a walk – and Francois had readily agreed. Progress was slow, particularly up the hill towards the Market Cross and then the Butter Cross, but his confidence grew as the sun warmed them, and they walked on, past St Mary's Church, and out on to the road to Ilketshall St Margaret. The road surface was uneven and Charlotte took care to guide Francois away from the ruts created by the carriages and coaches.

"We must not venture too far today, my Lord, but I will see that you walk regularly from now on when the weather is favourable," Charlotte said to her consort. "The physician says it is important to exercise and enjoy the air, and I can show you some of my favourite places."

"Thank you, mademoiselle, you look after me so well, so attentively." He looked ahead to where the road sloped upwards steadily towards St Margaret's. "But I feel I have walked far enough for today – my legs are not yet used to it. How can I thank you for your continued kindness?"

"You don't need to thank me, my Lord – you do so much for me, with my studies, and our conversations. I am the one who gains."

"Ah, one moment, mademoiselle."

In the ditch beside the road, nestling at the foot of an oak tree where its roots were exposed, he had spotted a clump of primroses, their cheerful faces pointing to the sun, and he went towards them and reached out.

"My Lord, be careful! You re not yet strong enough to step down there!"

But, stooping shakily and stretching to the limit of his good arm, Francois managed to pick three or four of the flowers, and a leaf, and bring them back to the roadside.

"There mademoiselle – for now that is the only gift I can give you, to thank you: the flowers of spring. May the beauty of your springtime never leave your face."

And the Frenchman folded his hand around Charlotte's as he gave them to her, and looked at her tenderly as she returned his smile and put her other hand around his. There was a hint of emotion in her voice as she said:

"Thank you, my Lord – but don't say, 'the only gift.' These flowers are beautiful, and I will treasure them because they are from you!"

Charlotte's eyes were sparkling. The two were standing very close, their hands still enfolded around the primroses, beside the oak tree whose leaf buds were promising imminently to blossom, beside that quiet Suffolk road beneath a wide blue Suffolk sky. Both seemed to be waiting for the other to speak.

"Charlotte..." Francois began.

"Yes, my Lord!" Charlotte's tone betrayed her expectant eagerness.

"Charlotte, I...Since I came to Bungay...my life...you..."

He seemed to be on the verge of pouring out his feelings, only to lose the courage. He drew a deep breath, before ending, almost disconsolately:

"I wish I was able to do much more for you."

The parson's daughter felt as if a spell had been broken, that a wish long awaited to be fulfilled had been dashed. Their hands parted, but she held on firmly to the primroses.

"My Lord, I have made you over tired. We will walk home now."

That evening, in the privacy of her bedchamber, she took one of the primroses and pressed it carefully between the pages of a book in which she kept the notes of tuition and work details that Francois had given her periodically. The others she placed in a vase on her dressing table, where she could see them as she lay down to sleep.

Francois continued to improve steadily over the next few weeks, and the walks Charlotte enjoyed with him became longer. They would walk to Ditchingham, or to Earsham, a village on the western side of Bungay, and also to Bungay Common, a short distance away through Back Street. Cattle and donkeys grazed there, and horses were pastured there too following their heavy day's work. Always they would talk about nature, and the flowers they saw, and the birds that sang, or about France, the studies Charlotte was undergoing – sometimes seriously, sometimes light-heartedly, sometimes animatedly, as close companions do.

On other occasions though, melancholy would again cloud Francois' countenance and he would fall silent, and seem to be unaware of Charlotte, lost in his own world. She would try to coax his thoughts form him, but he would be largely unresponsive, replying with a grunt or an unintelligible mutter. Occasionally he would talk about his family, and his anxiety for them, and she knew his heart was back in France with them.

John and Sarah Ives could see how radiantly happy their daughter was, and how she was often able to lift Francois from his depressive moods more quickly than they could. Her learning was progressing in leaps and bounds under him, her French was rapidly improving, and there was a new impetus, a new touch, to her piano playing – it was as if it was conveying subtle words of love to Francois as he stood by, and watched and listened.

Wherever they were walking, whatever they did, whenever they talked, Charlotte tried to read into Francois's phrases, or his movement, or demeanour, what his innermost feelings might be for her. Sometimes she felt he was trying to express them to her, but then he would hold back, and her expectancy would be frustrated again.

But most of all she just wanted him to stay in Bungay forever, and be there with her, in their family.

In early May the Frenchman was walking almost normally, and his arm and shoulder had gained full movement and increased in strength. He and Charlotte walked the full length of the river bank around the wide open common, which covered 400 acres of green pasture.

On one such walk, she skipped into an area of early buttercups, picked one of the bright yellow flowers and took it to Francois.

"My lord, let me see if you like butter! They say if the colour of the cup reflects under your chin, you like butter. Let me try – let me try, please!"

The Frenchman, amused, put his head back slightly, and Charlotte stepped close to him and put the flower under his chin.

"It is reflecting yellow on your skin my Lord! You do like butter!" she cried animatedly.

"I have always liked butter, my dear Charlotte," the Frenchman said with a smile. "Now let me see if you like it."

Charlotte put her hands behind her back and raised her chin. "Aha, you like butter more than the farmer who makes it!" he said, and laughed as she clutched the flower back. Their faces were close, almost touching. Suddenly they were silent, still, gazing into the pupils of the other's eyes, seeking a response, a sign of the feelings welling up inside them, each wanting to touch the others lips, but not being sure, not being certain of the re-action, and not wanting the moment to pass...

On another occasion they walked as beasts grazed in the warm sunshine, men came and went fetching their animals, or returning them to graze; others busied themselves cutting furze, or gathered shingle from the higher part of area. The cuckoo called, and skylarks soared and sang their symphonies.

Buttercups dotted the green meadow with bright yellow buttons, and beside the river the hawthorn was heavy with may blossom.

"Isn't it beautiful, my Lord?" said Charlotte, as they strolled. "See how the white blossom weights the branches so they are almost touching the surface of the river, as if the petals are taking a refreshing drink from the water."

The two stopped to admire the full-petalled whiteness of the blossom on the opposite bank at the foot of the steep hills which formed the side of the valley there. A vestige of the vineyards which once covered south-facing slopes as recently as a hundred years ago still remained, though now wild and uncultivated, and interspersed with oak, beech and elm trees which had begun to establish their authority there.

"The maiden blossom of the May gently kisses its attendant young stream, just as the lips of two lovers touch for the first time," Francois mused in French. Charlotte tentatively translated his words out loud.

"The young girl...the flower of May, lightly kisses the...the nearby river, as the...lips of two people in love touch for the first time."

"Oui! Bravo! That is almost perfect."

Charlotte, her white ankle length dress and bonnet matching the mayflowers, looked again into the eyes of her tousle-haired companion standing close to her.

"My Lord, no one has ever touched my lips with theirs. Will you...show me?"

She could not believe her sudden boldness, such forwardness unbecoming of a parson's daughter. Perhaps it was the idyll which surrounded them at that moment, the warm sun, the sky, the birdsong, the whole rustic scene in which they were a dot beside the river in the wide acres of the common, where the birds sang and the cattle occasionally lowed. But she kept her composure and held his eyes.

The Frenchman said nothing. Quietly, he took her hands in his, moved close to her, and brushed his lips lightly against hers. Charlotte's eyes closed as she savoured that exquisite moment of which she had dreamt so often over the past few months.

As her eyes remained closed Francois kissed her again, this time more firmly, and held his lips there for a few seconds before withdrawing them.

For a moment Charlotte thought she would swoon with joy. She could feel the warmth of this man so close to her, scent his body, his hair. She wanted him to enfold her in his arms and hold her there. She wanted time to stand still.

When finally she opened her eyes she saw his, with a new softness to them, still smiling. Their hands were still in each other's.

"My Lord...thank you...thank you," she managed to murmur.

"My dear Charlotte, thank you for the invitation to kiss you," he said softly. Then he straightened up.

"Now I think we should continue our walk," he said.

A spell, broken once more – but for Charlotte the glow of that moment remained through the day and long into the evening.

"Charlotte! A letter has arrived for you!"

Her mother entered the withdrawing room as she called her, and handed her the white envelope with red seal. Charlotte looked up from the book she was reading with a surprised look on her face.

"A letter? For me? Who could have sent it?"

"I have no idea! I couldn't recognise the seal. Open it and see."

Sarah hovered, interested in what the letter would reveal, as Charlotte broke the seal and unfolded the stiff white paper – at the top of which she saw the emblem of the Royal Navy.

My Dear Charlotte, she read,

My ship at this moment has docked at Portsmouth for two days before putting to sea again with Admiral Nelson's fleet. It did not leave me time to visit my parents, or to visit you, but I have time to write to you – something I have been meaning to do for some time, to ask if you have an answer to my invitation to you to accompany me to the summer ball. I do hope you will be able to accept – it would make me very proud if you would be my consort for such an occasion.

I have been thinking too about our last conversation before I left to rejoin my ship after Christmas, in which you asked about the difference in age between us. The more I think about it, dear Charlotte, the more I come to the conclusion that it matters not a jot, if our feelings for each other are good and true – as mine are most certainly for you. I do so admire you for the way you raised the matter so discreetly and maturely. I can only apologise for the fact that I was so slow in understanding the full implication of your question – now I realise you were referring to the age difference between us.

I have always had strong feelings for you Charlotte, since our first meeting at Bible study – now you are often in my

94

thoughts, and I look forward with great impatience to the time I can visit my home, and you, again, and take you to the ball. I know it will be a memorable occasion, and I do hope that in the ensuing months we can attend other occasions, as a couple, and explore the countryside together.

The letter continued with news of the latest manoeuvres of Nelson's fleet and what daily life was like on board ship. And it ended:

Now I must return to my duties, dear Charlotte, with you in my thoughts. That helps me to ensure the privations of naval life, that even officers must suffer to some extent, are easier to bear. I look forward fervently to seeing you in July.
With every affection,
Yours, Samuel

And underneath was added: Captain Samuel Sutton, HMS Martin, Portsmouth.

"Well, dear, are you going to tell me who is writing to you?" There was gentle impatience in her mother's voice.
"It's from Samuel – Samuel Sutton. He is asking if I have an answer to his invitation to the summer ball. His ship is at Portsmouth," Charlotte replied, vacantly, her mind racing at

what she had read. How could Samuel have got such an inaccurate impression from her question? How could he have read so much into it?

"Well, you will go, I'm sure. Papa and I are expecting an invitation to the ball. We will go together."

"No Mama – I don't want to go. Not with Samuel. I must write a letter to him letting him know I am not interested. I should have told him straight away!" This time there was agitation in her voice.

"It would lack good manners to turn such an invitation down without good reason, my dear." She paused before adding, knowingly:

"Unless, of course, there is someone else you would rather go with?"

Charlotte looked at her mother's inquiring expression, but said nothing, so Sarah added:

"Francois will probably no longer be her in July, my dear."

Her daughter stood up abruptly, her face contorting at the suggestion.

"Mama, don't say that! Don't! He will be here, I know he will! I love him you see, and he...he loves me!"

And she turned, and ran out of the room and up the stairs to her bedchamber, where she threw herself on the bed and buried her face in the pillow, confused and upset, not knowing immediately how to confront the prospect of two suitors vying for her affections – one who had now put his feelings in writing, and the other who in every way but that had been indicating his love for her. But the man she loved was the latter – Francois, not Samuel, handsome though he was, and kind and considerate, and making his feelings known directly.

As she calmed down and tried to think rationally she realised how it was that Samuel had misunderstood her inquiry about age – he would not have known that Francois was in her mind, and Samuel, after all, was similarly several years older than her, and clearly felt that was what she had been referring to. Charlotte chastised herself for her lack of discernment in the way she had raised the subject.

And her heart sank as another thought raced into her mind – if Samuel had misinterpreted her question so mistakenly, had she misinterpreted signs she had felt indicated Francois' attraction to her? It was an intolerable notion that she tried to put aside has quickly as it had arisen, but it obstinately continued to lurk in the recesses of her mind.

Before going to bed that night she prayed to God for guidance in her dilemma, and beseeched him to convey her love to Francois and move him to stay in Bungay with her forever.

Next morning, before going down to breakfast, she sat at her dressing table and wrote a letter:

My Dear Samuel,

Thank you for your letter, which was so unexpected, and thank you again for your kind invitation to accompany you to the summer ball, and for making known your feelings towards me – they are most flattering, and undeserved.

Samuel, I fear there has been a misunderstanding, over my inquiry, when last we met, and I apologise for my lack of foresight in putting it to you when I should have anticipated how you might receive it. From your letter, I know how hurt you will feel at this reply, but I do not want to deceive you. You see, when I asked you about the matter of difference in two people's ages I had in mind Francois, who as you know has been living here while recovering from injuries in a fall from his horse. We have become very close – I know he has deep feelings for me, and over the past months I realise I have fallen in love with him. I earnestly hope he will not return to France when he is fully recovered but will stay here in Bungay, with me. What the future holds I cannot tell at this moment.

I am so sorry Samuel – I know the chagrin this will cause to you, and I will continue to value your friendship and advice, and I hope we will be able to meet socially in the future.

In view of this, I feel it would be wrong of me to accept your invitation to the summer ball. I know that will greatly disappoint you, and in other circumstances I would have been pleased to accept. I do hope you will understand, and that you will find someone else to escort to the ball.

I do hope you will find it in your heart to forgive my naivety in this matter.

Yours ever,

Charlotte

She sealed it with the Ives' family seal, took it downstairs and asked Maria, as soon as she had finished her kitchen duties, to take it to the Three Tuns coaching inn at the top of Bridge Street hill to be put on the mail coach to London and from there to Portsmouth. Maria looked at her quizzically as she accepted the order. At breakfast she told her parents what she had done. Her father addressed her sternly.

"Charlotte, why did you not ask our advice before writing such a letter? Captain Sutton is highly though of in the Navy and from what I learn is likely to be elevated to higher commands. He would be a perfect suitor for you – yet you seem to think a penniless Frenchman who seems to have forsaken his country is the one you should give your allegiance to. What future is there in that?"

As Charlotte nervously picked at her breakfast plate her mother added:

"Your father is right, my dear. We know your affection for Francois – you have made that clear, and we have observed it, and his attraction to you. But his future is at best uncertain, while Captain Sutton comes from an eminent local family and is destined to reach the topmost rung of the King's Navy. He could give you a secure life."

"Papa. Mama – please don't scold me! I am greatly saddened at rejecting Samuel's invitation, but what sort of life is there for a Naval officer's wife while he is constantly away for long periods? And I feel nothing for him, apart from friendship. Francois has become part of me – he shares the same interests in literature, music, our countries. He stimulates me, excites me, moves me. I want to be with him, and I believe he wants to be with me. He loves me! Mama you have seen how he is – you approve, don't you?" she ended appealingly.

Sarah glanced at her husband, as if seeking approval for what she was about to say, before addressing her daughter again.

"Charlotte, your father and I have discussed the attraction there clearly is between you and Francois. We are pleased at the way he has tutored you, and given you confidence, nurtured your eagerness to learn. If he was to stay in this country we would be delighted. But your father is right – Francois may be from an aristocratic family but they have been scattered by the revolution in France and as far as we can see he has little to fall back on. Samuel would be able to provide you with a much more comfortable and assured future."

"And that, my dear, is much more important than matters of the heart, though at your age you will find that difficult to understand," her father added by way of emphasis.

Charlotte was close to tears, but managed to speak coherently in a breaking voice.

"I know you are advising me for the best, but I couldn't forsake Francois – I know he will stay, if you ask him. And in time he would take me to France, to meet what is left of his family. He just...he fills my heart. Mama, you must have felt that at my age, you must understand! That is why I have written to Samuel – it would be so unfair of me to encourage him when I have these feelings for Francois."

"Well, that is honest – that at least in your favour," said her father.

"Papa, I have prayed for guidance on what I should do. You always tell me that earnest praying will help when I am in trouble. It is prayers and God's guidance that led me to write the letter to Samuel – now you seem to be chiding me for it."

Tears began to spill from Charlotte's dark eyes, and her father got up and put his hands on her shoulders comfortingly.

"Reading the answers God gives to our prayers can be difficult – for all of us. The real answers are not always so obvious – perhaps we still await them. You should have consulted us before you wrote the letter, but it is written and that is that. As for Francois, he will make his own decisions when he feels the time is right. But for my part I still have reservations about the man."

Next morning, Maria arrived at the parsonage and let herself into the kitchen to begin preparations for the day, tidying the dresser, reviving the oven fire, assembling crockery and cooking utensils for breakfast. As she picked up a pile of towels from the scrubbed work table they brushed a folded paper underneath on to the floor. As soon as she saw it she realised what it was and gasped in annoyance with herself.

"Miss Charlotte's letter! I should have taken it to the coach! There is not another one until next week. I will be dismissed for my forgetfulness!"

In her panic Maria picked up the letter, opened the oven fire door, and threw the letter into the flames, which flared up immediately as they devoured the wax of the seal. In seconds the letter had disappeared.

"No one will know. It probably wouldn't have got to Portsmouth anyway and...and if it did his ship would've sailed," she tried to convince herself. "Anyway," her mind continued, "she's got that attractive Frenchman. I've seen 'em holding hands. He's so lovely. I wish he was mine. I could run away with him any day."

The meal had been enjoyable, and the conversation light and witty. Francois had entertained his host with stories of some of his students he had been teaching in the upstairs room, and of his meetings when translating French manuscripts at Beccles before his fall. But as Charlotte sat listening and enjoying the conversation, and joining in when she could, she sensed an unease behind Francois's light-heartedness.

It was two days after she had written her letter to Samuel, and she soon discovered the reason.

"Monsieur, my colleagues at Beccles are keen for you to resume your translations for them, and you seem to be close to a full recovery from your distressing injuries. Perhaps you would accompany me there next week, to carry on the work, which I know they are keen to see concluded."

The Frenchman looked at him, his face serious for the first time that evening, and glanced at Charlotte and Sarah before replying.

"Ah, Monsieur – I'm afraid that is not possible. You are correct when you say I am well recovered from my injuries, thanks to the care of you, Mrs Ives and Charlotte. I will be forever grateful for your attention. But because of that..." he looked at Charlotte as he spoke, as if to read her reaction to what he was about to say,"...because of that, I feel it is time for me to depart, to return to London, and eventually to France."

An audible intake of breath from Charlotte broke the momentary stunned silence that followed that remark, and a look of desolation clouded her countenance.

"But Monsieur…" Mrs Ives began to say.

"Madame, I must no longer take advantage of your hospitality which has been unfailing for so long. Nowhere that I have been have I received such care and friendship from anyone than that I have received in this house. I will always remember with fondness my time here. But I have had a letter from friends in London, where I can stay for a while. I will leave in one week, if that is acceptable to you – and to you Charlotte. I can finalise your studies in the next few days…"

"My Lord, I…Please don't go – you must not. I couldn't…"

But Charlotte, shaking with distress at the sudden disclosure, could not finish what she was saying. She stood up and ran out of the room. Her mother, stood up and said, pleadingly to Francois:

"Monsieur, you do not need to leave," and followed her out of the room.

Francois sunk his head into his hands, and then got up and walked to the other side of the room, concerned at the upset he had caused.

"Charlotte will miss you, Francois, more than I realised. We will all miss you. I have greatly enjoyed your company, your wit, your conversation. But I understand that you feel it is time to move on. Just remember that if things do not go well in London, you will be welcome to return here."

"Merci, Monsieur. I am most grateful. I am sorry to cause such chagrin to your most beautiful daughter. I have become greatly attached to her – in some ways we share the same dreams and hopes, and in another time and in other circumstances, perhaps…but that is not possible. She has helped to lift me from my depressions when nothing else could."

"What plans have you once you are in London?"

"I have no firm plans – I will be guided by destiny. But I have somewhere to stay and friends who will find me employment, and I will resume the writing which I am now able to do, now that I have two free hands. And I hope I will return to France when my beloved country is settled once more, and when it is reasonably safe to do so."

He hesitated, and then said: "Should I go to Charlotte?"

"No. My wife will attend to her. She is an emotional young lady. Having you here has given her a focus and the thought of your departure is upsetting. Leave it till the morning."

Deep in her heart, Charlotte had known that this man who came suddenly into her life and had given it such joy and meaning, could leave just as suddenly. She had tried to rationalise her feelings, to put them in perspective – even to tell herself she did not love him as she thought. But the time between his arrival and that moment had filled her with feelings which she had never known before, and she had convinced herself that Francois shared and returned those feelings too. As she lay there on her bed, once again distraught and sobbing, she could not get them out of her mind.

"They are real – they are! I'm here, feeling them. It's not a dream – he's not a dream. He's here, in Bungay, in our house, living here, part of my life that I cannot bear to lose! How can I make him change his mind, make him stay...make him hold me in his arms? I want that so much and I know he does too. My Lord, don't go, don't leave – please, please don't go now!"

Charlotte heard the door open, and she sat up immediately. Through her tears she hoped to see Francois – but it was her mother, and she lay back on the bed again, trying to stem the tears with her lace handkerchief. Her mother sat beside her as she lay there, and put an arm around her.

"Charlotte, my dear, I know what your heart is feeling at this moment, how it is aching but...try not to be so distressed. Try to understand that Francois needs to go, to return to his country, and..."

"I have tried, Mama, I am trying. I have told myself that I am being selfish in wanting him to stay here, and make his life here, with me. Every night in my prayers I ask for guidance, every night I pray for Francois and his family, and for his country to be at peace and harmony with its people. I ask God for the strength and courage to understand that, but I'm not strong enough to see my life ahead without him – there is so much more to learn from him, from his literature teaching, his language, his knowledge of the world, and...I think I am helping him, too...and...and I just cannot bear the thought of never seeing him again."

She was speaking quickly, gulping sobs as she did so, catching her breath. Her mother tried to be positive.

"He will try to come back to see us, I'm sure. He is a man of some standing, after all, and not one to leave and never be heard of again..."

"But how can you be sure Mama? How can you know?"

"Because I know how deeply you feel for him and I believe, from the way you both get on so well, how you are together, that he feels the same – you have convinced me of that from what you have said. A mother knows intuitively what a daughter is feeling, and my heart aches for you my dear, as your's does for him, in your sadness."

"The ache is different between the hearts of a man and a woman, from the ache between a mother and daughter," said Charlotte, with a profoundness beyond her years. Then she added:

"You say he needs to return, and I have tried to see that. But I see his melancholy sometimes, and his worrying countenance, and he has no set plans about what he is going to do, Mama. Why does he need to go now? All my being wants me to plead with him to stay – only the fact that I know I am being selfish holds me back."

Sarah looked at her daughter, who lifted her face to her for the first time as she continued to hold her in her arms. To her it seemed so short a time since she had held her as an infant, enjoyed the emotion of feeding her at her breast, of having her completely dependant on her as that tiny body fought to establish its being, and having done that, to gradually form her character. Now here she was, so suddenly it seemed, at that point in life when human feelings and emotions, and relationships with other people were coming into play, strongly and urgently, and needing careful guidance.

Yet despite what she had said to her daughter, she had to admit to herself that she was not convinced that Francois needed to leave, even if he was fully recovered. He had little for which he needed to return to France, with many of his family dead or imprisoned as the revolution decimated the country's aristocracy. He had no work to go to, while in England he could establish a living translating and teaching, and writing, in the knowledge that he could merge into the Ives' household as an adopted son.

She remained deep in thought for some time, as Charlotte's sobs began to subside, until eventually she spoke carefully and quietly:

"My dear, a commitment to someone is not to be lightly taken. If entered into rashly it can fade and wither as quickly as it blossomed. When a man takes a woman for his bride, both must be certain beyond any doubt that they can commit themselves to each other for their lifetime. You have attended a wedding so you will know the words that are spoken during that union of two people. It is a big step which will decide the course your whole life will take, my dear – my daughter of whom I am so proud.

"I will say my prayers, too, for you and Francois. If you are both prepared to make that total commitment, I would be entirely happy. As for your father, I am not so sure. But I will speak to him again, and if he is agreeable I will speak to Francois and let him know that if he has it in mind to make that commitment, we would be prepared for him to take you for his wife."

Charlotte sat up. In her innermost thoughts she had mused about Francois becoming her husband and the joy they would bring each other, but to hear her mother speak those words, in the way she did, made her heart beat faster in her breast.

She clasped her mother's hand in her's, radiancy replacing the tears on her cheeks.

"Mama, I have dreamed of that. I have tried to look ahead and imagine what it would be like and I know that is what I want. Do you think Francois would want that too?"

"You must be prepared for the fact that he may decline – that he may be set on moving on, on returning to France," her mother cautioned. "Your father is yet to be persuaded, too, though mainly, I do believe, because fathers are reluctant to release their daughters to suitors, even those who have good credentials and prospects. But he has much enjoyed the companionship and conversation of Francois while he has been here – it has been good for him to have male companionship here, not to mention someone he can share a glass of port with."

She paused, and smiled at her daughter's happiness and bright-eyed expectancy, confirming to her again the deep feelings she had for the Frenchman.

"I don't think it will take much to persuade him, my dear. I will suggest to him that we speak to Francois to let him know we would look favourably on my proposal."

Charlotte threw her arms around her mother and hugged her, nestling her head against her neck as she had once done as a baby.

"Thank you, Mama! Thank you! I just know Francois feels as I do. I know he will stay. I'm so happy!"

8

"Charlotte, I know you have something to tell me! Walking to Bible study this evening I thought you were going to burst! And during discussions you did not seem to be concentrating as you should – as you usually do, on the text for the evening."

Lydia was walking back from Bible study with her friend. It was a mild, late May evening, and instead of going straight home they took a detour through the streets, past the round-towered Church of the Holy Trinity and down towards the Staithe, to give them more time to converse.

"Do tell me what is filling your mind, you know you want to! It must be something important and happy. Confide it in me!"

"Lydia, no, I can't – at least not now. Wait a few days, and then you will know."

"There, I knew it – you have got something to tell! And I can also tell it is something that makes you happy, Charlotte! Do tell – please don't make me wait!"

And Lydia linked her arm through Charlotte's in a confidential, best-friend way, as they walked.

"Oh, you are quite right – it is so hard to keep it inside me when I want to tell the whole world. I want to tell the trees and the birds and the clouds in the sky, and the houses and the river, and I want them all to pass it on through their wings and their ripples and their chatter!

"But.... really I...!"

"Tell me! Just tell me, you don't need to tell anyone else!" Lydia squeezed her friend's arm closer still to her.

Charlotte stopped, and Lydia with her. They were on the path through St Mary's churchyard, with its tall, square tower, topped by pinnacles in each corner, looking silently down on them. Charlotte's resolve to keep her secret was wavering.

"Well...if you promise not to tell anyone – to keep it to yourself for a few days? You must promise!"

"I promise, I promise, I promise! Now tell!"

Lydia was wide-eyed with expectation. Charlotte could contain herself no longer.

"I'm going to be betrothed!"

Lydia squealed in excitement.

"Charlotte, how wonderful! And who is your suitor?"

"Francois, of course! I'm so happy!"

"Francois, you're house guest?" echoed Lydia in amazement. "Has he confessed his love for you? Has he spoken to your father?"

"No...no, not yet." Charlotte's excitement cooled momentarily. "But Mama has noticed the feelings I have for him, and the feelings he has for me. I love him so, Lydia, and I know he loves me. It has been agreed that Mama will speak to Francois, to tell him that she and Papa

112

would be happy for him to take my hand in marriage. She will do that shortly. And I know he will say yes. He has not spoken his love for me in words, but he has indicated it in so many others ways, during the time he has been here."

"And have you confessed your love for him?"

"No, not in words. It is the same for both of us – the feelings that pass between us. He will know from the way we are together the deep feelings I have for him, the rapport we share. You don't have to put voice to these things, Lydia, to know they are there in people's hearts and minds!"

Lydia looked doubtfully at her friend.

"I cannot understand, for it is something I have not yet experienced. But..." she hesitated before adding:

"Are you sure? Are you certain that he will accept your mother's proposal?"

"Yes, yes I am quite sure! I pray for it every night! I know he loves me. I know we will be married! He has no reason to return to France – he has lost his family and everything else there. Lydia, I am so excited, so happy. Are you happy for me?"

Lydia looked at her friend as she stood there, buoyant and exhilarated. It seemed that an aura of light surrounded her as the twilight gathered over the churchyard. She seemed so certain of her happy destiny.

"Of course I am happy for you, dear Charlotte. But you must promise me one thing?"

"Of course – what is that?"

"That you will ask me to be your bridesmaid for the wedding."

"You will be my bridesmaid, Lydia. I want you to be there with me, to share my happiness!"

And there, on the churchyard path, the two friends embraced warmly. Charlotte could not see the look of doubt on Lydia's face as they did so.

Two days later in that May of 1796, on the eve of his planned departure, Charlotte and Francois walked through Back Lane and on to the Common. The sun came out as morning cloud melted away and warmed them with its springtime rays. But their conversation was stilted, both concerned with their own thoughts. As they walked, Charlotte was frequently tempted to let Francois know that her mother was planning to ask him to stay, and to offer her daughter's hand in marriage; she so wanted to talk to him about plans for their life together, to tell him at last, of her love for him, and hear him confess his love for her. But she managed to contain her excitement and expectancy, to keep her emotions under control, and just enjoy being beside the man who had come to mean so much to her – without whom, now, she could not look into the future.

Eventually, as they walked through that peaceful meadow, where the beasts grazed languidly, unhurried, she was finally tempted to try to coax his feelings and desires from him:

"I will miss you, my Lord, when you re gone."

Francois turned to her, seeing the dark eyes that seemed to have a renewed sparkle about them over the past few days.

"Mademoiselle – Charlotte, leaving here, leaving you, is not a decision I have made lightly. It is hard for me...it would be easy to stay here, where I have been made so welcome. But I must go, I have to go, you must understand that. If it were a simple matter of staying with you, making my life in Bungay with you.... But...I have to think of my...my family in France, my mother, and sisters, my... But it is difficult to explain to you, why I must leave now before it is too late. Only know that I will miss this place where I have been made so welcome, been so well cared for, I will miss your parents..."

He stopped their gentle stroll, and turned to face Charlotte, taking both her hands in his as he had done once before in that quiet, rustic scene.

"...and you Charlotte, ma chere – yes, I will miss you as much as you will miss me – our close companionship, the way you have sustained me over these past few months. I will miss our love of the same music, the same art, the same literature, perhaps the same dreams..."

His voice quietened over the last few words, and he drew himself up to full stature, as one does when waking and stretching, before adding:

"But I have outstayed my welcome. Your parents, and you, have been so welcoming, so compassionate, so concerned for my welfare. Now I am well there is no reason for me to remain, except for the close, intimate friendship that has grown between us. But to stay because of that would be selfish on my part, much as I would love to remain in the bosom of your family."

The tone of his voice and what he was saying gave Charlotte a momentary doubt, a feeling that all would not be as planned. But she quickly dismissed it, and began again:

"My lord, you would not be selfish – only as far as the selfishness would be shared, because it would be what I want for myself. You must talk to Mama, she..."

But suddenly realising what she was about to say, she stopped abruptly, and the moment was saved as Francois withdrew his hands from hers. They had stopped beside a dyke running through the Common, beside which had sprung up growth and small bushes, among them briars, and he went to it's steep edge and stretched out to reach one of the first of the wild roses of late spring.

"Be careful, my Lord!" said Charlotte instinctively. But she need not have worried – her companion was regaining his full strength, and he plucked the rose and accompanying leaf on its stem, and stepped back towards her. He handed her the simple, four-petalled, pinky white flower with its yellow stamen.

"Take this Charlotte. It is a flower of springtime, and you are in the springtime of your life. You have brought the springtime to my life too. Take it, because I will always remember you, fondly, as the beautiful English rose I met during my adventure here, in England. Of all the people and times I have encountered here, I will remember you, and the feelings we had. Wherever I am, wherever I travel, whatever I do, wherever destiny leads me, I will never forget you, dear Charlotte."

And as she clutched the rose to her, he put his lips on hers with the gentlest of kisses, and held them there. Her eyes closed in the ecstasy of the moment, wanting him to never withdraw, wanting the kiss to become firmer, more urgent.

When finally he did withdraw his lips, their eyes met with an unspoken message neither could fail to read.

"Thank you my Lord – I will treasure this. But I still don't understand why it is so important, why you must go. Please don't go! Please stay with me!"

Charlotte was almost whispering her plea, doubt engulfing her again.

"I cannot, mademoiselle. I wish I could explain why it is imperative for me to leave now, before it is too late...I should explain...I...I ask you only to believe that it is for a very good reason that I cannot stay."

"I do so want to understand, but...if you do go, if you must go, will you...will you come back?"

Her eyes searched his for a sign of hope, doubt engulfing her once again – it sounded to her, at that moment, that his mind was made up. But just as quickly, she told herself that her mother's proposition would convince him to remain in Bungay.

Francois' reply, when it came, lacked conviction, however.

"Peut-etre, ma chere...perhaps...one day."

When they returned to the parsonage, Charlotte went to her room and lovingly pressed the rose into the leaves of her note book, beside the primrose, kissing the petals gently, lovingly, before she closed the page over it...

Dinner that evening was not as relaxing as Charlotte had hoped. Mrs Honeywood had worked hard to prepare a special meal as it was the last the French guest would eat with them, and Maria was bright as she served, frequently slanting glances at first Charlotte and then Francois, the hint of a knowing look on her face.

But the quality of the meal was lost on the four diners that evening. John Ives and Francois emptied their plates, but no sense of enjoyment flowed from it. Charlotte consumed occasional mouthfuls, but dwelt on them some time before eventually swallowing, and Mrs Ives did her best to eat the food before her, but was unable to finish it, her mind pre-occupied with how she would put into words the proposal she had for Francois when the meal was over. There was too much on her mind, and her inward nervousness conveyed itself to the company as they engaged in contrived conversation which ignored completely Francois's planned departure for London the following morning. It had, however, been the only topic of conversation between her and her husband the previous evening, when they had struggled to reach harmony on the subject of whether to invite their guest to take Charlotte as his wife, and to remain with them in Bungay. For her part, Mrs Ives was totally convinced that it was what her daughter longed for, and that Francois, with his background in the French aristocracy, was most suitable for her, despite his current situation as an émigré to England.

But while her husband eagerly confessed to liking the man, his company and his highly intellectual conversation, he had serious doubts about Charlotte's future with a man who he felt may ultimately be drawn back to his homeland, where he had lost his property and his family, and thus take her into a life which he felt was not suitable for her.

Eventually, however, he had yielded to his wife's view, and it had been agreed that she would put the proposal to Francois the following evening, on the assumption that if he agreed he would remain with them and cancel his arrangements to go to London.

Maria collected the plates and brought dessert from the kitchen – apple dumplings topped with fresh cream, which Mrs Honeywood knew had become a favourite of the Frenchman. But the two ladies again left theirs' unfinished, and after Maria had collected the plates, the cook came in to ask, with a diplomacy her expression betrayed:

"Was the meal satisfactory this evening ma'am?"

"Yes Mrs Honeywood, it was most appetising, thank you. Unfortunately Charlotte and I are...we're suffering - a little cholic."

The white lie seemed to satisfy the cook, and she withdrew with a nod. Charlotte took her mother's cue, apologised to the company, and left the room.

She hurried upstairs to her bedchamber. Francois had been gloomy throughout the meal, and she told herself that it was because he was reluctant to leave – he would be reconsidering his intentions following their conversation on the common. Nervous and excited at the same time, she went to her wardrobe and took out the dress she had decided to wear for her re-appearance when her mother re-called her to the dining-room. It was in cotton, with the full length green skirt drawn tight at the waist to accentuate her figure, and a bodice, picked out with a red, curly, ribbon-like pattern, buttoned to the neck and with a vertical frilled decoration to highlight it. She discarded the blue dress she had worn for dinner, and quickly got into it, checking in the mirror that it was neat and properly adjusted, before brushing her hair again, and re-vitalising the rouge on her cheeks and lips, though so flushed was she with excitement and expectation that it was scarcely needed. Finally, she tied her hair back with a red ribbon to match the pattern on her dress, and stood back to consider herself in the mirror again.

"Do I look suitable for my moment of betrothal? I do hope so. I know Francois finds me appealing in this dress – he has commented on it before," she said to herself. "Yes, I'm ready.

Now I must remain calm and composed. I'm so excited and it would be so undignified were I to trip or do something else unbecoming as I enter the room, which will be very soon. Surely Mama will be calling me soon?"

Soon after Charlotte had left the dining table, Mr Ives had withdrawn as well, leaving his wife and Francois together, on opposite sides of the table – much to the Frenchman's unspoken surprise.

Immediately he noticed that his hostess was almost shaking with nervousness, and clearly trying to gather herself together to say something. But it was Francois who initially broke the emotional atmosphere.

"Madame, I had hoped that we could all remain together so I could express…"

But he was interrupted as Mrs Ives, whose face had been firmly focussed on her hands on her lap, stood up, positioned herself behind her vacated chair, and spoke, with a great effort.

"Monsieur, my husband and I have noticed that Charlotte is greatly attracted to you, and that the two of you get on so well together in every way. We feel that you have similar feelings towards her, and that meets with our approval."

She paused momentarily, and then continued: "Furthermore, we have asked ourselves what reason you have to return to France. Most of your family is gone, your home has gone, your country, though peace is beginning to return, is still in some turmoil, you have no work to go to…But here, we can offer you a comfortable home, where you can continue with your translations and your writing."

Her voice softened in tone as she added: "Above all, we know you will make Charlotte happy. We would not stand in your way should you ask for her hand in marriage. I, on behalf of my husband and with the blessing of both of us, am offering you the opportunity, now, to do that."

Sarah smiled at last through her flushed cheeks. As the Frenchman opposite her stood up, and tears welled up in his eyes, she was convinced she had been right to make the proposal. He paused where he stood for a few moments, fighting back tears, of joy Sarah thought. Then he came round the table, and knelt at her feet, taking her hands and covering them with his kisses and his tears. As the tension drained from her, she wanted to convey the good news.

She pulled the bell-rope, and at the same time called out: "John, Charlotte! You can come through!"

But in the same instant that she did so, Francois cried out in a voice which at once was full of anguish, desolation and guilt in equal measure:

"Madame, wait! I cannot do this! I...I am already married!"
The last echo of her call stopped in Sarah's throat as she
heard those words. What was he saying? Married? No, how
could he be?

The blood that had bloomed her cheeks drained instantly
from them, and she flopped back into her chair in a faint.

Francois' wide-eyed, frightened look at her reflected his
myriad of feelings at that moment: fear, guilt, love, huge
sadness, compassion, cowardice – they all tumbled together
from his brain and through his countenance as he stood up,
tears on his cheeks.

With a last helpless look at the limp and distraught Sarah,
Francois turned abruptly and left the house, through the
hall, immediately, without returning to his room to collect
the belongings he had packed the previous night.

He was scarcely out of sight when Charlotte and her father
entered from the withdrawing room, summoned by the bell
and Sarah's elated call. Charlotte, in her moment of pure
joy which lifts one about to be betrothed to the highest
heavens, moved sedately, but her eyes were bright with
expectancy.

"Mama!"

But seeing as she spoke that only her mother was there,
added in a puzzled and inquiring tone:

"Where is Francois? Where is he? Did he...accept the
proposal?"

"Sarah – are you alright? What's happened?" her father said, almost simultaneously, as he saw her listless body, her head flopping on to her lap.

He hurried over to her and tried to sit her up. Seeing her ashen complexion and dilated eyes, he barked to his daughter:

"Charlotte, fetch the smelling salts, quickly!"

"Papa, what's happened? What's the matter with Mama? Where is Francois?" But she quickly brought the reviving salts as her father had demanded, and with their help, Sarah's colour gradually returned and she breathed normally again, further aided by a draught of cold water.

It was some minutes, however, before she was able to relate the dramatic turn of events to them.

"I'm sorry, Charlotte," she finished weakly. "I thought when he stood up and came and clasped my hands, that he was accepting our proposition. The next instant, he said he was...was already married. I don't understand why he had not mentioned his wife before. Had he spoken of his wife to you?"

"No Mama – no! I don't believe it. I don't believe he can be married! He would have told me! He must have gone up to his room – he must still be here. The proposal will have come as a shock and he will want to compose himself. He wouldn't have left – I'll go to him!"

And she ran out of the room and up the stairs. John Ives looked at his wife, anger in his eyes.

"In all the conversations I had with him – about France, the revolution, America, how he came to be in this country, his family – he never mentioned that he was married. Are you certain that is what he said, Sarah? If it is so, he has betrayed us, betrayed our hospitality and our friendship. I had a feeling all along that there was something about him that was not right, something he was keeping back – I mentioned that to you Sarah, did I not? This was it – that he was married, but did not mention it. Not something that would simply have slipped from his mind, you would think! A deliberate deceit, that is the only way I can look at it! What sort of honour is there in someone like that? He has deceived us, and deceived Charlotte."

At that moment his daughter returned to the room, now half-crying, her emotions in turmoil, her elation crushed by the realisation that the man she loved had fled.

"He's not there – he's not in his room!" she gulped. "But he can't have gone far. He's probably in the town. Yes...yes, that is it - he's gone for a walk so he can think, and he'll come back to me. I'm going to find him!"

"Charlotte, stay here!" her father commanded.

But for once his daughter ignored him, went into the vestibule, put on her coat, and seconds later her parents heard the door close.

"Charlotte!" her father called again. He moved towards the door to go after her, but then hesitated, realising that his wife, weak and in a state of emotional shock, needed him too.

Charlotte hastened up the hill in the twilight, and into the Market Place, calling as she went: "My Lord, my Lord! Where are you? Wait! Don't go! Tell me what the matter is! Francois!" at frequent intervals.

There were few people in the town that dark night, but occasionally she sensed a moving shadow, and would renew her calling, hoping against hope that it was Francois – only to be disappointed. One carriage passed her as she half ran past St Mary's Church and towards the fork in the road where one way would take her towards Halesworth and the other towards Flixton and South Elmham. She hesitated, tears on her face, frustrated, distraught, not knowing which route to take.

"He can't have gone too far – even though he has recovered he could not walk too fast," she reasoned with herself. And she turned back, took a short cut through the churchyard and took the road down past the Staithe which led towards Beccles, still calling in her anguish:

"My Lord! Where are you? Don't leave…please don't leave!"

Half walking, half running, she reached the Watch House, where Bungay parish joined the parish of Mettingham. There she stopped, breathless, exhausted from hastening, calling and crying. Her head slumped to her chest, and her voice was a pitiful whisper.

"My Lord? Where are you going? You've….nowhere…to
go. You didn't even say…goodbye."

She looked up, up the long hill that led up to the ridge of
the valley and out through Mettingham to Beccles. Was that
where he was now, half-way to Beccles? Surely he would
be as exhausted as her, and would have stopped. If she kept
going, she might catch him up.

 Charlotte took a few paces forward. But even in her
emotional state she realised it was futile, drained as she
was, and she stopped, and turned slowly in the near
darkness, and began to walk slowly home, her mind in
turmoil, trying to fathom the events of the evening, trying o
tell herself that her mother had been mistaken in what
Francois's re-action had been.

"She misunderstood him – that's it! Or she misheard him –
that could be it! Sometimes when he was down at heart, as
he surely was at the thought of leaving, his voice became
almost a mumble."

These and other desperate thoughts went through her head
as she tried to put out of her mind what her mother had said
– that he was already married.

"Dear God, wherever he is, keep him safe," she prayed
silently through her tears, as she walked.

Her father, anxious for her safety, met her half way, having
made sure his wife was fully revived and comfortable, in
body if not spirit. He put his arm round his daughter, who
readily put her head on his chest and whimpered "Papa!"

127

through renewed sobs. He led her home under the shelter of darkness, broken only by the candle glow from some windows of houses beside the main street, and down Bridge Street hill.

As the three sat in the withdrawing room, Charlotte on the chaise-longue with her head against her father's chest with his comforting arm round her, and Sarah in a rocking chair, it was too early to try to come to terms with what happened. Mr Ives mood was angry, his wife's guilty and apologetic, Charlotte's still tearfully grief-stricken and ready to forgive.

"He didn't say goodbye – if he had to leave he would have said goodbye. He'll come back, I know he will. He knows I love him."

"Charlotte my dear, I'm so sorry I raised your hopes – please forgive me," her mother said, somehow summoning the strength to speak through her state of shock.

"It seemed clear to me there were strong feelings between you, a strong attachment had been formed between you. I thought he would be happy at our proposal. It did not come into my mind for one moment that he might be married."

"No, and he did not mention it – not once!" said her husband. "He spoke often of his family and their plight in France, their imprisonment, mother, brothers, sisters, but not once did he mention a wife. That is unforgiveable! He had every opportunity to tell us and I can only conclude that he deliberately held back from doing so for...for whatever reason. He led us to believe that he was free to offer him our daughter's hand and he encouraged her in her feelings towards him. I will have much to say to him if he does return, and no mistake. But Charlotte, I don't share your hopes that he will."

"Papa, don't say that. He will, he will...Mama, what did he say to you, about his wife, did he name her?"

"My dear, he said nothing – only that he was married – it was the last thing he said. When I put the proposition to him he fell on his knees and kissed my hands, and wept. I thought that was because he was so happy at it, that he was accepting, that he was so overcome that he could not speak at first to say the words. I had already called to you when he cried through his tears, 'I am married.' I just..."

Now it was Sarah's turn to put her face in her hands and weep as she recalled those three words that had turned her family's hopes and happiness into despair and deep shock.

"It is shameful, after all the love and care and hospitality we bestowed upon him, to thank us in this way," said her husband, anger still glaring from his face. "As Christians we must pray to God that he is safe, and that he will return, but it is God he must answer to. And me."

"Papa, he has done nothing wrong in my eyes – he was never improper towards me. He never told me he loved me, though he knew I loved him. I believe he loves me but...perhaps it was my fault for interpreting that love into my hope that we could have a future together. He was so

good to me, so affectionate, and tender. I can't believe he
has left, I can't. He will come back."

As she sobbed into her father's chest again, her mother said
gently:

"My dear, you must prepare yourself for the likelihood that
he will not. Though what his intentions are one cannot tell."

She exchanged concerned glances with her husband, before
adding:

"It's late, and you are drained of energy. Got to bed, say
your prayers and try to sleep. Tomorrow we can all try to
look at it in a new light. But I regret my intuition that led to
the proposal has had such an unexpected and devastating
result, my dear."

Charlotte got up from the chaise-longue, her face tear-
stained, her eyes dull.

"Mama, is it possible that you misunderstood what he said?
What he meant? Perhaps he was saying something
completely different – not that he was married, but...but...I
don't know. I just know that he would have told me if he
was married. He would never deceive me."

"My dear, I'm afraid your trust has been misplaced. We
have all been misled. But I am still in a state of shock. It is
all so sudden, so unexpected. I fail to comprehend it, but no
– I did not mishear what he said. He spoke it clearly, in
spite of the shock of my proposal, which clearly left him
with no other course but to confess. I'm so sorry, my dear.
Just when we though we were going to make our daughter

happy, and secure her future, we are left feeling that we have been struck by a flash of lightning and a thunderbolt."

"It is not your fault, Mama – it is not anybody's fault. Perhaps it is God's will. But I will pray that Francois will return tomorrow, or the next day, and tell me that he is not married – that he is free to marry me. I believe he will come back to me. I must believe it."

And she kissed her parents, and retired to bed. After she had left the room, Sarah, drained of all emotion, managed the strength to say:

"I should apologise to you, too John. Your intuition was right – mine was wrong. I don't know how long it will take Charlotte to get over this; or any of us, for that matter. This is a most disastrous turn of events."

The next morning, Maria returned to the kitchen after taking breakfast to the family, a look on her face which she suggested she had something to reveal.

"I don't know what's happened Mrs Honeywood, but something has! Miss Charlotte looks as if she's been crying all night, Mr and Mrs Ives have faces as gloomy as rain at a picnic, and Mr Shatterbrain is nowhere to be seen. I thought he was leaving today, but it looks like he disappeared overnight. I wonder why?"

"Now then Maria, that's not for you to wonder – that's the master and mistress's business. Even so, it is very strange,"

Mrs Honeywood replied, as she stoked the fire in the range and adjusted the pots on it.

"Those two were very close – Miss Charlotte and Shatterbrain. I've seen them holding hands, and hugging each other, when I've gone in unexpected. Do you know what I think, Mrs Honeywood? I think, well, I'd say that they've lain together, and now she's expecting a child, and her parents have found out and he's run away in shame. I'd say…"

"Maria, that's enough!" Mrs Honeywood interrupted her sharply. "You're letting your imagination run away with you. No such thing has happened – this is a parsonage, remember, not a workhouse. Now take those cups through."

"Well, she wouldn't eat her breakfast the other day, and she's certainly not eating today. And you must admit he left very suddenly," the maid added sullenly. "I'd venture its something like that."

"Maria!" chided cook firmly again. But she wondered to herself, nevertheless.

Charlotte could eat nothing for breakfast. Joy had been snatched from her so cruelly and unexpectedly at the very moment she had thought her dreams would become reality, and the knot of desolation in her stomach made her sick at the thought of food. She had not slept throughout the night, her mind filled with thoughts of Francois, where he was, why had he not revealed before that he was married, what he planned to do – whether he would return to the parsonage to explain his actions.

Frequently she prayed through the long dark night: prayed that he would return to her, prayed that it has all been a mistake, that her mother had misunderstood – misheard perhaps - what he had said; prayed to relieve her of the hurt, the desolation, the humiliation of being rejected in such a way by the man she had looked up to with such trust, and confidence, and friendship. Often the tears would return.

But towards dawn, she resolved that she would continue the routine of the day that had been established: she would play the piano for an hour, and then study for an hour, in the forenoon, and in the afternoon would go for a walk, just as she had done so regularly – with Francois.

Though she could consume no breakfast, the decision lifted her spirits slightly. Sarah, who similarly had had little sleep, was encouraged when her daughter told her of her intentions. Mr Ives meanwhile, planned to take a coach to Beccles to try to discover whether Francois had stayed there overnight, or if anyone had seen him.

Half an hour later, Charlotte was sitting at the piano, playing the piece from Bach she had played for Francois soon after he arrived at the parsonage. She played it with feeling, as well as she had ever played it in the past, imagining him standing there, beside the piano, as he had so often, watching her, listening intently. And she hoped and prayed that he would walk into the room as she did so, and smile through his brown eyes the smile that she had come to feel was for her alone.

But he did not come.

Charlotte was left to comfort herself with the thought that while she was playing she felt his presence, that wherever he was, he would hear it somehow, and it would call him back to her, eventually.

She played for an hour, and then went and sat at the table and took up her passages of study. They had been looking at the work of Dante, which Francois had a particular passion for, and Charlotte tried to absorb herself in it, and feel the interpretations Francois would put on it. In her head she spoke with him, and discussed the work with him.

But still he did not come.

Eventually, disconsolately, she closed the books in front of her, fighting back the tears of disappointment. She could eat nothing at midday, and she and her mother said little as they sat at the dining table. They apologised to Maria when she came to collect the plates and found them still full.

Charlotte retired to her room and lay on her bed. The tears came again, but eventually tiredness brought with it the soothing balm of sleep...

John Ives had returned from his trip to Beccles with the information that Francois had boarded the mail coach to London that morning. Late the following afternoon, a messenger brought a letter, addressed to Mrs Sarah Ives,

The Parsonage, Bungay, with no imprint on the seal. Charlotte was in her room, and her husband out visiting the sick, and Sarah sat down quietly and opened it.

My Dear Mrs Ives, she read,

I write this with remorse and apologies in my heart, having left you so abruptly last night at a moment which you and Mr Ives and Charlotte had hoped would be such a happy one. The tears that I placed upon your hand were not for me, but for you, for the shock and sadness and anger I anticipated my revelation would bring you. I am full of shame and chagrin as I write this to try to explain my sudden and rude departure from such a welcoming home, such a hospitable family whose care and compassion I did not deserve.

I have to confess to you, Madame, that I am married, though it was not a marriage of my choosing, but the choice of my family. I married Celeste La Vigne five years ago, the year before I left France for England. It was an arranged marriage, you would say in your country. Celeste was an orphan, although of an aristocratic family, from Brittany, and had become a friend of my sister, Lucile, who introduced her to me. Her intentions for me were good – she felt Celeste had some wealth, and that I should marry her, though she was very young, not quite 16 years of age. Madame, my sister is very persuasive, and though I had much doubt about the arrangement, having only met

135

Celeste a few times, briefly, I agreed to go ahead. It was most unsatisfactory – her adopted family would not sign the papers when we married, because she was under age according to French law, but later they did sign.

It was a marriage, however, and I must honour it, though at this moment as I write this letter, in my emotion, I wish that it were not so, that I was free, so that I could have accepted your proposal. You will ask if I love Celeste: I cannot answer that, Madame, only to say that I must believe that in time I will come to love her as a husband should – that love will grow, as the love between myself and Charlotte grew in the months that I enjoyed the warmth of your hospitality. We found we enjoyed the same things – literature, languages, history, music. Our minds were as one, and I believe she loved me, though what she will feel for me now is distressful to imagine. In asking for your mercy, and that of your family, Madame, I can only make a plea to you to persuade your daughter that I tried to behave honourably towards her at all times – my last wish in this world was to cause her hurt and sadness, but now I realise I have done that through my weakness in not speaking to you of my wife.

You will ask why I had not mentioned this before, when I spoke of my family regularly, of their plight in France at the height of the revolution, and my fears for them. I have no answer to that question. I had only been with Celeste a short while before I left – perhaps I didn't want to remember her, perhaps I left France to leave her, but she did not deserve that, she had done nothing wrong.

Perhaps, Madame, it was because you so willingly took me into your family – me, poor, without a home, with little to commend me. Of all the people I have met in England, or on my travels anywhere, your family was the only one to accept me as I am and offer me everything I could have wished.

As to Charlotte, from the first day I met her I found her charming, beautiful, eager to learn, a gifted musician – she is surrounded in springtime. I came to have deep feelings for her – it was clear she had those feelings for me also. Madame, if the time was different I would willingly, eagerly, have accepted your proposal – she would have made me the most acceptable loving wife, and it would have been an honour to be her husband, and part of your family. But that is not to be. Please let her know of my deep affection for her, and in my sudden withdrawal I hope, in time, she will see that it was for honourable reasons – I will remember her with fondness always.

Now I have returned her love and care, and your hospitality, with rejection, and by fleeing your welcoming home, with no adieu. I ask your forgiveness for my miserable actions and the humiliation and embarrassment I have caused you. I will understand if Charlotte is not able to forgive me.

I leave shortly for London, to meet with my friend Peltier, who has made arrangements for me. I may never return to Bungay, but wherever I am I will never forget my time with you.
Yours
Francois

Sarah sat for some time with the letter on her lap after reading it, trying to absorb it, understand it – trying to find some sympathy for the Frenchman. But her anger was battling her natural Christian instincts.

"Forgive him! How can I forgive him when he has caused such pain and embarrassment, caused our beloved daughter such heart ache and deep sorrow, when he could have avoided it by telling us of his marriage at an early stage," she said to herself. "He had every opportunity – he talked enough about the rest of his family and his travels, every other aspect of his life. And he has admitted he was aware of Charlotte's feelings for him. How can I forgive him for that!"

Eventually, she got up and pulled the bell-rope for the kitchen.

"Maria, would you ask Charlotte to come down here, please," she said when the maid appeared.

Her daughter appeared a few minutes later, tired and drawn, her dark eyes dull, the surrounds red with crying. Her mother beckoned her to sit beside her.

"The mail office has just brought this."

For a moment Charlotte's eyes brightened as she looked at it.

"That's Francois' handwriting! Is he....?" She began. But her mother's expression stopped her from continuing.

"I think you should read it, my dear," she said in a consoling tone, which pre-warned Charlotte of its contents.

She read it, slowly and carefully, occasionally glancing up at her mother as she did so. When she finally laid it aside, she was close to tears again.

"I knew he had made for Beccles! I should have continued after him," she said.

"My dear what good would that have done? He had made his confession, and wanted to get away as quickly as possible. He could have told us long ago that he was married."

"Perhaps he...he had received a fierce blow on his head in his accident. Perhaps it affected his memory. His physical injuries are healed, Mama., but perhaps not his mind."

"His mind is perfectly well. It is no good making excuses for his behaviour. And the fact remains he has confessed to being already married."

She put her hand on Charlotte's. "I know you had great affection for him, my dear – perhaps you loved him. But now try to see him for what he is – he took me in, and no mistake, as well as you. Perhaps we should have listened to your father."

"I did love him, Mama – I do love him! I won't believe that he did this deliberately. He says he couldn't bring himself to tell us, that is all. Is that so wrong? With all that has gone on in his life, and his worry for his family, is it not understandable? I can forgive him. I will never love anybody else."

"I know you feel your life has been turned upside down, Charlotte – that you cannot look ahead without Francois being there. But with God's help, time will heal. We have all been terribly shocked by this – your father too."

"But I didn't...we didn't, even say goodbye? Surely he'll come back to say goodbye properly!"

And Charlotte's tears, which had flowed so frequently over the past few days, came again.

"My dear, you must make yourself believe he will not. We will not see him again."

"Don't say that Mama! We will, I know we will, despite his letter. I can't...I can't *not* see him again!"

Sarah's heart reached out to her daughter. She knew she was not to be consoled then – it was too early. The pain and anguish and confusion in her was still new, and raw, too strong to be readily healed. It would take time. So she made no reply, and the two sat there in silence, close, the mother still caressing the daughter with gentle, comforting strokes of her arm.

Over the next few days Charlotte barely ate, or slept. But she continued the routine that had been established with Francois – she played the piano for an hour, and then studied for an hour before lunch, and in the afternoon walked the paths and byways they had walked during his later convalescence.

During her playing she would imagine Francois standing there, beside the piano, leaning on it and watching her as he had done so often – so intense was her emotion that, concentrating on her playing, she would forget he was not there, and would speak to him – only to look up and see no one.

On one occasion, she was deep in one movement of Bach, the music enveloping her mind, when the door suddenly opened. She jumped up from the piano stool.

"Francois…!"

But her reverie was just as quickly dashed as she saw Maria enter, and in her disappointment she spoke harshly to the maid.

"Maria! What do you want? I've told you not to disturb me while I'm playing. Please leave!"

The girl was startled and taken aback by the anger in her tone, and could only whimper:

"I…I'm sorry, Miss Ives…I'm sorry," and turned to go. But within a few moments Charlotte regained her composure.

"Maria...no, I'm sorry – I shouldn't have spoken to you in such a way. It was unfair of me. I'm...I'm just tired. You've done nothing wrong."

The maid looked at the floor and then at her, muttered, "Yes, Miss Ives," and returned to the kitchen, as Charlotte returned to her stool and put her face in her hands.

The feeling that Francois was there with her was strong on her walks, particularly on the Common, where recent memories of their happy times were in the forefront of her mind as she strolled forlornly along the banks of the Waveney, stopping instinctively at the places they had lingered together.

At the spot where just short weeks ago the May blossom had been in full bloom and touching the surface of the river, the hawthorn was bare and green – the breeze and the moving on of nature had stripped the beauty from it, and as Charlotte looked at it she mused that the hawthorn, and the river there, must feel as she did, bereft of the blossom in her life, deserted, its soul stripped of the substance that had given it its beauty so short a time ago.

And she remembered that Francois had kissed her there, at that spot, and she closed her eyes to try to recreate that moment – to try to put away the feeling of rejection, of loneliness, that had pervaded her since she had last seen him. But the respite was fleeting.

When she returned home, she found her parents in earnest discussion, concerned looks on their faces, her father pacing the withdrawing room, her mother sitting, agitated. As soon as she entered, her father turned to her.

"Ah, Charlotte, as if Francois's suddenly unseemly departure was not enough, there is a rumour abroad in the town that the reason he fled is that he has impregnated you and you are expecting his child. I know, I know...."

"Papa, no! That is not possible! It is a sinful suggestion!"

As his daughter interrupted him with her affronted protest her eyes blazed and she turned to her mother for support, but her father continued:

"I know, we know, that is not the case – but somehow the gossip has grown, from what seed I know not, to the extent that it has reached the Bishop of Norwich, and you can imagine his consternation at such a suggestion concerning a clergyman's daughter. I have to go to Norwich for an audience with him, to re- assure him, to receive instructions on how to quell the rumour among the congregation...It is a most unfortunate situation. Have you any notion of how this gossip might have come about?"

"John, how could she possibly know," said his wife reprovingly as Charlotte looked at him with a pitiable look on her face. "People will have heard of Francois' sudden departure late at night, may even have seen him leave the house, drawn wild conclusions from it and gossiped about it, as the unintelligent do."

"Well, you know what the Bishop is like, sensitive to the slightest suggestion that something is not right with the clergy in his diocese, and this rumour reflects on me. I will need you, Charlotte, to write a note for me to take to the Bishop assuring him of your innocence, and that the gossip is without any foundation. I am sorry to have to ask you this when you are still so sad and confused at what has happened, but I cannot refuse the Bishop's request."

"Papa! You don't believe me! You don't believe I am not pregnant! You of all people, believe the gossip that is abroad! How could you? How could you?I have told you that Francois has always been honourable towards me, and I to him."

Her eyes were blazing with new anger and hurt. At that moment she wanted to strike her father – something she had never felt before.

"I...I hate you! I hate you! How could you think that of me! How could you? Well, let me tell you, I wish I was bearing his child – I wish it more than anything!"

Her father's angry face reflected her's, but before he could speak, Sarah interrupted:

"Charlotte, that is unfair to your father – neither he not I believe the gossip for one minute. We trust you in every way. But it is harming to our family and to the church, and you should not address your father in that way."

Charlotte heard her mother, but continued to glare at her father. Eventually she lowered her eyes and said quietly, icily:

"I will write the letter, Papa. I am so sorry for the embarrassment this has brought on you, but Francois' behaviour towards me was always without the slightest impropriety, and always honourable, and I will write that to the Bishop. I will do that now."

And she took her leave and went to her room, sat down and wrote the letter. Half an hour later she went downstairs and gave it to her father.

"Mr Dear Bishop," she had written,

I write to reassure you that the rumours you have heard about the relationship between me and Vicomte Francois-Rene de Chateaubriand, have no truth in them whatever. Throughout his time here he has been kind, solicitous and honourable in every respect towards me – he has never made any untoward approaches to me. He is a man of great intelligence and intellect, learned in languages, literature, art and history. It is my belief that one day he will become known throughout France, perhaps throughout Europe, either through his writing, or diplomacy, or in some other sphere. He is a man to be much admired.

I confess that I love him. I believe he loves me, and it is my earnest prayer that he will return one day, following his suddenly departure. Until very recently I was not aware that he was married, but even so our love has been honourable, not carnal, and it hurts me that anyone should think that it has been otherwise. I am not with his child.

Yours
Charlotte Ives

"I hope that will suffice," she said, with cold control, "and that the Bishop will see that neither his diocese nor your parish, Papa, has been brought into disrepute. Clearly that is the most important thing."

The she added: "I'm sorry, Papa, that I shouted at you in the way I did. It was wrong of me."

Her father took the letter, and embraced his daughter.

"I understand, my dear. Truly, I never doubted you. This whole affair has made us all angry and confused, and behaving in ways other than normal. We must all try to forget it, and renew our family life, with God's help."

"I know, Papa. And I will try hard. But I will never forget Francois; and despite the fact that he is married I will never stop loving him."

Then she turned to her mother: "I feel hungry Mama. I think this evening I will be able to eat."

9

VICOMTE Francois-Rene de Chateaubriand, consumed with guilt and shame, fled to Beccles after leaving the parsonage. He half ran, half walked up the hill and through the town and out past the Watch House to take the up and down road along the edge of the valley. Out in the countryside, with the night pitch dark, he often stumbled on the rough track as he hurried, anxious to get away, anywhere, from the shock, devastation and broken dreams he knew he had left behind him.

He had nothing with him apart from the clothes he wore – all his possessions he had left in his room in Bungay, and his overcoat which hung in the vestibule. Such was the drama, the confusion in his mind at the moment that he made his revelation that he could think only of getting away, and his papers, his own notes of work, his own manuscripts he had been writing, lay on his desk there.

Had Mrs Ives not made such an unexpected and sudden proposal to him, his plan had been to leave for Beccles in the morning, and catch the mail coach to London, and there meet his generous friend, Peltier, who had found accommodation and occupation for him. That was still his plan, but now he would have to find a place to rest and wait when he got to Beccles - in the churchyard, or among the bushes down by the river.

Even with his eyes growing accustomed to the darkness he could discern little ahead of him, and guided himself by keeping his eyes on the edge of the roadway. But one thing that was fixed clearly in his mind was the image of Charlotte, a beseeching expression on her oval face and her dark eyes bright as he pictured the scene of her mother revealing to her that he was a married man, and that he had run away rather than staying to make the confession to her. In the darkness on the uneven roadway as he made the best haste he could, he could not rid his mind of that silent, appealing image, however he tried. Occasionally he would stop, breathless, put his hands to his head and try to physically rub the picture away. But try as he might, it continued to torment him.

Vague shapes of houses and farm buildings loomed occasionally as he made his urgent progress, and at Shipmeadow, a small hamlet mid-way between Bungay and Beccles, he made out the church. There was a dim light in it, and he made his way through the lych-gate and the short distance up the path to the door, intending to go in and kneel before the altar and ask for forgiveness from God, and from Charlotte and her parents. But the door was locked, and he slumped down on the ground in front of it in despair, groaning to himself, trying to control his thoughts.

"I must go back to the parsonage, back to her, and ask for her mercy, try to explain why I had not told her I was married," he said to himself. "I will go back to Bungay, I must – I must have the courage to explain to Charlotte, her parents, face to face."

But almost as quickly doubt set in.

"But what would I say to them? How would I explain why I had not told them I am married? What would their response be if I could explain? Is it, Francois, that you are in love with this girl, and wanted to strike from your mind your memory of an arranged marriage? Were you trying to pretend it is not so, that you were free to marry that most beautiful, gifted, educated young English woman? Admit it to yourself, Francois! Yes, I admit it – mon dieu, I admit it! What more could I want than this maiden, a home with a most hospitable family, a life away from all the confrontations and responsibilities in my homeland. Ah, oui, j'espere, je reve…

"But I could not do that – how long could I deceive them, how long before the remains of my family, my wife, travel to England to find me, and I am revealed as a fraud, an infidel? I could not do that – and yet I could not tell them the truth and spare them the chagrin and embarrassment and hurt they are suffering at this very moment, as I sit here in the dark, a pitiful dog, my life in ruins, my destiny grey…"

There he sat, against a buttress of that stone grey flint church – for how long he did not know. He slept briefly, only to be awakened by the cold and discomfort, and the aches in his recently healed body caused by the unaccustomed exertion. He cursed himself for not at least snatching his overcoat as he left.

Eventually he got up, stretched stiffly, returned to the lych-gate, and tried to peer through the darkness in both directions, hesitating, uncertain. Should he return to Charlotte? In his tiredness and confusion, the urge was strong...

Then suddenly he turned towards Beccles.

Dawn was just beginning to break as the cold, tired, confused, hungry Frenchman finally reached Beccles, crossing the marshes over which hung a low morning mist, the tops of trees just visible above its even level as the sun emerged from the eastern horizon into a pale, cold blue sky. With the stout tower of the parish church to guide him, he made his way up into the town, overlooking the river valley, and knocked on the door of the King's Head Inn, shivering as he did so.

After a long wait, a dishevelled looking ostler unbolted the door and let him in. He had enough money with him for some food and drink, and having devoured it ravenously, he begged paper and a quill, and sat down on a corner bench to write a letter. He decided to write it to Mrs Ives rather than Charlotte – it was Mrs Ives, after all, who had put to him the proposition that had caused him to flee.

He took some time in composing it, wrestling with his conscience on what to say, how to say it. His aristocratic upbringing made him decide to write his apologies to Mrs

Ives and the family in a diplomatic and restrained way, choosing to indicate his strong feelings for Charlotte without confessing his love for her, which he felt would be too much for her to bear. Even as he wrote the letter, his heart was still urging him to return to Bungay to meet the family, to confess to Charlotte face to face and to plead for her forgiveness. But eventually he finished it, borrowed sealing wax, and asked that it be delivered at the messenger's earliest convenience.

Francois had not long finished the task when he heard the sound of heavy hooves and wheels on the rutted road, and through the window saw the mail coach from Yarmouth to London drive into the yard in front of the stables. The four powerful horses drank greedily from the water offered them, and were uncoupled and tethered loose for a while to rest before continuing the journey.

It was 11am when the coachman finally flicked the reins and the team of four obediently eased their wheeled burden away from the King's Head to resume the journey to London, with the weary Frenchman huddled into his uncomfortable seat as the vehicle clattered over the cobbles and out southwards through the town.

Still Charlotte dominated his thoughts, still one part of his mind urged him to go back to Bungay, while the other told him that would be futile and unwise – that destiny was calling him to London, and that eventually he would return to France to resume his life there, with the bride he had not chosen, with his family greatly reduced by the revolution, with his home sold, his country and its government unrecognisable, his future uncertain.

In a different time, he would have stayed, and his life with Charlotte, in Bungay would have been certain, secure, and fulfilling...

London gave Chateaubriand no respite from his misery, no easing of the shame he heaped upon himself, no reducing in his longing for Charlotte – to see her face to face again, to hear her voice, her eagerness and love of the classics, to watch her as her hands moved effortlessly over the piano keys, producing the music which filled the room with the compositions he had come to love.

He found Peltier, who had organised rooms for him near Holborn, and translation work to provide him with the means to live.

"It is good to see you again, mon ami," said Peltier cheerfully, as he settled him into the primitive accommodation, with a minimum of furniture and facilities. "Et tu, Peltier," muttered Francois. "But I am not in the mood for conversation. My mind is confused, I can only think of Charlotte, the daughter of the family who were so kind to me in Bungay following my fall, and took me into their home as a member of their family. Monsieur, you would not see a woman as beautiful as Charlotte outside Eden – her hair, her eyes, her delicate skin, her enthusiasm, her personality....so attractive. And her mother offered me her hand in marriage – she had seen how attracted she was to me, a penniless émigré; she invited me to remain in England, to live with them; she offered me the life of the English gentry...

"Oh, Peltier, why did I get married to Celeste? Why did I allow myself to be forced into a marriage I had no appetite for? It was not of my asking or wanting! I have only seen Celeste for a few months! And I had not told the Ives that I was married – they thought I was free to take their daughter, Charlotte, a young woman who would fulfil the dreams of any man.

"When I told Mrs Ives I was married, I fled the house right away, not waiting till the morning. And how have I left this family who did everything for me? I have left them desolate, humiliated, and Charlotte heart-broken. I have behaved miserably towards them."

"You are being too hard on yourself, Francois – you told them of your circumstances as soon as you were offered their daughter's hand. That was honourable, was it not?"

"It was too late – I could have saved them the suffering and pain, and I had every chance – we spoke of my family often. Their plight was in the newspapers. It is my own selfishness that has caused the Ives such embarrassment."

The Frenchman had been pacing the room as he spoke, face to the floor, agitated. Then he said:

"Mon ami, I am going out – I don't want to see anyone or speak to anyone. I do not make a good companion – my company is no help to anyone. My head and my heart are muddled."

He thanked Peltier for organising his accommodation, and left abruptly.

Over the next few days, which ran into a week, Francois sought only solitude, where he need speak to no one, concerned only with dwelling on the image of Charlotte which filled his mind: the things she had said to him, the places they had walked, the conversations they had shared, the companionship they had enjoyed, her family life of which he had become a part.

He was unable to focus on anything, or anyone, neglecting his work, seeking out instead solitary places to walk, or sit morosely, cursing his fate. He sat in obscure places, shunning areas where they were people, cursing himself, and calling Charlotte to him in his mind. She was everywhere he went, everywhere he sat and mused, morbid and melancholy.

When he did see people he ignored them. Every so often a fellow émigré of the Revolution who he had known from his previous stay in London would greet him.

"Francois! How are you. It is…"

But he would hurry past, without replying and without acknowledging recognition. He wanted no one to disturb the images and memories of Charlotte that consumed him every hour of the day.

Sitting against a tree in a meadow near Hyde Park, two days after leaving Bungay, he started to write a letter:

My Dearest Charlotte,

What words can I write that would be adequate to convey to you my sorrow and regret for the great sadness I have caused you? I can only imagine your feelings when, at the height of your happiness and expectation, I deserted you, and fled like a miscreant from his evil deeds. I cannot ask your forgiveness, and I would not be worthy of it – you had given me so much joy, and a focus to my life, yet I so cruelly rejected you.

Only know my dearest, that I loved you...I love you...though I am not free to give you that love. I should have spoken of my wife, Celeste, who I left behind in France, but I lacked the courage – I was thinking only that it would affect your feelings towards me, which I wanted only to encourage.

You are part of my life that I will remember with supreme fondness – the sweet memories of our walks in Bungay, our mutual love of beautiful things – literature, music, nature, religion.

You fill my thoughts ever hour now I am here in London – I long to be with you in Bungay again, to be close to you. A hundred times I dream that I am not married, that I am

free, that I will return to Bungay and accept your mother's proposal, that I will resolve to spend the rest of my days in Bungay, and that we will have a family of our own.
Charlotte, dearest, I will come and see you again. I will. I feel I cannot go a minute more without starting my journey back to you. Your picture fills my mind – without you I am bereft of the spirit of life, because you have become that spirit to me, you are the sustenance I need. I will board the next mail coach to Beccles. I…"

Francois' quill had been in full flow, driven by his emotions. But he stopped, got up and walked slowly as he read what he had written, out loud to himself. Suddenly, he let out a howl of agitation and frustration, screwed the letter up in both hands and flung it to the ground.

"I can't do this! I can't write this! I can't go back to Bungay! I can't forsake my wretched marriage!"

And he sat down heavily again beside the tree, and put his head in his hands.

Trying to write to Charlotte had been no help to him. Still he saw her in anything of beauty that came into his sight – the bright rhododendrons in Hyde Park, the late spring sun sparkling on the Thames, the song of the nightingale in Berkeley Square, buttercups in a rural meadow, the gentle sound of a harp wafting from a large residence…

The last reminded him of Paris before the Revolution – then, the composers of harp music and makers of harps were in great demand among the aristocracy, and he had enjoyed recitals in many withdrawing rooms and salons in the capital. But many of those musicians and craftsmen were among the émigrés in London – he knew some of them, and mused that it was one who was now lovingly coaxing the strains of a sonata from the harp strings.

That was a fleeting respite from his torment. Almost immediately he pictured Charlotte at the harp, saw her slender fingers skilfully plucking the strings, glimpsed her ankles as her feet worked the pedals, saw her arm lovingly cradle the instrument into her shoulder, her face close to the strings and eyes half closed in rapture and concentration. How he longed to be that harp, embraced by Charlotte, feeling her sweet breath on his face, his arms drawing her closer still...

He could not erase the image of the English maiden from his mind. He was not inclined to try, in those long days and nights after he left Bungay – there was an ecstasy about the torment it brought him, an inverted comfort. There were many times when he sought pain and discomfort, purposely lying down on beds of thistles, or nettles, or dank ditches he came by on long, lonely walks out of London into the countryside. In his troubled mind they were a certain exquisite antidote to salve the purposely applied agony and pain, and when they became intolerable there was always the vision of Charlotte approaching him, leading him away into a comfortable meadow decked with daisies and buttercups, and embracing him lovingly there.

Many were the times when, during long, restless nights without sleep, he resolved to journey to Bungay the next day, to catch sight of her, to be in her vicinity without talking to her, to watch, as she walked on the common or in the town, her graceful movement, her flowing black hair, the demure expression on her face – the vision that had no equal, in his mind.

Each time, he stepped back from putting that intention into action. There were other occasions when, sitting in his room alone, he again wrote long letters to her, laying out his thoughts, and feelings, his admiration and love for Charlotte, and his intention to see her again. But each time he tore it up in exasperation, and chastised himself afterwards for not having the courage to send it.

Francois could concentrate his mind on nothing else. He would re-create everything he had said to her, and she to him, every note of work he had written for her; he would recall every musical work she had played for him, and every walk they had taken during his convalescence, every conversation they had had.

In his few moments of rational thinking he reasoned that if he could re-create every moment spent with her, he would be able to put them all at the back of his mind, and begin to move on. Then, on the occasions when exhaustion did bring sleep to him, in a meadow, or his room, or sitting in the corner of a tavern, she would come to him in his dreams...

He was back in Bungay, elated, climbing into a carriage outside the parsonage. With a companion he did not know, they were driven to the small round towered church of Ilketshall St Margaret, where John Ives was the Vicar. They alighted, and his companion led him into the church, full of people, immaculately dressed, turning and smiling at him as he walked down the aisle.

Then the organ was playing, music he recognised, and everyone was standing up. The altar in front of him was bathed in brilliant sunshine, and behind him he sensed people approaching, but dare not look round.

He closed his eyes momentarily, as if in a dream. When he opened them, Charlotte stood close by his side.

"Charlotte?" he whispered. Tears filled his eyes, as he took in the radiant vision, dressed in a flowing white gown, with a matching headdress and veil over her face which could not conceal those dark familiar eyes and the tender smile of love. He glanced down at the bouquet she carried – a mixture of wild roses, primroses and buttercups.

"Do you, Francois-Rene de Chateaubriand, Viscount of Combourg, Brittany, take Charlotte, Ives, spinster of the parish of Bungay, to your lawful wedded wife, to have and to hold, from this day forth, for better, for worse, for richer, for poorer, in sickness and in health, as long as you both shall live, so help me, God?"

John Ives was in front of them, leading the vows. So full of emotion was Francois that at first he could not speak. Bu eventually he managed, huskily, "Oui – I do."

"And do you, Charlotte Ives, take Francois-Rene de Chateaubriand to be your lawful wedded husband, to have and to hold from this day forth, for better, for worse, for richer, for poorer, in sickness and in health, to love, honour and obey, as long as you both shall live, so help me God?"

"I do."

Charlotte turned to face Francois, and lifted her veil. Love, fidelity and honour shone from her eyes, a certainty of her trust in their future together.

"Gracious Lord, we ask for your blessing on this man and this woman joined together here today, that they may have a full and loving life together. Give them peace, happiness and friendship, and in your bounteous goodness bless them with children and grandchildren."

The organ struck up a triumphant wedding march. Charlotte and Francois, clasping each other's hand tightly, turned and faced the congregation, and began the walk down the aisle as husband a wife, fulfilling their dream.

Out of the corner of his eye, Francois caught sight of Celeste, standing beside the aisle, tears tumbling from her dark eyes. Then suddenly, without warning, they were blazing with anger and power, her face contorted, she stepped forward and struck out, as he raised his arms instinctively to protect himself...

...Francois let out a cry of terror, and found himself sitting bolt upright in his bed, sweating from head to foot. Dawn was breaking, but he could see only the aura of love on Charlotte's face, and the grimace of revenge on Celeste's. For the first time he realised that the two women shared the same black hair, dark eyes, and oval faces.

That image of Charlotte was with Francois wherever he went, whatever he was doing. As he continued to shun friends and fellow emigres in London, they began to think he was mad – something he himself feared in his lowest moments. But the vision of Charlotte was there always, to lift him from his deepest depression and melancholy.

Many more times he began to write letters to her, sometimes to apologise and try to explain, sometimes to tell her he was returning to Bungay, to meet her – long letters, with thoughts and memories of his time in Bungay, his feelings for her, confessing his love, asking her to understand. But each was never finished – he became angry and frustrated at himself, unsatisfied with what he had written, unsure that he was able to be honest about the intentions expressed in them. On most occasions he tore them up and disposed of them, berated himself fiercely, ands fell into deep melancholy.

His urge to travel to Bungay surged through him often. More than once he boarded the mail coach to Yarmouth, or Norwich, only to lose courage and focus quickly, and disembark at the first staging post, and walk the long miles back to his rooms. He avoided meeting people, shunned crowds and gatherings, was unable to concentrate on his writing, unable to focus on anything – only Charlotte, and her beauty, and the times he had spent with her.

Even Peltier despaired of his erratic behaviour.

10

At the parsonage the mood remained subdued for some time, despite the best efforts of John and Sarah Ives to lift their daughter from the depth of her sadness. After writing the letter to the Bishop she had begun to eat again, but her piano playing lacked its previous inspiration and feeling, and she took to playing works *penseroso* rather than the lively, vibrant works which she had played for Francois.

She continued to walk in the places they had walked, dreaming that he would suddenly be there, and enfold her in his arms and profess his love for her, to assure her that he was free to marry her after all, and eagerly accept her mother's proposal. Each time there was someone at the door she would hurry to the vestibule as Maria went to open it, praying that it was Francois; each time she was crestfallen when it was a parishioner with business with her father, or one of his friends.

Each day too, she hoped there would be a letter for her from him, professing his love, telling her where he was, what he was doing, to give her belief in her hopes. She visited the mail office regularly to inquire whether there was such a letter. But the days and weeks went by, and there was none.

Sometimes Charlotte would begin letters to Francois, writing down her feelings for him, asking for his, telling him she was not angry with him, and wanted to understand

163

why he had left without saying goodbye. Writing those things down made her feel better. But with no address to put on the letter, no idea of his whereabouts, her despair quickly returned, and she discontinued her writing.

Often, in her room, filled with the thoughts of Francois and what might have been, she would read again the notes of work he had written for her, and open the book in which she had pressed the wild rose, and the primrose he had picked for her, such a short time ago it seemed, when her world was happy and expectant, and he was often by her side. And she would draw the pages up to her lips, and close her eyes and kiss the delicate petals, as he had kissed her that bright May day.

Each night, and in church, Charlotte prayed for Francois – that he was safe and well, and comfortable. She beseeched God to watch over him and asked that she be in his heart and mind, as he was in her's. She took comfort from her prayers, feeling closer to Francois through their common beliefs.

And, through her religious integrity, she prayed for Celeste, too.

A week after her father's concern about the rumours abounding in the town that Charlotte was expecting Francois' child, John Ives, grim-faced, called Maria into his study. She stood in front of him, wide-eyed and shaking, not knowing what he was about to say.

"Maria, you will know very well that there is gossip among the townsfolk that my daughter is with child. I cannot emphasise too highly that that is not the case, and I have been working to find out where such cruel rumours came from. Now I have been told that you, and your parents, have been heard saying that, gossiping about Charlotte and her state of...of health. And that she is due a child. Is that correct?"

Maria's shaking increased and her face contorted as she burst into tears.

"No!" she sobbed. "No, sir! It's not true. I was....just...talking to my parents about Mr...Mr Shatterbrain leaving so suddenly, and...well...it was just...they said perhaps he had gone because...because Miss Charlotte was...well, was..."

"Yes, Maria, I'm sorry to cause you upset, but you must understand the upset this has caused to Charlotte and Mrs Ives particularly. Your parents were heard talking about it openly at the market on Thursday, and now it seems everyone in Bungay believes Charlotte is...with child, and the Bishop is most concerned."

Maria's head was down on her chest, with her hands covering her eyes, her body shaking with her crying.

"I'm s-s-sorry, sir, I didn't say...people got it....wrong..."

"I understand that, Maria – people do read into what is said more than the words contain, and that is why it is wrong to speak about something, particularly people, you know nothing about. I now have to placate the Bishop, who could have me removed from this living. Do you understand that?"

"Yes, sir...I'm sorry...I know how much Miss Charlotte loved him, Mr Shatterbrain...I didn't mean to upset no-one."

Mr Ives sighed heavily.

"It's too late for that now, Maria, much too late. Now do try to stop crying."

The maid lifted her head slightly, without looking directly at Mr Ives.

"Yes, sir."

Then, as a thought suddenly seemed to enter her head, her eyes screwed up again, and she stammered:

"Will I...will I have to leave....will I be dismissed, sir?"

Mr Ives stood up and came round to the front of his desk, beside the contrite girl. He spoke in a gentler tone.

"Maria, this episode has caused me considerable embarrassment in the parish, and much extra work. But God calls on us all to forgive, and I preach forgiveness through Him. You are young. I earnestly hope and pray that you will learn a lesson from this Maria. But you can remain in your position here."

"Oh, thank you sir, thank you. I won't be so foolish again – I promise I won't. I'm so sorry for all the trouble I've caused."

"Very well, Maria. I know you are genuinely sorry. Now return to Mrs Honeywood in the kitchen."

The Bishop of Norwich, though exasperated, was equally forgiving when he visited Bungay, and after a brief philosophical and informal lecture to Mr Ives on the need for house staff and servants to be properly tutored in what was expected from them when they took a position in such a place as a parsonage, he readily accepted the offer of port and the two men soon fell into discussions of a more worldly nature.

In Bungay, the populace soon found new outlets for their gossip.

As the days moved into weeks, Charlotte gradually adjusted to life without Francois, though she continued to believe fervently that he would return one day, when he was ready. She drew comfort from the relics she had of their time together - the flowers, the notes, the music – and the memories, and continued to pray for him. She eagerly read the newspapers, in case there was news of the activities of émigrés in London which might contain mention of him. But she found none.

Her parents were disinclined to discuss Francois in any way, considering his stay there an episode in their lives which had now finished, and tried to encourage Charlotte to feel the same. Privately they chided themselves for not having ascertained that he was married, though Mrs Ives told herself that she had given him many opportunities to do that during discussions on his family back in France. They had done their best, as a Christian family, to make him welcome and comfortable, and in most ways he had been an appreciative and contented guest.

Charlotte continued to hope for a letter from Francois, and would regularly check at the mail office to see if one had arrived – only to be disappointed each time.

Then one day in the middle of June, after she had toiled up the hill to the Market Place in the heat of a summer's day, with the warmth reflected off the buildings on either side of the street, she entered the mail office once again, glad of the dim coolness of its interior after the brightness and dust outside.

As her eyes adjusted, she saw the master of the office standing by the counter, a cheery smile on his face.

"Ah, Miss Ives, your patience has been rewarded – there is a letter for you today!"

Her heart leapt at the words, but she tried to remain demure, and wait patiently as he retrieved it from the room behind the public office. But the master cannot have failed to notice the disappointment on her face when she saw it contained the emblem of the Navy on it.

"I hope its good news," he said.

If it had been from Francois, she would have opened it there and then, eager and expectant to find out where he was, what news he had, and if he was returning to Bungay. Instead, she took it home and read it in her room.

My Dear Charlotte,

It seems many months since I wrote to you, and had been hoping for a reply, but on the occasions when my ship has been in port, and I have hurried to the mail office, there has been none.

It has made me wonder whether you received my letter and, in case that might be so, I thought I would write again, to see if you yet had an answer to my invitation to accompany me to the ball at Ditchingham Hall next month.

I have been thinking of you much on my voyages – the picture of you in my mind helps me to tolerate the privations of life on board His Majesty's fleet, though conditions for us are much superior to those on many other vessels. If you would do me the honour to accompany me it would make me a proud man, Charlotte – I imagine us dancing together, and the other guests admiring the beauty of the woman with whom I am dancing.

It is now certain that I will be able to be there, and I hope you will enable my dream to come true. If you do feel disposed to write with an answer, I will look forward to it eagerly.

Yours,
Samuel Sutton
Captain, HMS Albion

Charlotte read the letter with some puzzlement – she had replied and asked Maria to take the letter to the mail office, and the service had a high reputation for its dependability. Now she would have to write again with the news that would disappoint Samuel, when she had thought that task was long over.

That evening, when they were sitting in the garden by the river, with the air still warm, cows grazing in the meadow on the opposite bank and swifts and swallows darting and weaving above them, she told her parents of the letter.

"The mail service is usually most reliable," said her mother, as she concentrated on her embroidery. "But I wonder how reliable the organisation of it is at ports. Nevertheless, it is thoughtful of Captain Sutton to write again."

"And the situation has changed since you sent your original reply," added her husband, pointedly. "Perhaps you may feel now that you are able to accept his generous invitation."

"Papa, the situation may have changed, but my feelings have not, and neither have my hopes. I still hope and pray that Francois will return, and I do believe he will," said his daughter fervently in reply.

Sarah put down her embroidery, and turned to Charlotte, a pained expression on her face.

"My dear, I know how deeply hurt you have been, but is it not time to put thoughts of Francois behind you – it is nearly six weeks since he left? And with the revelation that proceeded his flight, do you think he would have the audacity to return here, now? What could he do? What could he say, to you or us, that would change anything, even if your feelings, or his, are unchanged. That would not alter the fact that he is married, and can have no intentions towards you."

Her husband took the cue from her inquiring glance towards him.

"Your mother is right. He could not expect to be welcome in our house after what has happened, and in time he will be just a memory. We do urge you to accept Captain Sutton's invitation. It is not to suggest that he will ask your hand in marriage, but it will help you to look forward, and not backwards."

"Papa, I am trying to look forward, I am. But no, Francois will never be just a memory – he will always be there. Wherever he is and whatever he does, he will always be part of my life. I understand your reproaches, your anger at him, your feelings of humiliation, but he never meant to bring that upon you, and he means so much to me...so much."

"We only ask that you give Captain Sutton's invitation some thought before you reply. Accompanying him to the ball is making no commitment," said Sarah. "You cannot turn from any commitment or activities because of your feelings for Francois."

"That is wise advice," her husband added, gently. "Francois could only return here as a friend, not as a suitor."

Charlotte looked at both of them. The rawness of her love's sudden departure, at the very moment when her hopes had soared so high, had faded, if not her feelings for him, though still she could think of a permanent future with no one. At last she said:

"I know you are thinking of what is best for me. I must try to see everyone's point of view."

And she kissed them both, and went indoors to bed.

"Maria should have taken her letter to Samuel to the mail office," Sarah observed after she had gone. "Charlotte had written declining Captain Sutton's invitation."

"I shall not chide her for it. She should have taken it if she said she would – the fact that it did not get there, for whatever reason, may prove to be a blessing in disguise for all of us."

In her room, Charlotte again opened the book containing the pressed flowers, and tenderly touched the delicate petals Francois had touched as he gave them to her. It brought him closer in her mind, made it easier to recall the days and weeks and months they had spent together – wonderful memories she would always hold dear.

"My Lord, where are you? What are you doing, who are you with? Are you well, have you good accommodation?" she whispered to herself. "If I could know these things it would make it easier to understand. If I could hear your voice, see your face close, just once more…"

But she was an intelligent young woman, trying to be practical amid the strong emotions she felt. In the weeks since he had left she had tried to step back and look clearly at their relationship, and now she did so again.

Everything about him – the way he looked at her, and spoke to her, the little gestures he made to her, the look in his eyes, his whole demeanour, made it clear that he was strongly attracted to her. Many were the occasions when she had felt that he had been about to enfold her in his arms, embrace her tenderly, lovingly, in an expression of his ardour. There were times when he had started to tell her something, and then seemed to lose the courage. Were those the times he had wanted to tell her he was married? To confess his love for her but to say their love was impossible?

Or had he been waiting for her to confess her love for him? She had longed to say the words, "I love you, my Lord." But she too had lacked the courage, the confidence, to speak them.

Despite all the signs from the way he was with her, even when he had gently touched his lips on hers, beside the river on the Common, he had never told her he loved her. Had she read too much into the way he was with her, misinterpreted the signs? Were they born simply of the affection of a companion, out of gratitude for the friendship

and care she had shown him; she was, after all, the only
companion he had had during his stay in Bungay – was it
not inevitable that she should have his undivided attention,
that she should be the recipient of his small gestures and
gifts, when he had no one else on which to bestow them?

And yet her love for Francois - for love it was on her part,
she was certain of that - could not have been born from
nothing, without any response to nurture the seed, she
reasoned. If there had been an aloofness about him, with no
hint of feeling of any kind, would he not have been to her
simply someone she dutifully helped to recover from
injuries sustained in a fall, a compassionate and selfless
duty she would perform for anyone, that would not have
caused the deep pain in her heart when he left so suddenly?

Something substantial had nurtured the love she had – the
day dreams of choosing a wedding dress, of walking up the
aisle of her father's church, on her father's arm, with the
smiling congregation on either side, of seeing Francois
standing there in front of the altar, waiting for her, of seeing
his smile of pure happiness as he looked at her, of speaking
their vows of love, and faithfulness and honour, for a
lifetime, before God; of becoming his wife, and having his
children.

Yet he was married – he had been through that process with
his wife; no matter that it was an arranged marriage he had
had no particular appetite for. He already had a wife to
honour and care for, and was not free to offer his affections

to another. For some time after Francois's confession to her mother, Charlotte had denied to herself that that was so, had told herself that it was a mistake, that her mother had misunderstood what he had said. Even when she saw Francois' fleeing letter, with the confession in writing, she had shut it out of her mind, would not let herself believe it, had prayed that in his confusion he had written it as a fantasy.

Now she was coming to terms with the truth, with reality. She would not deny her love for him, but he could not be part of her future.

The last rays of the evening sun were glinting through the window as she knelt at her bedside to say her night-time prayers, and seemed to penetrate her clasped hands and closed eyes as she prayed. From outside a dove cooed its message, and the light and its song of peace filled Charlotte' head, merging and forming words in her mind:

"Remember me, my beautiful English rose, but do not be sad. Live your life, as I will mine in the knowledge that you will find happiness and fulfilment. Do not wait for me – I cannot come. Only remember I am with you always in my heart…"

The last rays of the sun slipped from the window, the dove's cooing ceased, the picture in her hands and mind went suddenly dark. Charlotte jumped up, and ran to the window, just in time to glimpse the silhouette of a dove flying beyond the trees and away…

She turned back, blinking, trying to absorb the moment, and sat down again on her bed, for some time, marvelling. Then she closed her book, which was still open on the counterpane, got into bed, and fell asleep.

In the morning she wrote another letter to Samuel. This time she took it to the mail office herself.

11

T he couples were lined up, waiting for the music to begin; and when the orchestra commenced, the men bowed, and the ladies curtsied, before joining arms to dance a minuet in the large well appointed ballroom at Ditchingham Hall, as others stood or sat around the fringes, talking and watching the activity. Above them the high ceiling, painted in a tasteful yellow, was ornate with stucco work, rich covings and bosses, and large chandeliers hung from it, all part of the richly colourful scene, enhanced by the colours of the ladies' gowns and the gentlemen's embroidered frockcoats and waistcoats. It was July in that long, hot summer of 1796, and the doors of the ballroom were flung open to provide air, and present a panorama of the ornate, immaculate formal garden, reached from the veranda steps, and containing a number of statues among the boxwood hedges, rose gardens, and lawned areas. Some of the guests at the summer ball strolled there in the cooler evening air, glad to be free of the stuffiness of the ballroom for a while. Beyond the garden was a lake, well stocked with fish, and backed by a copse of oak, birch, elm and evergreen trees.

With the dance concluded, Samuel bowed to Charlotte, and led her back to the table where they were sitting with her parents.

"Thank you Charlotte, you dance delightfully, as if you have danced many times before," said Samuel.

"I have danced very little – I have a lot to learn, but I am enjoying the occasion. I have not been to a ball before – it is a new experience for me," she replied.

"But you move so gracefully. I must take you to others. Ah, they are now calling a polka – something much more lively! Are you ready to dance again?"

Charlotte smiled a natural smile at the captain, and accepted his invitation as the music struck up again, violins, harpsichord, cello and viola in perfect unison. Sarah looked on approvingly as they danced.

"She is beginning to sparkle again I feel, though she is not as she was before," she observed to her husband.

"She has more energy – she has lost her listlessness; and I noticed there is more meaning to her piano playing lately," her husband replied. "I think she is beginning to forget about the Viscount."

"No John, she will never forget Francois – her feelings for him go too deep. But I think she has come to terms with them in the last few weeks, and is beginning to find the right place for them in her mind. Agreeing to come to the ball with Samuel has given her life some focus again. She was quite enthusiastic in choosing which gown she should wear."

"Yes, he is an agreeable young man, with considerable prospects in the Navy. I'm told he is highly thought of –

that chap Nelson, who I have been reading great things of in the newspaper, is said to be considering him for one of the ships in his fleet."

"That will probably mean he is away even more than he is now – he is seldom at home," said his wife with a sigh. "There seem so many sea battles to be fought at this time, against the Dutch, or French, or Spanish, or all of them together. Why can't England settle her differences with other countries with diplomacy rather than cannon?"

"France can't settle her internal differences without fighting and executions, it seems – that's why the Viscount came over here in the first place, along with many others."

"Are not things becoming a little more settled there now? I wonder if he has returned there yet, or whether he is still in London."

"Still in London, according to the account of my friends at Beccles – but I don't expect him to come anywhere near Bungay again."

Charlotte and Samuel returned to the table, Charlotte fanning herself vigorously following her exertions. She danced much that evening, not only with Samuel, but with her father, and other admirers taken by her looks and asking for a place on her card. All too soon it was midnight and the ball was ended; carriages arrived to convey the guests to their homes, and Samuel dutifully accompanied Charlotte and her parents to the parsonage before returning to his own home, and after offering to escort Charlotte to Bible study the following week, before he returned to his ship.

She had accepted the offer, and thanked him for taking her to the ball. Her gratitude was sincere – she had enjoyed the occasion, and experiencing the atmosphere of a local society event, attended by all those from large halls and estates in the surrounding area, listening to the orchestra, admiring the fashionable ball gowns, and dancing the popular steps of the day. She was tentative at first, having had few opportunities to dance at such an occasion, but her confidence grew.

And she had enjoyed Samuel's company, she admitted to herself as she prepared for bed later. He was attentive, strong, led her well through the dances and was animated and interesting in his conversation. She told herself again, as she had when they first met, that he had attractive features without being handsome – assured in the way he moved and carried himself, but with modesty, and without aplomb. It was easy to be natural, and relaxed, with him.

But when she got into bed, tired after the evening's excitement and exertions, and closed her eyes, she imagined what it would have been like to be at such an occasion with Francois, to dance with him, feel his arm around her, leading her gallantly and expertly across the floor, the two of them lost among the other dancers, engrossed in each other, and the warmth of their feelings...

On their way back from Bible study a few days later, the hot weather suddenly broke, a sharp thunderstorm cooling the night air and forcing them to hurry down the hill to the parsonage before they became drenched by huge raindrops. But they managed to escape the worst of it as they hurried through the porch and into the vestibule for cover.

"Samuel, you must remain here until the storm passes – you cannot walk home in such a storm," Charlotte advised. "I will see if I can find you refreshment while you wait."

Samuel smiled in acceptance of the offer. "Thank you," he said, as they moved into the withdrawing room. "The storm will pass before too long. But Charlotte…"

He hesitated, as if considering, before going on, "Charlotte, it gives me the opportunity to speak with you about the future – we scarcely had the opportunity at the ball, or earlier this evening. Now we have a few minutes."

They sat side by side on the chaise-longe as the captain continued:

"When first I wrote to you it was to apologise for not understanding your question about the difference in our ages, and to assure you that if our feelings were the same, and our interests, age was not an important issue. I have thought much about it since, about us, my dear Charlotte. Some months have passed since then, I know, but they have not diminished my feelings for you and…and I am anxious to know whether you feel the same."

Inwardly, Charlotte tightened. It was a matter she had feared Samuel would raise at some point but had hoped to avoid. She had written her views honestly in the letter she had sent, and now, with the mail not getting through to him, had to find the courage to let him down gently, face to face. She chose her words carefully.

"Samuel, I enjoy your company, and value your friendship. And I adored going to the ball – it was all so exciting and new to me. As to our conversation about the difference in age between two people, I think there was...a misunderstanding. It was foolish and unthinking of me to ask your advice on such a matter. You see, it was...I was...It is difficult for me to say this when I know it is going to hurt you, Samuel."

He put his hand on hers. "Tell me, Charlotte – I will try to understand."

She looked at him, with an expression half of sorrow, half of pity. "When I asked you that question, I was thinking of the Frenchman who was staying with us here at the parsonage at the time. I had formed a...a close attachment with him, and he with me, I believe, and I had earnestly hoped..."

"I had heard that he left quite suddenly. My parents had been told there was much gossip in the town afterwards. It must have been very difficult for you, and Mr and Mrs Ives," Samuel interrupted sympathetically.

"Mama suggested to him that she and Papa would not stand in his way if he should propose marriage to me – it was then that he told her he was already married."

Tears brightened Charlotte's eyes again as she recalled that moment, and Samuel pressed his hand more firmly on her's.

"I was not aware of such details – it must have been most distressing for you, and so hurtful."

"Yes, I was heartbroken, and hurt, and angry – but it did not change my feelings for him, Samuel. Despite all that, I still love him."

"But because he is married, you have no hope of a future with him."

"No, I am beginning to come to terms with that. But you see Samuel, Francois will always have a big place in my heart, always. I will never forget him and I believe he will always remember me, wherever he is. It will be the same for him. How could I accept the advances of another man in such circumstances? I would have to be honest with him, and tell him my true feelings."

Samuel withdrew his hand, and stood up. "I must confess I was not aware of your strong feelings towards the Frenchman," he said. "It would be dishonest of me not to say I am also hurt and deeply disappointed; but the misunderstanding over your question was on my part, not your's – I should not have been thinking so selfishly. Forgive me."

"Oh no Samuel, it is I who should ask your forgiveness – I who was in the wrong. You must not blame yourself."

Samuel, who had been looking down at the floor, raised his head, and smiled ruefully at her.

"I had hoped this conversation would have turned out in a different way for…for both of us.

"You say he will always be in your heart – you have often been in my mind, also, wherever I have sailed, wherever I have quartered. For me, that won't change.

"Tomorrow, I leave again for Portsmouth, and expect to be away for some time – months, perhaps years. Much can change in such a period, much may happen to either of us, Charlotte. Only grant me this favour – that when I do return, I may call on you, to resume this friendship that we have begun and which in such early times has come to mean much to me. Will you grant me that consolation?"

"I will, Samuel – your words are most flattering. I will look forward to when you return. I hope in time you will understand."

Samuel took his leave, and as she had done once before, she watched him stride across the bridge and towards Ditchingham, until he was out of sight. This time there was not such a spring in his step. As she turned and went indoors, she mused to herself:

"Was it really less than a year that he first came to Bible study, and I found him attractive?

"So much has happened, so many new feelings have tested me, in those intervening months..."

Charlotte gradually recovered her enthusiasm for her music, her art, and her studies of English and European literature, and the French language. Her piano playing had a renewed expressiveness, and she learned new pieces, coming to enjoy entertaining house guests with recitals of work by the established and new composers. She had a determination, a resolve, to improve in everything she did, and her thoughts of Francois were her impetus – he was constantly in her mind, through the notes and relics he had left, and still, sometimes, she would imagine him standing at the piano as he used to. And she continued to wonder, in her quieter, melancholy moments, where he was, and what he was doing, whether he had returned to France, and his wife – whether he thought often of his time in Bungay, whether he would return there one day. She still prayed for him each night, and in church, and in her weaker moments her whole body ached for him, and she yearned for him to be with her again, close, comforting, loving.

But Charlotte began to see her life in perspective too, accepting that their relationship could never be resumed, that thoughts of him should not hold her back in her progress in life, that their love could only be a memory, and she began to involve herself in her father's church work, and in voluntary work for the poor and destitute in Bungay.

In the ensuing few years, the newspapers contained regular reports of the frequent manoeuvrings of the English Navy, in the North Sea and the Mediterranean, against the fleets of Spain, France and Holland, and even Sweden. Charlotte read them in the hope of seeing news of Francois, only to always be disappointed. But there was regular news from the Admiralty, and one day in the autumn of 1796, she was pleased to read, in the Times:

The Admiralty announced yesterday that Lieutenant Samuel Sutton has been promoted to command the sloop Martin in His Majesty's fleet.

Some months later, early in 1797, in another Admiralty report, there was another mention of him:

HMS Martin, under the command of Captain Samuel Sutton, has been commissioned to convey the Duc D'Anjouleme from Leith to Cuxhaven. A few weeks after that she read that he had been put in command of HMS Aligator. There was something about seeing Samuel's name mentioned in The Times, that gave her a sense of pride, and pleasure, that he was winning recognition and promotion in the Navy, and she found that he was talked about in social circles.

It was two years after they had last met that Charlotte received a letter from Samuel, informing her that the fleet was back at Portsmouth, and asking her if he could come to see her while he was ashore. She wrote and said that he could, and a week later, Maria announced him after answering the door.

Charlotte and her parents welcomed him warmly, and they conversed for some time about his duties in the Navy, his travels and his experiences. Charlotte watched him as he spoke – his expressions, his mannerisms, the way he laughed when something amusing was mentioned, and she was aware of him watching her in the same way as he listened to her conversation.

Later they walked on the Common – a place that was a regular haunt for Charlotte, somewhere she found relaxing, spiritual and, even two years after their parting, where she sensed the presence of Francois, lifting and supporting her.

She found Samuel good company. His long voyages, bereft of female company, made him impatient for something other than the often banal, earthy talk that went on among the crew, even the officers, as they tried to forget the privations and boredom of life at sea. Yet he enjoyed the life, and the responsibilities and spoke much about it, though ruing the fact that the time away meant he had little opportunity for social activities.

"My fellow officers who are married speak often of their families at home, what they plan to do when they are ashore; and of their children, and the way they grow up while they are away so that they barely recognise them, but it must be just as difficult for those at home," he said, as they enjoyed summer's warmth beside the sultry river, amid the scents of the rural meadowland.

"I can understand the feelings of longing to be home," Charlotte agreed. "I have never been far form Bungay – it is difficult to imagine it otherwise. But sailors are doing their duty for their country, protecting her shores, are they not, and must take great satisfaction from that?"

"That is certainly the case with the officers, but not with all of the ratings, I fear. For most it is earning a wage, often a pittance, and they are in the Navy because they are forced into it, or have no other way of providing for their family."

"And you are proud of your country, Samuel? I can tell that you are."

"I am proud to serve in His Majesty's Navy, Charlotte, and proud to serve my country. It makes up for the many drawbacks. But I often wonder if I would feel the same if I had a family, who I would leave at home for long periods. I do not think my pride would be compromised, but I believe there would be a reluctance, a constraint on my career, though one I would dearly love to have. I do hope to marry and have a family, one day."

He looked at Charlotte, and she sensed a pointedness about his last remark, as if it heralded something more specific.

"I'm sure you will," she said, lamely. He looked at her intently, and when he spoke again there was understanding in his tone but also a sureness about what he wanted to say.

"Charlotte, it is some time since last we met – I have been away for two years, and before we left we were both aware of each other's feelings. In that time I have thought much about you, and my feelings towards you have not changed – you know I am greatly attracted to you, and though we share lives that are widely different, we have the same understanding of many things.

"I know your feelings have not changed, towards the Frenchman. I accept that they never will. But I wonder Charlotte, if they might have changed towards me, that you might have thought of me sometimes, too, in my absence?"

"From time to time there has been mention of you in the newspapers, Samuel – of your promotions, and your command of ships, and it pleases me to read them, and that your career is successful, that you are well thought of by the Admiralty. At other times, yes...yes I do think of you, and I looked forward to your return, and the opportunity to meet with you again."

Samuel was unsure about the reply – it seemed to him to lack warmth and affection, and might have come from one of his senior officers in addressing him. But he continued, enthusiastically:

"There is a big difference in our ages – nearly 20 years, but as we have said that should not be a barrier between two people who are otherwise suited, as I believe we are. You have been honest with me about the Frenchman, and how much he fills your heart, and that that is unlikely to change.

Nevertheless I know you accept, however hard that may be, that a future for you and him together is impossible.

"I know that any other man could only be a consolation for you, my dear Charlotte – but should you ever consider it, I would be happy to accept those circumstances if you felt able to accept me – I would willingly be a poor substitute if it meant being at your side."

They were standing on the bank of the river, at its furthest point from the town, with the tower of St Mary's Church on the near horizon, and close to where Francois had once picked a wild rose for her. She recalled it every time she passed that spot on her walks, and despite her respect and affection for Samuel, he almost seemed to be intruding at that moment. But just as quickly she felt guilty at such an unreasonable thought, and perhaps that guided her reply.

"I could not expect you to be a substitute, Samuel – you deserve so much more, someone who could love you fully and unreservedly, without someone else in their mind. That would not be right or proper."

"Then you plan to remain a spinster, Charlotte, with no desire for children of your own? That would but an unfair compromise on yourself, on your life, your fulfilment. Don't put that burden on yourself."

Charlotte was slightly taken aback at the reply. It came gently and caringly. As a woman a desire for children had risen in her periodically, and she imagined at those times the joy of cradling a baby in her arms, and suckling it at her breast. It was a strong and natural innate urge, but one she managed to suppress each time because she felt, now, that it would never happen. But the remark coming from a man gave it a poignant focus, and made her realise fatherhood was as important to a man, though in a different way, as motherhood was to a woman.

"It is not a burden I proscribe, rather one that circumstances have proscribed," she said after some thought. "I could not impose those circumstances on someone else, that would be impossibly selfish."

"But if someone else was prepared to accept that, for the sake of being with you, and was prepared to accept that he did not have your whole heart, for the sake of loving you fully himself, would you accept him, if in every other way he was acceptable?"

Again Charlotte pondered, trying to gather her thoughts, knowing that Samuel was earnest and sincere. But she could not find the right answer that was true to her feelings and yet not a rebuff to him. At last she said, in a tone of exasperation:

"Oh, Samuel, I don't know! How can I know? All these questions are confusing me!"

She turned her gaze from him. They had stopped walking during the conversation, but now she resumed her steps. Samuel was quickly by her side.

"Forgive me, it was wrong of me to press you. I should be more considerate – I have no wish to upset you."

Charlotte stopped again, a feeling of guilt quickly chasing her exasperation.

"No, it's I that should be sorry – my re-action was uncalled for. Samuel, allow me time to…some time to ponder carefully on what you have said and my response to it. It's simply that, sometimes, of late, I don't know how I feel…what I feel…what I want."

Samuel, looked at her, an anxious look clouding his face; and then he smiled acceptance.

"Of course," he said.

Once again his stay was short – he returned to his ship in Portsmouth two days later, having thanked Charlotte for her companionship, and re-assured her that she was often in his thoughts.

The evening after his departure, Charlotte sat with her mother in the withdrawing room, Sarah sewing and Charlotte doing some embroidery.

"Samuel's visit was so short," said Sarah. "Our fleets seem so busy, in many places. Why do nations look upon others as enemies?"

"He is committed to his country, and to the Navy, Mama. It must be so hard for the families left ashore when husbands and loved ones spend so much time at sea."

"And in many cases they have no choice in the matter," her mother observed, laconically. Charlotte put her work down for a moment, ignoring the comment and picking up on her own last remark.

"Mama, I feel Samuel may make a marriage proposal next time he is ashore. He has been questioning me about my feelings."

Her mother looked up from her sewing, immediately inquisitive.

"Oh – what has he said?"

"He knows the feelings I still have for Francois – we were talking about that, and he asked if that meant I would never consider taking a husband, and that in such circumstances, if I were to consider it, he would be prepared to marry someone he loved, even knowing they loved someone else."

"That would not be good grounds for a life-long marriage, my dear. What did you say to him?"

"I said that would not be fair on the man, and it would not be proper for a woman to agree to a marriage in those circumstances. But I began to get confused. Finally I agreed to think on what we had both said, and what our views were."

"Well there is no question of you marrying Francois, or any likelihood of seeing him again, Charlotte, and there will be other suitors, eminently suitable. Samuel would be most acceptable to me and your father – he is a good man with a splendid career. As for Francois, it is two years since that dreadful evening when I put that proposition to him, and it still gives me nightmares. I have no wish to remember it, nor Francois, though I pray that he has returned to France, and to his wife."

"It has made little difference for my feelings towards him, Mama. Samuel asked if I intended to be a spinster all my life, without husband or children, knowing that Francois could never be mine. I know I have to think deeply about that. I do try to put him to the back of my mind, but with no greater success now than two years ago."

"There is no dishonour in remaining a spinster, my dear. But you have so much to offer a husband, and children."

"Perhaps, Mama," said Charlotte, doubtfully. "I value your advice always – would it be fair, if Samuel were to propose and I were to accept, both knowing that part of my heart will always lie elsewhere?"

"That would be up to the one taking on that burden – it would be a most honourable thing. But of course in time, once you are in a marriage and all the care, and love and duty that entails, you may find your feelings for Francois eventually subside."

"Neither my heart nor my head give me confidence that that might be the case, Mama."

Charlotte sighed deeply. Her mother put her arm around her shoulder.

"Samuel may well be away for many months, even years, again. We can only wait and see, when he returns, whether he will make a proposal," she said.

12

Over the coming months and years Charlotte, and her parents, were kept informed of the manoeuvrings and engagements of the Navy through the newspapers – The Times and the London Gazette.

Charlotte marvelled at the way they received information on happenings off Spain and in the Mediterranean, and in the North Sea, so soon after it happened; and she found herself becoming concerned for Samuel's safety as ships he commanded continued to be in the forefront of battles, and she prayed for his safe return to the shelter of England.

The sinking of enemy ships and the loss of life among them, as well as among the English crews, troubled her greatly. She learned that Samuel had become captain of HMS Monarch, and later HMS Prince. As they were involved in various skirmishes, she tried to imagine his feelings at watching enemy ships going down – the mixture of triumph, and sorrow and fear in equal measure that he had spoken about during his last visit.

He mentioned such feeling in letters which occasionally reached her when he had the opportunity to write – missives in which he sometimes sounded buoyant, sometimes depressed, sometimes remote. Each stressed, too, how much he was looking forward to the opportunity to visit her again, and expressing his deep affection for her.

She took those messages to her heart. But, reading of the continuing enmity with France and battles which seemed to be looming, brought thoughts of Francois to the fore again, and her concern for his welfare, and she wondered where he was, whether he was back in France, and prayed that he would not be seconded to the French Navy and be put at risk.

In her idle moments the thought did not escape her that the Englishman desiring to be her suitor was on the opposing side of the country of the man she truly loved.

The change of century was close at hand when Samuel next had the opportunity of travelling to Suffolk to visit Charlotte. He heralded his intention with a letter in which, for the first time since their last meeting, he asked if she had been thinking about their conversation when they were last together, and whether she had come to a decision.

"I look forward with great anticipation, dear Charlotte, in the hope that you may have something favourable to tell me," he wrote.

She sighed as she read the letter. She had thought about it, tried to rationalise her thoughts, to think about what marriage to a man who she had great admiration and affection for, but who was away so often, would be like, and how that would compromise her continuing love for Francois – an unexpressed but deep bond which had no future but which was nevertheless still real and vibrant and guiding her everyday thoughts. In replies to his letters she had made no mention of the conversation either, simply writing of her studies, and her music and art, and the topics discussed at Bible study, which she still attended with great regularity, and adding that she looked forward to seeing him when he returned.

She had been delaying giving serious thought to what her answer to Samuel would be, should he propose – perhaps she had taken too much to heart her mother's words at the end of his last visit, to wait until the time came that he did propose. But she was certain that time was now close at hand, and she must have an answer for him to which she could confidently feel committed.

"When I first met him at Bible study, I felt attracted to him, and happy walking by his side – I remember lying in bed and thinking about him, hoping I would see him again," she said to herself, as she now lay in bed again, five years later. "But then I did not know Francois, my Lord – he came suddenly into my life, and brought me joy, knowledge, learning, companionship and love – yes, he brought me the love of a man, for all those months...such sweet and memorable times, just being with him, hearing his voice, watching him, admiring him, depending on him. I look back now and it seems as if it was just a reflection beneath the surface of the Waveney – the reality of the May blossom and flag irises and swans above, our love the dream, just below, unreal, but as exquisite as the springtime. He made me feel like the springtime, all the time, but the best part of that season always – the freshness, the excitement of what is to come, the brightness, the expectancy. And I felt I was the only person in the world who really mattered to him, that he could depend on me, as I came to depend, so much, on his being there – for ever. I really thought he would be there for ever."

She opened her eyes in the darkness of her bedchamber as her thoughts tumbled along.

"But I was young then. Was I innocent, too easily taken in? Should I have been wary? Did I read too much into the way we were? Should he have told me he was married, before my feelings and hopes formed? If he was feeling the same, Francois should have told me – yes, he should not have let me fall in love with him. He was keeping a secret from me. And yet he was not to know my feelings, at first at least – and when he began to realise them, he couldn't bring himself to disappoint me. He could not have known how deeply I felt for him – I did not tell him because...perhaps because I could not be sure he felt the same, and I would have embarrassed myself, and him."

It was the first time Charlotte had seriously asked herself that question, even after all this time. Now she did – she asked herself if she had misread all the signs, or exaggerated them in her mind; whether, in fact, it was simply his friendship, and the rapport they had built up in spending so much time together.

But she quickly dismissed that.

"No, it was much more than that – he felt the same as I did, I know…my woman's intuition knows his feelings ran as deeply for me as mine for him. He had found something he never had with Celeste. Even if he thought, in agreeing to marry her to please his sister, that those feelings would come in time, they had not had as much time together, to develop such feelings, as he had had with me."

But now he would, she admitted - if he had returned to France, he would be with her now, to resume his marriage, and to be faithful to Celeste, to care for her, and love her the best he could, knowing his true love, the girl he called his English rose, was back in England, and that marrying her was impossible, and would be wrong.

And suddenly, as one thought ran into another as she lay there in the dark, wide awake, it dawned on Charlotte how parallel their situations were – for that was just what she was contemplating: to agree to marry someone she had spent little time with, knowing that her deep love was for another man to whom marriage was impossible. She may have spent even less time with Samuel than Francois had with Celeste.

Somehow she knew that her love would commit himself as best he could to Celeste, would care for her, provide for her, give her the support she needed. Give her all the love he could.

And she knew, then, also that across the distance between them, over the rolling slopes of Suffolk and Essex, over the downs of Kent, across the sea and away over Normandy to Brittany, carried by the winds, or the flight of the swallows; yes she knew somehow, they would give each other the spiritual strength to carry out what she now saw as God's will.

Francois would not know that she was to marry, and yet she knew in her heart he would expect her to do so, and would be wanting her to be fulfilled in a life they could not share together, despite their love.

"My Lord, my love, we commit ourselves to this because of our love. We commit ourselves to the happiness of Celeste and Samuel, not as a consolation, or a penance, but as a tribute to our love," she whispered out loud to herself.

Charlotte knew, now, what her answer would be should Samuel propose marriage to her. She knew in her heart, too, that it came with the blessing of Francois.

Two days later, Samuel arrived at the parsonage, and he did propose, an understandable nervousness leading him to speak rather more quickly than he intended.

"My dear Charlotte, I think of you so often during my long weeks and months at sea – the thought of you keeps me going, though I am committed to my career and my duty to the fleet, and to Admiral Nelson. I have much time to think while I am away, and I have drawn the conclusion that we are well suited in intellect and outlook, we share the same views on many things, we have a committed allegiance to God – in short, we are right for each other."

He paused, and took her hand in both of his, looking at her with an intense and loving countenance.

"I fall short of you in looks, I readily confess – your beauty, your poise, your exquisite smile, the way you laugh, I have nothing to counter those qualities. I offer you a plain man by comparison, but one who would earnestly, eagerly and willingly commit himself to you in every way that God calls for.

"Charlotte, you have been honest with me and told me your continuing feelings for Francois, and I know you feel you cannot give me your heart entirely, but I am happily prepared to accept that because I do believe, as your husband, I could make you happy, if you would accept that."

"Samuel, I could not ask you to take me in those circumstances – it seems most unjust, because it would be a sacrifice on your part."

"If it is a sacrifice as you say, it would be the most welcome sacrifice I could imagine. I would see it as a joy," Samuel replied. Charlotte studied his face, now full of anticipation, for a few moments before replying.

"You are right that we have much in common, we please each other in many ways. If I agree, and if Papa agrees, I too am convinced we can be happy, and I will work hard to put my feelings for Francois at the back of my mind. It is unlikely I will ever see him again, or hear from him again, in any case."

For a fleeting moment her smile faded and her eyes dimmed as thoughts passed through her mind, before she regained her focus.

"You will continue to be away for long periods, and I would try to become accustomed to that, and keep myself busy in the ways I do now."

"Then...you would agree to accept me as your husband, and make me the proudest officer in the King's Navy?"

"Yes. Yes, Samuel, I agree."

And Charlotte smiled a genuine and loving smile as, for the first time, Samuel embraced her, and held her close.

"Thank you, thank you my dear, dear Charlotte. I will speak to your father immediately."

Later that evening, John Ives and Samuel came into the withdrawing room where Charlotte and her mother sat reading. Charlotte stood up as her father approached her and took her hands in his.

"As you know, my dear, Samuel came to me and asked for your hand in marriage. We have spoken in depth, and I have told Samuel that I have every confidence in accepting his proposal – and I know it has your mother's approval too. I am very happy, and delighted for both of you," he said.

Sarah stood up, beaming. "So my daughter is betrothed, and I am so happy, dear!" she cried.

All four embraced each other in turn, and spoke animatedly and light-heartedly for some time, before the men withdrew to enjoy a drink of porter in celebration.

"We are delighted that you have someone of such standing in the country to take as your husband, my dear, but are you quite sure you want to commit yourself to Samuel?" Sarah inquired when they had gone. Charlotte did not hesitate.

"I am quite sure, Mama. He will make me a good husband, and I will make him a good and dutiful wife."

"And Francois? Is he no longer in your mind, so you can give your whole heart to Samuel?"

"Francois was part of my life – a part of which I will always have fond memories, and will never forget. But marriage to Samuel will be a new and fulfilling chapter, Mama, and I am anxious to turn the page."

Sarah smiled, content with the reply. Later, she thought back to the day four years previously when her own proposal for Charlotte's future had brought such a devastating and heart-breaking result, and compared it with the happy outcome this time.

When a new dawn, with the turn of the century, came a few days later, amid great celebrations and hopes of continued success for the empire and the English Navy, Charlotte looked forward on the first day and wondered what the nineteenth century would mean for her and her plans – and wondered where Francois was, and prayed that he was happy. And she wondered whether they would ever meet again as the world moved forward with expectation into the unknown of a new era.

The voyages, confrontations and battles at sea continued for the Navy as they had in the last few years of the previous century, so that Samuel was scarcely ashore and no early plans could be made for a wedding. His reputation as an astute commander continued to grow, and after a short spell as flag captain to Sir Charles Cotton he became captain of HMS Alcmene in the early days of the new century. A year later his ship joined the North Sea fleet under the now Rear-Admiral Horatio Nelson, popular with officers and crew on every ship he commanded. The Swedish fleet was at sea and posturing aggressively at that time, and the Alcmene assisted Nelson in the capture and distribution of the Danish line of defence at what was to become known as the Battle of Copenhagen.

Nelson rewarded Sutton with the command of HMS Amazon, and he continued to serve as Nelson's flag captain in the Baltic. Two years later he was given the command of the 104-gun HMS Victory, one of the Navy's best equipped fighting vessels, and with ominous reports of battles with the French Navy looming Nelson was appointed Commander-in-Chief of the Mediterranean fleet. Two days later he hoisted his flag on the Victory, with Captain Sutton his flag captain.

From time to time Samuel was able to send letters to Charlotte with news of his manoeuvres and his thoughts on how well campaigns were progressing. At other times Charlotte followed progress by reading the newspapers, and there was a feeling of pride, mixed with fear, when she learned that Samuel and HMS Victory had captured the 32-gun French vessel Embuscade and her crew of 187 men.

"Samuel writes of life on board ship and his feelings at the moment they are encountering enemy ships on a rolling sea, and fearing for their fate, but even so I cannot conceive how grim and uncertain and cheerless such times must be," she said to her mother on one occasion. "And so many seamen are killed. One wonders whether the prize is worth all the sacrifice."

"I think they would say that the prize is protecting our shores from enemy invaders, and who could gainsay that," her mother replied. "We have been doing that for all of our history – so many have tried to conquer these islands, but our men have always resisted with great courage and stoutness of heart. Now Samuel is among them, trying to do the same. We must continue to pray for his safe return."

Charlotte had confided in Samuel her fears for his safety and he had comforted her by saying the King's Navy was equal to any fleet anywhere on the seas. She knew that to be true, but it was nevertheless a distraction to never know quite which area of the high seas he would be in next.

In the summer of 1803, it was the Mediterranean to where Samuel sailed Victory to rejoin Nelson off Toulon, and there, through continuing bouts of ill-health, he exchanged roles with Captain Thomas Hardy, of the frigate Amphion, with Hardy taking over HMS Victory. In command of that ship, he continued to be actively employed in the most important of Nelson's commands, and manoeuvred his vessel skilfully to assist in the capture of another French ship, La Mercedes, witnessing the spectacular sight of it blowing up when a well aimed cannon hit her gunpowder store.

Some months after that incident, Charlotte received a letter from her husband-to-be.

"My Dearest Charlotte,
You will have learned from my last letter that HMS Amphion and her crew under my command, together with three other ships of the fleet, captured four Spanish frigates in the Mediterranean. You also may have read of this in the newspaper. It has turned out that the Spanish vessels had a bounty on board of considerable value – hundreds of thousands of pounds, perhaps as much as one million pounds – an amount so vast as to be unimaginable. As captain of the Amphion I should be entitled to a good share of that. The matter of how it should be divided has come under considerable discussion and those who are not entitled to a share are trying to claim one nevertheless. But

I know Nelson believes I should benefit significantly from the bounty and will use his influence in my cause, if he is in any way able so to do.

This has been a long campaign my dearest, and it has left me feeling tired and listless. I have been suffering palpitations, and shakiness of the limbs, and I am feeling my responsibilities lying heavily upon me. I fear it may be as the result of the yellow fever I contracted some years ago in the West Indies – the physician said at the time that that is an illness of which I may never be free completely. I long to be home again and able to see you once more, my dear betrothed – I know that alone will quickly return me to full health. It is the thought of you that keeps me cheerful amid the battles, but once my share of the bounty is secured we will talk seriously about arrangements for our marriage.

I hope this letter finds you well and happy. Do not worry about me, dearest Charlotte, as I'm sure my health will recover in time.

Yours forever,
Samuel

But Samuel was not able to return to his home even for a short break, and his health did not improve. The English and French fleets continued to evade each other in the Mediterranean for some months, but among the crew of Nelson's ships there was a growing anticipation that a major battle was imminent and every vessel available was summoned to gather in readiness in the autumn of 1805. Amphion, which had put into Lisbon for a spell, sailed via Gibraltar to join them but Samuel could not summon the nervous excitement of an impending battle as he had previously – that overwhelming feeling of excitement tempered by a little fear had been replaced by a fear which had no excitement to spice it, and his bouts of palpitations and extreme tiredness increased.

He felt obliged to report his concerns to Nelson, who was immediately compassionate and understanding, stood him down from his duties and gave the command of Amphion to Captain William Hoste. As the decisive battle between the English and French and Spanish fleets loomed, Samuel travelled back to Portsmouth, a feeling of failure leaving him depressed, and heightening the severe exhaustion he had been unable to dispel.

A week later, Samuel and Charlotte were re-united. She immediately noticed how pale and drawn he was, and expressed her concern as she ushered him into the withdrawing room and sat him down on the chaise-longe.

"My dearest Charlotte, it is so comforting to see you again and it lifts my heart. It should have been my duty to be with the fleet at this moment – my heart is here, my mind in the Mediterranean – but I have not the energy to give any activity its proper due."

"Then you must rest completely, Samuel, and let your parents and I care for you and return you to full health. The hard life and privations of the Navy, and your conscientiousness which have led you to give so much of yourself to your duties, have brought you to this. You must see the physician and see what he recommends for you."

"I have seen the ship's physician many times and he has had difficulty diagnosing the nature of the ailment. But being able to stay here for a while will be the medicine I need, I'm sure, and I have been granted extended leave. Nelson used his influence to arrange that. He is the most considerate of commanders to all his officers and men, from the top rank to the lowest crew member. Our country should be proud of him. I pray that he may have a long life."

But his prayers were not answered. A week later, in October, 1805, as Samuel recuperated at his home, where Charlotte and her parents visited him frequently, the English fleet of 27 ships, under Nelson's command on HMS Victory, engaged the larger combined French and Spanish fleet in the Mediterranean off Cape Trafalgar in a bitter battle which the English won decisively, sinking a large number of enemy ships without the loss of a single vessel of their own, thanks to unusual tactics employed by Nelson which took the enemy by surprise.

But in its moment of triumph the fleet lost its beloved commander.

When the news reached Bungay in the newspapers, Samuel was lifted by the victory, but left deeply distraught and saddened at the loss of his commander.

"He was such a fine man, such a skilled commander, Charlotte," he said as he read the report. "The whole country will welcome the battle won, but will grieve greatly at Nelson's loss. His crew, every single man in the fleet, loved him, they really loved him, as I did, and were prepared to die for him – as some did. They will be mourning the loss as if he were their own father."

Charlotte could feel the emotion rising in him as he continued: "I should have been there – what help was I to him, sitting here ailing when he and his whole fleet were there, fighting against that tyrant Napoleon for the sake of their country? Damn this wretched, wretched illness! Damn it! That yellow fever has put a curse on me which will remain with me till I die! I should have stayed, sailed with him, fought beside him – I might have saved him. I should have been with him in his last moments, not Hardy, fine captain though he is! I'm a coward Charlotte, and no mistake. I could have stayed!"

His betrothed laid a sympathetic hand on his arm as he threw the newspaper aside and stared grimly at the floor.

"Samuel, Samuel! You are not a coward. It was Nelson's wish – he was thinking of you and your welfare when he ordered you ashore. Perhaps," she added after a pause, "perhaps he saved your life, and that was Nelson's will,

God's will. Be that as it may, dearest, I'm glad that you were here, and not in the forefront of battle."

It was a genuine thought, borne of her heart. She was beginning to feel closer to Samuel as every day went by, and pleased that they she was able to visit him regularly.

But silently in her heart, also, she offered a prayer that Francois had not rejoined the French Navy, that he was not in the forefront of battle, and beseeched God to keep him safe, wherever he might be. The thought that Francois and her husband-to-be were on opposing sides in this dreadful war of supremacy continued to trouble her, and the news of the English victory, joyous though it was, was tempered by thoughts of the Frenchman she loved.

Samuel smiled at her wanly, and thanked her. "I'm glad, too, that I'm here with you – but I wish too that I had been able to do my duty to my country."

He picked up the paper again. "It says here, that as he prepared the fleet for engagement, Nelson signalled to them: 'England expects that every man this day will do his duty.' And I was not able to answer that call – I was not able to do my duty. Damn it! Damn it!"

"Nevertheless," he added more cheerfully, after some moments' pause, "it was a valiant achievement. We did not lose one ship, and it appears we sank or scuttled more than half of the 33 of the treacherous French, and Spanish. They are warmongers, not a race deserving of any compassion. What was left of them made a hasty retreat to port with their tails between their legs. They won't have the appetite for another battle in a hurry. Villeneuve, who led the French fleet, was among those captured, according to this account."

"Not every Frenchman is a warmonger," Charlotte could not help herself remarking. But added quickly: "Does it mean that the war is close to an end - that the king's Navy will not have to join battle so regularly with France?"

"While Napoleon is leading his country he will not readily admit to defeat, but he may concentrate on waging war on land, on the continent, rather than at sea. We must, however, always be in a ready state for any aggression he attempts," Samuel replied.

"I wish there could be more peace between countries. We are so close to France and Spain – why cannot we be friends?"

"War and peace, peace and war – those two opposite bedfellows are so inextricably intertwined. I fear it is the nature of humanity. And so many good men perish in war for the cause of peace. Yes," Samuel sighed heavily, "and none more so than Nelson. God did not allow him so much as a moment to enjoy his victory and his greatness. His body will be returned to Portsmouth, Charlotte – I must be there when it arrives. May he rest in peace."

"Only if you are well enough to travel," said Charlotte, firmly.

13

N ews of Admiral Horatio Lord Nelson's glorious victory at Trafalgar brought joyous celebrations throughout the country, and Bungay was no exception. Flags and decorations were put out on houses and shops, and the King ordered Nelson tokens to be struck and distributed throughout the land.

The feeling spread that the battle meant that Napoleon was beaten and that the prolonged war against France, and their leader in particular, would soon be at an end. Nelson was declared a hero at his death, and events in tribute to him were held in his name. The French as a nation were condemned, and derogatory sarcasm and other aggressive, satirical names aimed at them were voiced loudly in some quarters, particularly when too much ale got the better of them as they made known their feeling of triumph.

"Who rules the waves? Britain rules the waves!
Who rules the knaves? Bony rules the knaves!
They will never be saved

was one chant taken up and repeated endlessly over the following days. Charlotte winced inwardly when she heard it and felt a pang of anxiety, despite welcoming the pleasure and improvement in health that the victory seemed to bring out in Samuel. And she felt almost a sense of relief when a more sombre atmosphere descended on the country when Nelson's funeral service took place, memorial services were held throughout the land and glowing tributes were paid to his career, his generous leadership and his compassion.

Samuel was well enough to travel to Portsmouth to see his body arrive and show his respect as it was borne through the town. Later he paid his respects as Nelson lay in state at Greenwich for three days, before his coffin was taken by barge to the Admiralty, to remain there for the night before his funeral at St Paul's Cathedral on January 9th, 1806.

Charlotte accompanied Samuel to the funeral service, where he was among seven royal Dukes, 32 admirals, and more than 100 captains paying their last respects to a great leader. The coffin was escorted to the cathedral by 10,000 troops and another 30,000 lined the route as vast crowds clamoured to get a glimpse of the cortege. Samuel had written a letter of condolence to the Admiral's widow expressing his admiration at his courage and generosity, his deep sorrow at his death in battle, saying that he would be forever grateful for the help he had given him, Samuel, personally in many ways.

Later, at the Admiralty, he had discussions with senior officers about his health and his career, which resulted in his being given a posting on shore for two years.

"It is a decision I can only accept, though with some reluctance," he told Charlotte on his return. "I had hoped to return to sea, with the fleet, but I confess to having little appetite for that life presently. I have yet to regain my full energy, and having spent more time here beside the Waveney, of late, and having you visit me regularly, has made me contemplate life in a different prospect. One day perhaps, I shall return to captain one of His Majesty's ships, and resume my pride in that role, but for now, I shall sit at a desk at the Admiralty."

"I know how you must feel, Samuel, but in my turn I must confess that I am pleased that you will not be spending long weeks at sea and months away from home, and my not knowing what is happening to you. Perhaps you will be able to travel back to Suffolk regularly?"

"That is my hope, dearest Charlotte. And something else has come to me which will be to our advantage – being on shore will mean we will be able to plan our wedding with some certainly. Would you agree to our marriage taking place next summer?"

"Oh, yes, I would!" Charlotte's excitement was genuine. "We have been betrothed for such an uncommonly long time, and friends are regularly asking when my wedding day might be. We must talk with Mama and Papa about it at the first opportunity, and I will give thought to the style of my wedding gown, and the flowers, and the invitations, and…! Thank, you Samuel, thank you! I perceive your frustration at your illness and your sadness at being unable to return to sea for the time being, but Mama always said something good came of disappointments, and I believe this to be the case now!"

Samuel's heart lifted at her eagerness and enthusiasm, and he embraced her and held her close.

"I have had many happy times in my life, but our wedding day will be the happiest of all," he whispered to her.

"It will be a happy time – I'm so looking forward to it," she murmured in reply.

Charlotte and Samuel were married at the church of St Mary's in Bungay on a warm April day in the spring of 1806. The whole congregation smiled approvingly as she walked down the aisle, her slimness accentuated by the simple white dress gathered tightly at the waist, and short train – white was not the favoured colour of the period, but Charlotte had read somewhere that white was first worn by a bride in Brittany in the 15th century and had insisted she would wear it too, though red was the popular colour for many brides.

"White is the best colour for my complexion, and my hair, Mama," she had said, as she had her first fitting for it. "Don't you think so? And I shall wear a single wild rose in my hair."

She did, making a special trip to the common on the morning of the wedding, to choose a perfect flower. It drew admiring whispers from the ladies as she passed them, glancing nervously from side to side during her slow progress, to join Samuel, dashing in his full Naval uniform, before the altar.

John Ives conducted the ceremony, a proud father presiding at the marriage of his only daughter, and leading bride and bridegroom patiently through the responses and the vows to the moment they committed themselves to each other for the rest of their lives.

Samuel answered eagerly, clearly, "I do" when invited to confirm that he took Charlotte as his lawful wedded wife, to love, honour and to cherish, forsaking all others, to the end of his life.

"And do you, Charlotte, take Samuel as your lawful wedded husband, to have and to hold, for better or worse, for richer or poorer, in sickness and in health, to love, honour and obey, as long as you both shall live, and therefore I plight thee my troth, so help me God?"

Charlotte turned to look at Samuel through her veil, meeting his unwavering eyes as they gazed back at her, serious, but with deep love in them. She paused for some moments, longer than the congregation would normally expect, focussing her thoughts on her life ahead, confirming to herself this was what she wanted. Finally she said, clearly and with conviction:

"I do."

Later the wedding was celebrated back at the parsonage, where the guests, who included some of Samuel's Naval colleagues, drank a toast to the couple, proposed by Mr Ives, as everyone looked on happily, Sarah Ives with tears of pride in her eyes, and some regret that her daughter was leaving the home where she was born, as Samuel presented his wife with a gold ring, slipping it gently on to her finger, and kissing her.

"This is the bond between you and I, my dearest Charlotte. I give it with all the love in my heart, and pray that our marriage will be fulfilled throughout our lives," he said. And the gathering applauded enthusiastically.

It was a gay and happy occasion, a day of humour and laughter and Charlotte, breaking with convention, played the piano, and sang, to entertain her guests, who all had the opportunity to congratulate her and her husband individually, and wish them well in their life together. John Ives made sure all the male guests rarely had an empty tankard of ale as he acted as host, and had generous portions himself throughout the day. Samuel, whose health had improved considerably, though he had not fully regained his original strength, was attentive to his bride and the guests, Sarah was the busy and discerning hostess, anxious that everyone should enjoy the day and remember it favourably. Mrs Honeywood and Maria were invited in to help with cooking and serving, and additional staff were also taken on for the day.

That night, at Ditchingham Lodge, which they were to make their home with his elderly parents, Charlotte and Samuel consummated their union in their four-poster bed. Charlotte was somewhat nervous, Samuel was excited, about that moment when, having joined their minds and hearts, they would join their bodies in the final confirmation of the vows they had made before God.

Samuel was gentle with her, caressing her body tenderly with his hands, and gently kissing the soft white skin of her face and neck, before gently covering the nipples of her breasts with his mouth and manoeuvring his body close to her's so she felt his strong thighs against her's, his stomach against her's – and felt, too, with a quickening of her heart, that he was fully aroused. She sensed, too, her own body responding, a moistening of the very font of her womanhood, as his firm manhood pressed expectantly against the mound above its opening, ready to respond and take her virginity as his bride, now relaxing as the feelings began to build within her, moved against the warmth of his muscles, the senses of both of them heightened by the scents of their own bodies, pressed close and signalling in their own unspoken ecstasy that they were ready for the moment.

When Samuel penetrated her, tentatively at first, then more firmly, she let out an involuntary gasp as he broke through the final barrier and entered her fully, a sound deep in his throat signalling the joyful surge of the new, longed for moment, the exquisite mystery finally revealed as he entered a woman, his bride, for the first time. Then their bodies were moving together, rhythmically in unison. As he moved deep into her, Charlotte closed her eyes, her hands caressing his back, feeling his weight on top of her, delighting in that first experience of giving her naked body to a man.

As the movement of their bodies, now gently perspiring, gradually increased, as the sensations intensified, the vision of Francois flittered into Charlotte's mind – briefly at first, but then returning. She tried to block it out, tried to open her eyes to see Samuel's face close to her's, to be true to his image and his love as the indescribable feelings deep in her abdomen, continued to increase. But somehow her eyes would not open, nor could she blot the image out of her mind; and then...then she did not want to, as she anticipated the moment when her body would lose control of itself. She wanted it to be Francois there, moving with her, she wanted it to be his manhood insider her, firm and triumphant, his breath against her face, his thighs against her's, his arms around her back, his buttocks she now clenched and kneaded with greater strength at every movement of their increasing rhythm; his eyes looking into her's and becoming glazed as the joyous, surging, exquisite moment erupted spontaneously through their bodies, shuddered and rippled to every corner of their being, taking control of every sinew, every pore, every fibre, every sense.

Suddenly that moment was there.

"My Lord! My Lord!"

Charlotte's aloud cry was instinctive – she had no control over her body or her voice as the racing urgency of their movement took them over the edge into the bubbling cauldron of mutual orgasm, into the warm raging torrents of potent, pent-up energy released at last, into the ultimate joy that God had designed for a man and a woman to express their love.

For a moment she thought she was going to faint. But as their bodies gradually stopped moving, relaxed, as they regained control, their desire sated, Charlotte finally opened her eyes. It was Samuel's face close to her's not Francois' – he was smiling, his brow glistening as he kissed her lips and neck again, gently, as he had at the beginning of their love-making.

"Thank you, my dearest, beautiful Charlotte – thank you for that moment, thank you with all the love in my heart."

She smiled back, content, fulfilled, relaxed, and sleepy after a long, memorable, happy day. But she also felt great relief that Samuel was not aware of the subject of her spontaneous utterance.

And she felt deep guilt that she was relieved at that.

14

"Celeste! Ma belle!"

Francois opened his arms to receive the wife he had not seen for eight years as she entered the room at the house he had rented in Paris since his return from England, embraced her and tenderly kissed each cheek, before standing back to look at her.

"Francois!"

She gazed at him too, looking him up and down, remembering the man she had married rather hastily, and had known for such a short time before he had left France to avoid being pursued by the zealots who were hunting down the aristocracy as the Revolution took hold.

Now, with a fragile stability in place, he had slipped quietly back into his native land, along with other returning émigrés, taking the boat from Dover to Calais, but taking also the precaution of obtaining a false passport, under the name of Lassagne. He had smiled laconically to himself as he received the document as he noted it was his third identity in his travels – Chateaubriand, Comburg and now Lassagne. But he had felt it wise security.

The Battle of Trafalgar was still five years away when he made the journey, shortly after the new century had dawned. After arriving in Paris and finding accommodation with the help of friends, he had written to Celeste, his sisters Lucile and Julie, and others, to inform them of his return, and each visited him in turn in the ensuing weeks.

Since fleeing in chagrin from Bungay and Charlotte, and since the guilt and regret and depression that followed had abated, he had spent time in London among other émigrés, including Peltier and Hignant, and had engrossed himself in writing – work which helped him to stabilise and put in perspective his feelings for the parson's daughter. His urges to return to Bungay in the hope of catching a glimpse of her had gradually receded. Even so, she was never far from his thoughts, and the vision of her had given impetus to his work.

Celeste was not the reason for his fleeing. Now there she was in front of him, dressed soberly but fashionably in lilac, with the bodice of her dress buttoned to her neck, accentuating her slim figure and pale complexion. She had changed little since he had last set eyes on her, despite the ravages of several months imprisonment during the Revolution, and the harshness of life to which the aristocracy was not accustomed.

As he studied her, the vision of Charlotte returned to the front of his mind, and he was startled to realise that there was a marked physical likeness between the two – Celeste's hair was long and fair, but her oval face and dark eyes, though not as dark as Charlotte's, and her high cheek bones all provided a remarkable resemblance. Was that, Francois found himself wondering, why he had been so attracted to

223

Charlotte, that somewhere deep in his mind he had seen her as Celeste and taken comfort from that? But he dismissed it: Celeste's temperament was much more abrasive and cajoling, while in Charlotte he had found someone who shared his love of literature, music and history, subjects Celeste had little interest in. It remained to be seen whether the experiences of the Revolution had affected her outlook on life, or mellowed her coquettish personality. And would his experiences in England prevent him from resuming his relationship with the wife he had taken under circumstances unsatisfactory in the extreme? Would he hold her responsible for the regrets he still held, despite his rationalising, for being unable to accept Mrs Ives proposal?

"You have not changed since we were last together, despite your adventures – in outward appearance at least."

Celeste's remark brought Francois out of his reverie.

"Celeste, ma cherie, you are as beautiful as I remember you – perhaps more so. France and her troubles have kept us apart for a long time, but seeing you entering this room has helped to lift the memories of the privations I have endured since leaving these shores. Another phase of my life – our lives – will now begin."

"We have had different journeys, very different since you left me here. Before then I did not know you well, we had little time. With God's help we will now have the time to learn more about each other – if that is what you want?"

Celeste looked at him from lowered eyes and the final remark seemed to carry a question. He gave his answer.

"That is what I want. You remind me of many of the good things I have experienced over the past few years while I have been away. We have much to tell each other. Come and sit down."

Husband and wife embraced again, tentatively, lightly, as if unsure of each other. Such was the gap in time since those arms last enfolded, it was as if it was a totally new experience, and the embrace was fleeting, before they sat together on the sofa, with the clatter of hooves and carriage wheels outside in the Paris street the background to their sharing of their lives since last they were together.

On his journey from Calais to Paris Francois had been shocked and depressed at the physical state of his homeland. The worst of the Revolution, its fighting, killing and desecration of land and buildings, took place several years before he returned, and yet the results of it were starkly evident on either side of his carriage as it made its way through the countryside. In Paris the legacy of the Revolution was even more apparent in the dirt of the streets and the demeanour of people as they went about their business, poorly dressed and, it seemed, poorly fed. He sighed heavily as he looked on, and instinctively compared it in his mind with the England, and London, he had left behind so recently. Inevitably, too, he thought of his days spent in the Ives household in Bungay, and cursed himself again for leaving, for having to leave, that comfortable and welcoming home because of the way destiny had dictated the first 30 years of his life. For a while he descend again into one of his melancholy moods, muttering angrily and frustratedly to himself as he looked around him and made his way to the accommodation friends had found for him. Had he not been dressed so respectably, in contrast to the fellow Parisians around him, onlookers could easily have taken him for one of those who had stayed to fight instead of fleeing, and suffered the same poverty as a result.

Now, having settled in to life in Paris, and met relatives and old friends, he shook himself, with effort, out of his bout of moroseness, and began to look ahead.

He renewed old contacts. The French aristocracy had proved resilient, he discovered, and he soon found work editing The Mercure de France newspaper. And the writing he had done in Bungay, and later in London, was well received throughout the country, and Europe. By 1802 he had won fame with his book, The Genius of Christianity. One of the effects of the Revolution was an upsurge in religious beliefs, and Francois, to his surprise, found himself sought after and feted – people wanted to discuss his work with him and he was busy addressing meetings on his work on the Christian faith. In many ways it was not complimentary to it, but it served to boost further the revival of religion in France.

It came to the notice of Napoleon Bonaparte, head of the country following the Revolution, who saw it vital to his political progress to win the favour of the Catholic Church. Francois was summoned to see him at his office in the Champs Elyses, where they conversed for some time about his book. It was clear that he felt it would be to his advantage to involve Francois in his political plans, and when Bonaparte offered it, he accepted the appointment of secretary of the delegation to the Holy See in Rome.

"I say that I was offered the appointment, but Napoleon made the offer in such as way as to make it almost impossible to refuse. He is a man of great determination – to gainsay him would be a foolish thing to do, at least at this stage in my political career," he told Celeste later.

Even at that early stage, Francois saw that it provided a good opportunity to embark on a political career, and through that to serve the country he loved, and work to make it respected throughout Europe once more.

"But I do not intend to be the poodle of M Bonaparte – I will not be persuaded to follow a policy if I feel in my heart it is not right," he added.

His words were put to the test before too many years had passed. Having been appointed as minister to Valais in Switzerland, he angrily resigned in 1804 after Napoleon ordered the execution of the Duc d'Enghlien, a fellow aristocrat and émigré following the fall of the Bastille in the early stages of the Revolution. He was one of those involved in the unsuccessful bid to invade France following the fall of the monarchy. Francois realised the charge against him was false, but his protests, and those of other influential statesmen, failed to persuade the stubborn Napoleon against his execution.

The interruption to his career as a statesman, still in its infancy, gave Francois the chance to concentrate on his writing – he needed to earn a living, and he returned to the subject of his previous noted success, religion, resolving to write an epic, based on the persecution of the early Christians by the Roman empire. He travelled widely, in 1806, in search of information and the feeling for the area in which the work was set, from Asia Minor to Spain, from Greece to Palestine and Egypt.

The animosity between Francois and Napoleon continued however, and became more intense when, on his return to France, he published a severe criticism of the First Consul. Rather like Rome's Nero, he fiddled while France burned, he claimed in it, and warned the country that a new Tacitus, the Roman senator, consul and governor of Asia, could emerge in France to counteract his power. Napoleon, who once saw Francois as a useful ally, banished him from Paris as a result, and he went to live on an estate called La Valle des Loups, about seven miles south of the city.

Sometimes these setbacks would bring on further bouts of melancholy and depression and at those times, despite the encouragement and support of Celeste, the image of

Charlotte would return to him, and he would recall his days and months with her in England, and wish again that he had been able to stay. Always he would admonish himself out of what he called "the abyss" of depression, and away from the atmosphere and business of the city he returned to his writing, which brought out the forthright and rebellious part of his nature. His work brought accolades from all over France and Europe, and in 1811 he was elected to the Academie Francaise. The speech he prepared for the ceremony of his adoption gave him the opportunity to publically voice his deep-seated criticism of the Revolution. Wisely, he accepted the advice of his influential friends in Paris, and delayed his acceptance until after the Bourbons had been restored to power and Napoleon had been forced to leave France's political stage.

After Emperior Napoleon's abdication, with the monarchy restored and the Bourbon Louis XVIII returned to the throne, Francois used his steadily growing influence in France to support the Bourbons, and for a few years remained popular. His advice was sought after, his speeches valued at meetings and he guided the progress of his country subtly from a position of influence close to the Royal court. He wrote a pamphlet in 1814 condemning Napoleon and the path he had taken France along and, with his expressive phraseology and gift for the written word, ridiculed him. The people loved it, and several thousand copies were published to meet the demand.

But with Louis XVIII forced into exile during the Hundred Days War the following year, as Napoleon came out of exile in a new attempt to regain power in France, Francois followed him, and was appointed ambassador for Sweden. But his exile did not last long. With the defeat of Napoleon's France at the end of the 100 Days he returned to Paris, where he voted for the execution of the treacherous Marshal Ney, who had remained loyal to Napoleon following his abdication and was a key man in the Army which was formed to fight in his abortive attempt to lead France again. He was elected a peer of France and State Minister.

His penchant for speaking his mind soon got him into more trouble, however. When he criticised the King over an issue in which the Chambre Introuvable was dissolved, he was disgraced again, lost his role as state Minister, and joined the ultra-royalist Opposition in support of the man who ultimately became Charles X – the former Duc d'Angouleme and the man who, though he was not to know it, Charlotte's future husband had transported from Leith in Scotland to Cuxhaven some years before as captain of HMS Martin. Francois also became one of the main writers for Le Conservateur, the pro-royalist publication.

The statesmanship of Francois meant his advice continued to be sought after over the next five years in which France enjoyed comparative stability, and his articles in Le Conservateur were eagerly awaited and avidly read by the population. But he fell out of favour again in 1820 when he sided with the Court following the murder of the Duc de Berry, and served something resembling another exile as he was sent to Prussia as French ambassador there in 1821.

Then, in the spring of 1822, he was appointed ambassador to the Court of George IV of England, and took up office in London...

15

Charlotte sat in the room at Ditchingham Lodge she had set aside as her study, where she could write, play the piano, sing or read, and gazed out over the panorama before her. In the foreground, perhaps 200 yards from where she sat, the Waveney meandered its peaceful course among the meadows, a pair of swans, serene in their beauty, scarcely moving as they allowed the gentle flow to carry them slowly along.

On the horizon she could see the rooftops of Bungay, and the tower of St Mary's Church, highlighted by the late afternoon sun, standing proudly and steadfastly above them, as if sentinel and protector of the people living and working there. If she looked carefully, she could see the home where she was born, The Parsonage, at the bottom of the Bridge Street hill, where her parents still lived.

And between those two near and far boundaries was the Common, with the cattle grazing, a few sheep, and goats, and donkeys among them – statues, it seemed, or toys, like the wooden farm animals her father had made her to play with as a small child in front of the blazing inglenook fire.

But as she looked Charlotte, lost in her thoughts, was oblivious to those. She saw only two people walking there, a young woman, probably in her teens, and a man, somewhat older. They seemed deep in intimate conversation, and would stop now and then as one pointed out something to the other – a bird, or a flower, or the sound of a fish breaking the surface of the river as it snapped at a fly. At one point the girl knelt down and picked a flower, and seemed to offer it to the man, and they laughed together. Then their faces moved so close that they were almost touching...

"A silver penny for your thoughts, my dearest."

The voice made Charlotte start, and broke her reverie. As she turned from the brightness of the common scene to the comparative shadow of the interior of the study, Samuel moved towards her and put his hand on her shoulder.

"Oh, Samuel! I was quite somewhere else. I didn't hear you enter. I'm quite shaken."

"I apologise – I didn't mean to startle you, particularly in your present condition. But you seemed so far away and I was reluctant to intrude into your thoughts."

Charlotte turned her body back towards the window.

"I was just enjoying the scene, and thinking of...I mean to say, we are so lucky to have this wide view to enjoy from our home – the wide blue sky, the greenness, the Common where I have walked so often."

Samuel spoke slowly, almost whispering: "I have come to realise that you are...in love with..."

A pause in his sentence led Charlotte to glance fearfully at her husband, and she was relieved as he continued.

"...you are in love with that Common – those acres of marsh and reeds, and bushes, and cows, and beasts, and sand and gravel. You spend much time there."

"It is the atmosphere of peace, and...and comfort, and spiritual feeling that fill me when I walk there," said Charlotte, quickly regaining her composure. "I do so miss my daily walks there, now I am deep into my confinement. Not being able to leave the house is such an imposition, such a limitation. Sometimes I am beside myself, and so tempted to walk out of the house and down to the river. But I know that would be quite an improper thing to do."

"And it is for the best," Samuel nodded in encouraging agreement. "Perhaps two more months, the physician believes, and you know the baby himself is telling you the same. So be patient my dearest – it will not be too long before you can introduce our son to the outside world - and the common, in due time."

Charlotte leaned her head into her husband's shoulder, and put one hand on the swelling abdomen covered discreetly by her smock.

"You call our baby 'son' already – you seem so sure?"

"It is simply my hope, as it is for any man that his first born is a boy."

"I share that hope – I want it to be a boy also," said Charlotte. Then added, almost as an afterthought, but tenderly: "For your sake, Samuel."

He kissed her forehead lovingly, and left the room. Charlotte turned back to the window, and the scene before her.

But the couple she had imagined there, in the grazing meadows beside the river, had vanished.

It was early May in 1807, and a new sound was heard throughout Ditchingham Lodge – the cry of a new born baby. Charlotte's confinement had no complications, and the birth was natural and not unduly prolonged. It left her exhausted but happy as she cradled her son to her breast, with Samuel, overcome with delight and pride, sitting on the bed beside her.

In the high emotion, the physical effort, the pain and finally the relief as the baby slipped into the world, and the coaxing nurse announced, in a matter-of-fact way: "It's a boy!" Charlotte found herself instinctively, silently, saying to herself: "Francois – let me call him Francois. It should be his firstborn!"

The tears that rolled down her cheeks at that moment of a woman's complete fulfilment were not just because her baby had been born safe and well, and with a loud and healthy cry.

But the momentary appeal was gone. Later, when she was comfortable, and the baby sleeping for the first time in its cradle, she offered prayers of thanks to God for his safe arrival, and once more pleaded for forgiveness for her wrongful thoughts.

God signalled his forgiveness through the face of Samuel when he was summoned to see her and his son – his beaming smile, the modest pride which was obvious in the way he entered the room, the awe in which he gazed at the baby, and the thankfulness in his eyes as they met Charlotte's, told her that. Her husband's happiness was reflected in her's, and they embraced and congratulated themselves.

They named the baby Samuel Ives Sutton, after his father and maternal grandfather, and watched over him with love and care as he established himself, taking easily to his mother's breast, watching her, after the first two weeks, with steadfast blue eyes as he suckled, and soon warming their hearts with his first smile of recognition.

As they settled into bed one evening, with the infant sleeping peacefully in his cradle beside them, Samuel turned to Charlotte and said:

"When I was on long voyages at sea, with all their discomfort, and hardship, and an abiding fear that I may never return home, I was comforted by the thoughts and hopes, dreams perhaps, that this day would come – even before you agreed to marry me, my dearest; that one day I would be here, in our home, with the wife that I love, comfortable and happy, with our son beside us. I feel blessed by God that he has brought us to this."

"I too am content, Samuel. You provide well for me, and care for me – I feel cherished. And now we have a son who one day will go on to have a career equal in success to your own, though I will fret for him every day that he is away."

"My hope is that he will follow in my footsteps, either in the King's Navy, or his Army. But I will not impose that on him if his aptitude lies elsewhere."

Samuel paused, as Charlotte closed her eyes, and then added:

"Do you ever bring to mind the Frenchman, Chateaubriand? Do you wonder what became of him?"

Her eyes flinched slightly at the remark, but did not open, as she replied:

"I know he returned to France eventually. On occasion in The Times there is mention of him, and the success he has had with his writing – and there are suggestions, from what I read, that he is beginning to get involved in politics. Having fled the Revolution, and knowing his thoughts about that, it would not surprise me if he played his part in helping his country in that way."

"Do you still have regrets that he left Bungay, in the way that he did?"

Charlotte, who had been lying on her back, turned towards her husband. Her voice was gently reproachful.

"Dearest Samuel, it is more than ten years since that day, and much has happened in my life since then – good things. You have said how much our situation makes you happy –

it makes me happy too. When I see his name mentioned, yes, I do think of him, and remember his as a good and honourable man, but unsure of his destiny. Now I feel sure he is back with his wife, and beginning to fulfil his own ambitions, and if that is so, I am pleased."

"But do you still have any feelings for him?"

"Samuel, my feelings are for you, and our baby Samuel, and our life here. You make me truly content - that is what is important to me now, and will be always. I thank you for your love and care, and try to return it in full measure."

"You do so, more than I deserve. Forgive me. It is not that I doubt you – I just want to be sure that I make you as happy as you make me. Let us sleep now."

He kissed her, and turned to sleep on his side. Charlotte lay on her back, her eyes wide open in the dark, for some minutes before sleep enveloped her also.

16

W hat Charlotte had not told her husband was that she eagerly read the columns of The Times at every opportunity, and had done so for some years before their marriage, in the hope of reading something of Francois – where he was, what he was doing, the influence he was having in the ever-changing political scene in his country. She read of the success of his work, *The Genius of Christianity,* how Napoleon Bonaparte courted him for support after he had became Emperor as a result of his writing, and the courage he had shown in opposing him over the issue of the execution of the Duc d' Enghlien.

His visit to Rome, his appointment in Switzerland, were all recorded, as were other aspects of his work. Charlotte found herself feeling a reflected sense of pride at his stature – and a sense of anger, on his behalf, when he was banished from Paris following his criticism of Napoleon over his policies.

After Samuel was born, she ceased to read the papers so avidly for a while as she gave him all her attention. A year later, their second son, who they named William after his paternal grandfather, was born to bring more joy to the Sutton household, where the staff became enlarged with the addition of nursemaids, and where the presence of infants brought a family atmosphere and growing activity.

"The boys have made this old house younger," Samuel told Charlotte one day. "It echoes with their crying and laughing and gurgling. It is enjoying having children about its rooms again."

Charlotte smiled at her husband's happiness. He no longer went to sea, which pleased her and relieved her of the anxiety that was always with her until she knew he was safely back on shore; and though he was still away for periods of weeks at a time on naval business at the Admiralty in London, or in Portsmouth, he was also at home more often than in the days he had captained warships, and so was able to see his sons growing up. He was appointed a Deputy Lieutenant, and magistrate, for Norfolk and Suffolk, which meant fulfilling engagements close to home. And Charlotte felt contentment and pleasure at that.

Three years after William's birth Charlotte was in confinement for a third time, and in July, 1810 the family was blessed with a third son, John, named after Charlotte's father. In the ensuing months she took her sons regularly to the Parsonage to see her parents, and her father delighted in playing with Samuel, who was showing an innate intellect and sharpness even at six years old.

One day, at the approach to Christmas of 1811, her father suffered a bad bout of bronchitis, and was weak and confined to bed. His mind seemed confused, and, struggling for breath, he said to Charlotte:

"Do you ever see that Frenchman, Shatterbrain? You remember him, he stayed here once, a long time ago."

"Papa, of course not! How could I? I haven't seen him since he left abruptly, as you will recall. Why do you ask?"

"No, no reason. I was thinking about him, that is all. Enjoyed his company, you know, enjoyed his conversation. He was a scholar, a man of great intelligence, and wit. Enjoyed a drink too. If you do ever see him, give him my best regards, won't you?"

Charlotte took his hand as he lay there, now looking old and tired beyond his years.

"Papa, Shatterbrain, as you call him, returned to France many years ago – I am certain I will never see him again, much as it would please me to do so. He enjoyed your conversations too, as I remember."

"Yes, well, if you do see him..."

"If I do, I will let him know you remember him fondly."

Charlotte looked at her father with a worried expression, and returned to her mother downstairs, where she was with the children.

"I fear Papa is ailing badly," she said.

"The physician has given him medicine, and seemed hopeful that it would improve his health," Sarah replied. "I am concerned, and no mistake, but he is in God's hands."

Their prayers seemed to be answered. By Christmas he was back to rude health, enjoying the season with his family and grandchildren, fetching holly and ivy to decorate the hall and the festive table, and ready to celebrate in the way he most enjoyed – with a tankard of porter.

Charlotte and her mother relaxed at seeing him so well – better, it seemed, than before he fell ill, and he was in the same spirits as the New Year was celebrated.

Then, two weeks later, a message arrived at Ditchingham Lodge, informing Charlotte of the death of her father, suddenly and without warning. Shocked and distraught, she hurried to the parsonage to be with her mother, to console her in her grief. She was scarcely able to speak, but managed to tell her that he was suddenly convulsed with pains to the chest, and died in the drawing-room a few minutes later without being able to say anything.

"He had seemed so well since Christmas, full of his usual energy. Now he has gone, so suddenly, so suddenly," Sarah sobbed.

Samuel returned immediately from London and took control of the funeral arrangements in his compassionate but efficient Naval way, so that Charlotte could remain with her mother.

Later, after the funeral and interment were over and mourners had gathered at Ditchingham Lodge, Charlotte was in conversation with Lydia, who was now also married and lived in nearby Ditchingham House, from where it was easy to continue their childhood friendship.

"Charlotte, how are you? I cannot imagine how deep your grief must be – particularly as your father died so suddenly."

"Thank you, Lydia – I am managing quite well, and so is Mama. He had been ill before Christmas, but had recovered so well. It came as such a shock to us all; it gave us no time to, to say goodbye to him, that is the worst part of it. But I'm still puzzled at something he said to me while he was weak and suffering, just before Christmas."

"Why, what was that?"

"He asked me to remember him to Francois – I believe I told you once he stayed with us in the 1790s while recovering from an accident. It seemed so strange, mentioning it again like that, without any - any reason."

"You did tell me about him – that you had hoped to marry him, and your feelings when he left so suddenly. It was a long time ago. Perhaps your father had been fitful, or delusional, and his mind had gone back to earlier days. That does happen sometimes."

"He was tired and weak. But he seemed so earnest about it. Did he think then that he was dying – and if he did, and if it was his last wish, should I take steps to pass on the message to Francois?"

"I don't think that would be wise, Charlotte. It was not the last thing he said, and it was a remark made for no particular reason. I don't feel it would have been in his mind for you to pass it on, even if he fully realised what he was saying. Unless..."

Charlotte looked at her friend inquiringly as she paused.

"Please take no offence at this Charlotte; but in all the years of our friendship, during our conversations, you have mentioned Chateaubriand – Francois – often: that he is doing this, or that, that he is meeting this person or that person, that he has gone to this country or that country. And you told me some of your feelings for him during the time he stayed with you.

"I wonder – is it perhaps that you have been seeking a reason to contact him again, and see your father's remark as that reason?"

Charlotte lowered her eyes. Her hands played with the handkerchief on her lap.

"Papa was very angry with him when he left. That is why his last words were so strange. I need no reason to contact him," she said unconvincingly.

"But you would like an excuse to contact him?"

"It had occurred to me that I should write a letter to him, conveying Papa's message, that is all. It was his last request to me."

"Is that all?" Lydia urged gently.

Charlotte suddenly put her face in her hands, and began to sob.

"No! No, it is not all! I cannot get Francois out of my mind, hard as I try. I thought I could, but I cannot! I yearn to see

him again, just to see him, to be in his presence. Each time I see his name in the newspaper it gives my heart a lift – it makes me feel closer to him. I want to be closer to him."
She took a deep sobbing breath.

"It makes me feel so guilty – I shouldn't be feeling these things, so long after he had left. I thought in a few weeks, or a few months, I could put it out of my mind – I have tried so hard to do so, Lydia, so hard. I try my best not to pick up the newspaper when it arrives, but it is like a magnet, and draws me to it. I curse the day that printing was invented! Had it not been so there would be no newspapers and I would not have been tempted to read them, tempted to feel closer to Francois.

"It is all so unfair - to Samuel I mean. It is as if I am being unfaithful to him in my mind, yet he is so good, so honourable, such a caring and considerate husband, so proud of our sons He has such hopes for them. And... I do... love him...with almost all my heart. But not with my whole heart, you see, as I should. There is part of me that will always love Francois, always, part of me that will always want to be with him. I have tried to pretend that it is no so, but I cannot pretend. I pray to God to take Francois from my mind, to help me be true to Samuel, completely true to him, but He has failed me. I have failed Him. Oh, I feel such an awful being, not worthy of anyone...I am weak – weak-willed. I have not the mental strength to put Francois behind me, and out of my mind for good..."

"Charlotte, Charlotte, you must not persecute yourself so. You are grieving so for your father, you are in such a high state of emotion because of that. Do not chastise yourself. You are a good and dutiful wife, and mother, and daughter – that is important. What is in your mind can hurt no one, as long as it remains inside you."

Lydia had moved closer to Charlotte as she tried to soothe her in her turmoil, but her tears continued to flow.

"Francois would have called these things my daemons. But now I have told you. I have confessed my feelings."

"And that will help – it always helps to tell someone, and it will remain with me alone."

"There is something else I must confess. I still have notes he made for me for my studies, notes in his handwriting, and...and flowers he gave me on our walks, and other memoirs that have meaning for us. Even now, I get them out from where they are hidden, from time to time, just to look at them, and touch them, and remember. I do not have the fortitude to resist that."

Lydia listened, trying to understand her friend's turmoil, trying to sympathise and advise at the same time. Now she tried firmness.

"Then you must burn them, to put them out of temptation's way, and in doing so your feelings for him will be consumed by the flames also. You must throw them on the fire. I will help you."

"No! No, I cannot! I cannot let them go. They are all I have of him."

"Charlotte, sometimes a serious condition requires a strong medicinal potion. Look on it as that."

"No, Lydia! Please, no – not yet. I could not bear that."

"Perhaps the time is not right – not when you are mourning so deeply. We will talk about this again in a few months."

With a big effort, Charlotte stemmed her tears and mopped her face with her now sodden handkerchief. For the first time she was able to look at Lydia face to face, her eyes red.

"Yes, yes – perhaps. Lydia, you are such a loyal friend. Thank you, for listening and for your confidence. I must try to compose myself and return to the other mourners. In my selfishness I have shown no thought for Mama, and how badly she is grieving."

Later that evening, as she said her nightly prayers, the thought returned Charlotte that, somehow, her father had known what she was feeling, still, for Chateaubriand – that it was a message from God, through him, to contact the Frenchman, just once, so they could make their peace and say the goodbyes to each other that had not been possible on that night sixteen years ago...

However, as life gradually returned to normal over the following weeks and months, she resisted that temptation, great though it was. Two weeks after her father's death,

Samuel arranged for Charlotte, their sons and her mother, to spend some time in an apartment in Portsmouth he rented for them while he was working there, so they were close to him. He felt they needed time away from Bungay, to come to terms with their loss. Charlotte loved him for that – his thoughtfulness, and concern for their well-being, and his desire and effort to lift them out of their grief.

As for herself, she strove hard to put Francois out of her mind. Caring for her three sons, even with the help of their nursemaid, and visiting her mother more frequently now she was on her own, kept her occupied, and for a while she was able to turn away from searching the columns of The Times for news of him.

But that was not always possible. In the social circle of which she was part, politics and the affairs of nations were often the topic of conversation, and she was aware of Francois' continued strong opposition to Napoleon, his support for the Bourbons, his exile in the footsteps of Louis XVIII as Napoleon made a renewed attempt to run France, and the monarch's return following that short-lived episode of France's continuing change and instability.

"I learn that your French friend is now a minister of state," Lydia remarked one day, when they were taking tea together. "One wonders if he will eventually become King, or Emperor, whichever state of politics that poor country is in at the time!"

"Lydia, don't mock! He is an ardent Royalist and would never become Emperor, and to become king would be impossible. But I had not read that he had an appointment as minister – I'm trying not to read of him, so that I can devote my mind to the boys, who are growing up so fast. Samuel is now nine years old, and increasingly handsome. He is having teaching in mathematics and literature, and I am teaching him and William to play the pianoforte. They are both making good progress."

"I should not have mentioned Francois – I apologise," said Lydia, taking note of Charlotte's attempt to change the subject. "But England's involvement in France, particularly through the Duke of Wellington in recent times, means it continues to be much talked about.

"Now, I am so pleased the boys are progressing well, though I knew they would, with such intelligent parents. Your father would be proud of them too. It must be four, five years since his death?"

"Yes, four years. One does come to terms with the loss eventually, though he remains in one's mind – he still seems to be there, using his guiding influence. It is difficult to explain, but it is a comfort to me. I suppose it is the same as it is with Francois – he will always be there. And yet it is different. I know I can never see Papa again, until I myself join him in the life hereafter at least, but Francois is still alive and living in this world, and to be with him, stand beside him again, is possible. I know it is wrong, Lydia –

wrong to want that so much, and since Papa's death I have managed to keep those thoughts at the back of my mind. I think I have them under control, but deep inside me somewhere that possibility flickers, and try as I might, even after all these years, I cannot extinguish it."

17

D ays with their little changing routine, months with their changing needs, seasons, with their changing colours, years with their changing challenges went by in the Waveney Valley.

St Mary's Church continued its watch over the common towards Ditchingham, where from the Lodge Charlotte drew succour from the view and the contours of the common land unchanged since time began, and walked there, often, with her family, and remembered.

The Sutton family continued to be a close and loving one, with Samuel, William and John developing well towards adolescence. Their grandmother, Sarah, who doted on them, eventually moved into the Lodge with them as she became frail through her increasing years, and enjoyed their regular company.

It was succour to her to hear the children's voices through the house as they played, and got into scrapes; or to hear their tentative playing of the piano under Charlotte' tuition; or watch them running around in the garden and adjoining meadows, flying their kites, or bowling a hoop, or playing at soldiers. Sometimes they would attempt to put on a dramatic sketch they had written themselves, using costumes they found in forgotten wardrobes. William, as the eldest, was always the leader, directing his brothers in their roles, or intervening if there were quarrels. He was

251

following in his father's footsteps, Charlotte thought, as she too observed their activities. One day, he would receive a commission in his country's forces, she felt sure – though the idea made her fearful.

Samuel Sutton's Naval career continued to flourish – he was a respected senior member, with influence at the Admiralty, and in July, 1821, his standing was recognised with his promotion to Rear-Admiral as he moved towards the close of a distinguished career at sea and on land.

"Samuel, I am so pleased for you. This is richly deserved," Charlotte told him when he received the letter of confirmation. "You have served your country well – you have loved and cared for your country, as you have loved and cared for your family, and I know your country loves you as well as we love you."

But over the next few months Charlotte became pre-occupied with concern for her mother's health. Sarah had become increasingly tired, and began to lose her appetite. Her physician prescribed her different potions, which helped for a time, but was unable to provide a certain diagnosis for her troubles. Through the autumn of that year she rallied for a time, but towards Christmas, her health began to deteriorate again.

"I am so worried about Mama," Charlotte said to Samuel that Christmas. "She is becoming weaker by the day. I fear she will not see another year. The physician is at a loss to know what best to prescribe for her. I am beside myself with worry and fear. What can we do?"

"The physician has done his best, and we must continue to care for her as best we can," her husband replied. "She has a strong constitution and may rally when the warmer weather returns. We must continue to pray that that will happen."

The winter, however, proved to be cold and harsh, with severe frosts and snow lying on the land for several weeks. Looking out from the window, Charlotte saw a shroud of white enveloping the Common, and shivered and prayed that it was not a portent. There was even ice forming along the sheltered banks of the river.

The family fussed around Sarah, keeping her warm in bed, and, when she was downstairs, insuring she sat close to the inglenook fire which was kept well fed with logs. She was resilient, and chided them good-humouredly for their concern, and said there had been many winters more harsh than that one.

But having got through without too much discomfort to March, when an unusually mild southerly wind and three days of bright sun quickly dissipated the frost and snow which had resisted in town and countryside for so long, she suffered an unexpected relapse, had no appetite for food, and steadily weakened. Despite the family's earnest prayers, supported by those of the congregations at St Mary's Church and St Margaret's, Ilketshall, Sarah was re-united with her beloved husband in the early spring, ten years after his death, as Charlotte laid her head, weeping quietly, on her still breast.

She gathered her three sons around her to tell them, and hugged them to her, for comfort for them and her. When her father died, they were too young to fully understand; this time, with Samuel fifteen years old and John nearly 12, they did, though they were solemn, and not quite sure what to say.

Charlotte's husband, comforting, compassionate and re-assuring, once more made the necessary arrangements for the funeral and interment, and arranged for an obituary notice to be included in the columns of The Times. To her own surprise, Charlotte controlled her grief outwardly much better than she had on her father's death, until the service itself, when the words of the Vicar, the message of the hymns and the heartfelt condolences of the congregation broke through her weakening self-control and her tears were unrestrained.

Charlotte did not leave the house over the ensuing days and weeks of mourning. With the funeral over, the heaviest atmosphere of grief was lifted, but a sombre atmosphere pertained, and the natural boisterousness of Samuel, William and John, particularly following the completion of their daily lessons, was restrained. They understood a period of respect and reflection was needed, and that made their parents proud, though there were times when Charlotte silently hoped that their laughter and noise would return to break the atmosphere.

A week after the funeral, she was sitting in the withdrawing room, and picked up the latest copy of The Times, believing it was the day that her mother's obituary would be published. She scanned the long, grey, almost unbroken columns of text as she turned the pages, looking for the appropriate section, when suddenly, her eyes passed a headline at the top of one of the columns, and immediately focussed on it. She sat up straight in her chair, with an audible intake of breath.

FRENCH AMBASSADOR

Paris. It was announced in Paris yesterday that Vicomte Francois-Rene de Chateaubriand has been appointed France's Ambassador to the Kingdom of Great Britain. Vicomte Chateaubriand, who has been his country's Ambassador to Prussia for the past year, will take up his appointment at the French Embassy in London at the end of this month.

Charlotte read it twice, to take it in fully. For several months, during her mother's illness, she had rarely looked at the newspaper, and Francois had been, for the most part, at the back of her mind. Now, suddenly, he was there with her again.

"Francois is coming to London. It will be the first time since he left me – since he left Bungay – that he has been in this country, the first time he has been so close since then," she said to herself. A feeling of excitement welled up in her, and for a moment the subdued air of mourning left her.

Then her eyes moved to the opposite page, and the obituary column, where her mother's death was duly recorded: *"...Sarah Ives, nee Williams, widow of the late John Clement Ives and mother of Lady Charlotte Sutton, wife of Rear Admiral Samuel Sutton..."* was how she was described.

The names of two people she had loved, there before her, side by side – each bringing such contrasting emotions: on the one hand the love for a mother now taken from her, and the intense grieving the loss had brought to her; on the other, the love for a man she knew had loved her, who she still loved, a man she had hoped and prayed she would have the chance to see, to converse with once again, even now, all these years after the dream of marriage to him had been so cruelly dashed. A man at the height of prominence in his country, and in Europe.

Charlotte kept her eyes fixed on the columns of the paper as her mind wandered. It took her back ten years, to the days shortly before her father's death, and one of the last things he had said to her: "If you ever seen him, give him my best regards, won't you?"

He had been weak and ill, and his mind confused, yet it was his last request to her. Now, by chance, or fate, or accident, the notice in the paper of her mother's death had brought to her attention the news that Francois was about to come to England. In her emotional state, Charlotte tried to work out in her head whether this was co-incidence, or confirmation, indirectly through her mother, or her father's wish that she should contact Francois once more.

She could make no sense of it, and eventually she shook herself out of her reverie, and closed the newspaper. But the news had brought thoughts of Francois to the forefront of her mind again, and hard though she tried to dismiss them, they kept returning to haunt her: images of him standing by the piano at the Parsonage as she played and sang, of walking with him on the Common, of the way he looked at her over the dinner table while he was in conversation with Papa, of the way Mama had established a rapport with him, and made him feel part of the family. She tried to keep her feelings in perspective, telling herself that the distress of her mother's death and trying to comfort her sons through the loss of their grandmother, were leading her to think illogically; that coming to terms with her mourning would also enable her to come to terms with the foolishness, indeed the wrong, of any aspirations to visit Francois in London.

But despite everything, those thoughts persisted.

Two weeks into the period of mourning, Lydia called at the Lodge. She had attended the funeral service, but since then had stayed away out of respect. Now she felt it was time to visit, and offer her female companionship to Charlotte in a household in which, apart from the servants, she was surrounded by men – her children and Samuel.

"I'm well, thank you, and pleased to see you," Charlotte said in answer to Lydia's natural and concerned inquiry. "Samuel has remained here as much as he can, and the boys seem to understand, though it is my belief that William is feeling the loss of his grandmother most – he is very quiet and withdrawn much of the time. But we have talked to him about...about the process of life and...death, and they are intelligent children. They need time to come to terms with the loss, as we as adults do."

"And you – are you coming to terms with it?" Lydia inquired. "Is it less hard than the loss of your Papa?"

"I feel, in some ways, that it is harder. When Papa died I still had one parent left – now I have neither. On the other hand, having lost her husband, Mama depended on me more and more for her companionship, particularly over the past year. But I gain comfort from God, and my prayers, and each day that goes by is easier."

She paused, and looked earnestly at Lydia as they sat in the study overlooking the Common, before continuing.

"Besides, though it fills me with guilt, there is...I have...something else is troubling my mind."

"What can that be?"

"Francois Chateaubriand, is back in London." Charlotte said it quickly, as if, had she paused, she would have held back from saying it.

"In London? The last information I read he was in Prussia."

"He has been appointed France's Ambassador to King George, and is now in office at the French Embassy. The news was in the paper recently," Charlotte explained, more calmly.

"And you are moved to go to visit him," Lydia said in a matter-of-fact way.

"Oh, Lydia, you read my mind so well. Yes, yes, I am! You are quite right! I am trying so hard to resist it, I know it would be wrong, I feel I would be betraying Samuel. There is guilt inside me just to think it. But the urge in me is so strong, Lydia, so powerful – it is getting the better of me."

"But you must resist it, Charlotte, with all your mind. What would it achieve? What would you do – what would you say to him? He is a married man. Besides, you have not seen him for...how long? Twenty-five years at least, you have had no contact. In all probability he will not remember you, and will wonder who you are."

Charlotte did no flinch at the coldness, the unintended hurt in that phrase.

"He will remember me – I know he will," she said firmly, but almost inaudibly.

"But I ask you again, what will it achieve? And after you have seen him, what then? Will you call on him regularly? It is impossible! Charlotte, I am your close companion. I advise you for your own sake not to visit Francois. You must forget about him."

"Lydia, I have tried! No one but God knows how hard I have tried, and there have been times when I have felt I was succeeding in that. I know you are right, and you are advising me as my most valued friend. But..."

The emotion was now welling up in Charlotte, but she kept it under control as she continued:

"You ask what calling on Francois would achieve. My hope is that, seeing him as he is now, a different person in many ways, moving in different, exalted circles, with age taking its unceasing toll, I believe that would help me to forget. His age is advancing - he is in his middle fifties.

"I hope you can understand, Lydia. Have you visited a place that you enjoyed as a child, where you loved the atmosphere and the buildings and the views, the warmth and the blue skies; have you been drawn inexorably to visit that place many years later, believing it would give you the same feelings, the same memories – but found it cold, and much changed, and seemingly altogether different to the place you knew once, long ago? So that when you left it again, you had no desire to return? That is how I believe it will be if I visit Francois again – that he will be much changed, and that the strong desire inside me to see him, to talk to him, to be in his presence again, will be gone."

She stopped, and looked at Lydia with an appealing expression on her face, seeking re-assurance that it would be so.

There was silence for some moments as Lydia held her eyes. She got up from where she was sitting behind Charlotte, and stood to face her, before replying. Then she said:

"I can understand the theory of what you are saying, Charlotte. But a person is very different to a place, though I grant you places have souls. Are you earnestly hoping that that will be the outcome of your visit – or might it be an excuse for it?"

Charlotte lowered her eyes. Her face took on a troubled expression.

"I am trying hard to be honest with myself, and true to my family. I value your advice Lydia, but the urge to visit Francois is so strong. I thought I had controlled it, but it has returned more urgent than ever. Do you remember me telling you that, just before Papa died, he asked me to pass on his regards to Francois? That might have come from the delirious mind of a dying man, but it was his last request of me, and I have not been able to fulfil it. Now, when I was reading the newspaper to find the obituary on Mama, there, almost beside it, was the news of Francois's appointment as

Ambassador. Is that not a second message to me that I should visit him, now the opportunity is there?"

"Oh, Charlotte – my closest friend, I want to support you and encourage you. But was this truly their wish, or are you reading these messages into two unconnected incidents, twelve years apart, to support your desire, at a time when the loss of your dear Mama has left you again in such an emotional state – as did the loss of your Papa? I can only advise you as I see it from the outside. My belief is that if you visit him once, you will be moved to do so again, and a third time. I urge you to be strong, and resist this temptation, for the sake of you and your family – I beg you most earnestly not to do it."

"But if I do not, I will never know – never know what he...felt, what he thought. Lydia, you know how hard I have tried to put him out of my mind completely, and for the most part I have. I have a happy and loving family, a beautiful home, good friends, a life many people would envy. I am well blessed. But twenty-five years since Francois left, he is still there in me. He used to talk to me about his daemons – the word he gave to his periods of depression and melancholy, of which he could not rid himself. Now, he has...may God forgive me for saying this...he has become my daemon. The man I first loved has become a blight on me, and the only way to rid myself of that is to visit him, just once. It would be only once, Lydia,

I promise you. But I cannot stop myself, now the opportunity has presented himself."

Charlotte was now weeping quietly to herself, dabbing her eyes with her handkerchief.

"Charlotte, I beg you again to resist this temptation, however strong it maybe. You cannot predict the effect it may have on you and your family – and imagine the chatter in Bungay's society were it to become known that you were associating with someone known to have left the town in disgrace, however long ago it might have been."

There was a hint of anger in Lydia's tone – and in Charlotte's instinctive reply.

"He did not leave in disgrace – he left with honour!" she snapped. And in the next breath she apologised.

"Lydia, forgive me, I know you mean well."

She looked up at her friend, her face pale.

"Nevertheless, I shall visit Francois," she said, defiantly.

18

"Charlotte, my dearest, I have been called to the Admiralty on business again. This role as Rear-Admiral is proving busier than I anticipated."

Samuel had opened a letter which had just arrived, and was sitting at the table in the withdrawing room, reading it. He tutted agitatedly

"It means I must travel to London in two days' time. I may have to be there for a week."

His wife, sitting opposite, looked up at him, sympathetically.

"I understand, Samuel – your work for your country is important. It has to be done."

"Yes. Charlotte, I know we are still in the period of mourning for your mother, but perhaps it might be good for you and our sons to travel with me, to see fresh surroundings, have a change of air. It might be a comfort to you, help to heal your grief. I could find accommodation near the Admiralty for you."

"Do you think it would be proper, and respectful, to do that during mourning?"

Charlotte did not want to appear too eager at the suggestion – but the idea of travelling to London instinctively strengthened her resolve to visit Francois. Here was the opportunity to do so – it seemed to her that she was being encouraged by providence, and that her intentions were right.

"Proper respect for those who have passed on must involve an understanding that they would not want the lives of those left behind to stand still," Samuel replied, gently. "Besides, you have seemed particularly pale and pre-occupied during the last few days, my dear. I believe a change of air may do your health good, as well as your mind."

He was a practical and pragmatic man – qualities which had brought him respect throughout the Navy, and traits which Charlotte admired too.

"If you feel sure, then we will travel with you," she smiled. "I will let the servants know of our plans, and ask them to prepare the things we will need for our stay."

A bloom had appeared on Charlotte's pale cheeks as her heart quickened at the prospect that the opportunity to meet Francois again was close to becoming reality.

Samuel arranged for an apartment for his family in the fashionable area of Mayfair – he himself had accommodation at the Admiralty, but would have time to spend with his wife, Samuel, William and John. They were eager and excited about the trip, and high-spirited on the long journey, for which they joined the London coach at the Three Tuns Inn in Bungay, and which included four stops at other coaching inns along the route for a change of horses and an opportunity for respite for the passengers.

For Charlotte the journey was one of excitement, apprehension, nervousness, guilt – all those motions rolled into one, with each coming to the fore in turn, as her plans and their possible problems tumbled through her mind. When should she call at the Embassy? Should she send a message in advance? How would she find it – she was not familiar with London, though she had travelled with her husband there before? Should she take her sons with her to meet Francois, or arrange for them to be taken to visit the sights in the capital? What if Francois was not at the Embassy? It would be a busy role which would take him to meetings and receptions regularly. Her heart sank at the thought of that eventuality – that the opportunity to meet him, which had presented itself so readily, may be snuffed out by circumstances which she could not foresee.

She had decided that she would tell Samuel of the planned visit – that would be only right and honourable. But should she tell him beforehand, and risk the possibility that he would forbid her to see him, or wait till afterwards, and tell him of the outcome? If it was the latter, would he be angry, with good reason, that she had not told him in advance? That at least she discounted – Samuel's nature was to remain calm and understanding at all times, though he would make his views known to her, and would reproach her if he felt hurt, or betrayed. Charlotte did not want that – he cherished her so well, was a great comfort to her in times of stress, and to sadden him in any way by her actions would compound her feelings of guilt.

All these things occupied her mind on the long journey to London, under dull, cloudy skies which dropped heavy showers of rain at intervals, making the rhythm of the carriage even more uncomfortable. But she was scarcely aware of it.

Overriding all her mental turmoil was the feeling that she was on her way to London, to where Francois was, where she would meet him, see him, be in his presence for the first time in twenty-five years.

It was a meeting that was pre-ordained, one she could not step back from now, even if she wanted to. She knew, somehow, that he would be there when she called.

The next afternoon, the rain had ceased, but the scent and taste of it was still in the air, giving a freshness to the morning, though the sky, or what Charlotte could see of it high above the tall buildings which crowded along the side of every street, was still grey, with just a hint of brightness appearing fleetingly high above the tall chimneys. There was an oppressive atmosphere, which she felt matched her mourning attire of black, complete with a veil. She would have liked to have worn brighter colours, more cheerful designs, but she knew that would be disrespectful and highly irregular and she stayed true to the memory of her Mama.

Samuel and William accompanied her to the Embassy – she felt they were old enough to do so and would understand, but John remained at the apartment with their nurse. She had spoken to them in recent months of Francois, and of his time staying with her and their grandparents at the Parsonage while he recovered from an injury sustained in a fall. She spoke of him naturally, as a friend she had not seen for some time, and told them of some of his adventures after leaving France. Hearing that he was now in England, and they were in London, it was a good opportunity to visit him, and renew his acquaintance, she had explained. But she had not spoken of the reasons for his sudden departure from Bungay.

They decided to walk, rather than call for a carriage, though Charlotte soon wished she had not made that decision. The pavements, such as they were, were dirty and wet, with the debris of people and horses and the general scent of staleness in contrast to the cleaner and relaxed streets of Bungay, and though she had been to London before she was not familiar with the streets and the turns she needed to make to reach the Embassy, even though it was just a short distance away in Knightsbridge. Samuel and William tried to work out where they should turn, but after two or three false trails down intimidating backstreets, where beggars and gaudily dressed women stared at them with expressions of aggressive suspicion, Charlotte began to become agitated.

The directions given by the commissionaire at their apartment had seemed simple and straightforward, but the further they went, the more the unfamiliar streets, and the throngs of people, the rattle of carriage wheels and the clatter of horses hooves on cobbled surfaces seemed to crowd in on them, surround them, seemed to fill her head with noise and her mind with doubt and fear, so it seemed impossible to know where they were going.

Charlotte stopped, and put her gloved hands over her ears, squeezed her eyes tight shut, contorting her face.

"Stop!" she cried to her sons. "Stop! I cannot go on! I don't know where we are! I should not be here! We should not be here! We must go back!"

Samuel took his mother's arm.

"Mama, don't fret! William and I will look after you! We cannot be far from Knightsbridge and the Embassy. We'll ask for directions."

He spotted a carriage, which had just set down passengers, and the driver was about to climb back on to his seat.

"Could you tell me how far we are from the French Ambassador's office my good man?" he asked boldly.

The man, who had a gaunt face with one badly shaped eye, and one brightly sharp and wide open under a scruffy top hat, looked him up and down with a bemused expression on his face; then looked at his mother and brother, standing nearby and looking on timidly.

"I'd say I'd take you there for a fare, sir," he said at last. "But I'm an honest Cockney and it would not be right to take silver from country folk such as you, for such a short journey."

He pointed his whip down the street.

"See that building down there, on the left hand side, stone-built? See where I mean? That's yer place —no more than 200 yards. You'll see the plaque beside the door: Embassy Francais."

"Thank you very much," said Samuel, gratefully. Unknown to them, they had unexpectedly wandered into Knightsbridge.

"You see, Mama, we are nearly there already. I knew we could not be far away."

His mother, who had regained her orientation and opened her eyes again, sighed with relief. Together the three, more used to the quiet streets and lanes and open fields of the countryside, made their way across the busy thoroughfare, and along to the address they sought.

In no time they were standing in front of the tall, three storey building wedged between brick buildings on either side, with the front door reached by three steps. As she looked up at it from street level, Charlotte was seized with apprehension; doubts and misgivings came flooding back to her once again. Her mind bubbled with conflicting hypotheses:

"If he is in, within two short minutes I will be standing face to face with Francois again. What will I say to him? What will he say to me? Will he recognise me? Heaven forefend the embarrassment should he not do so! Will I recognise him? Will he be angry with me for calling, and dismiss me as soon as he sees me? Now I'm here I'm not at all sure I should go in! Perhaps Lydia was right – I should not see him, I will only make a fool of myself, and regret it forever. We should go back to our apartment, and keep my memories of him intact – seeing him, if he has aged greatly, might be worse than not seeing him. I'm fearful that I will let myself down in front of him. I'm frightened – frightened to walk up those three short steps to ring the bell. I cannot do it! I cannot move! Please God, I should have listened to Lydia – she would be triumphant if she should see me now! No, no – she would not, that is unfair to her, she would be sad on my behalf, despite what she felt. I shall gather the boys together and we shall turn round and leave now...

"Mama, you are shaking so! Are you ill, or is it too cold for you?"

Samuel's voice broke into Charlotte's mental turmoil, and she took her eyes from the imposing pillared portal and black front door on which they had been fixed unblinking for some moments.

"No – no Samuel, I'm not ill, though it is a little cold. It is just that this is an occasion, a meeting, I have thought about a lot, seeing an old friend, and I own that I am a little nervous.

"Now come along, up the steps and ring the doorbell for me."

She had told her husband she planned to visit Francois, and his re-action had surprised her – he had encouraged her to do so, had seemed keen on the idea. He had told her that recalling memories of times gone by, of happy days and old friends, could have a salving effect on her, could help lift her spirits through her mourning, and she would visit Francois with his blessing.

His re-action came as a relief to her, but also increased her feeling of guilt. And when he had left her at the apartment the previous day, to go to the Admiralty, after seeing them settled in, she could not help noticing a feeling of reproach in his eyes that he tried unsuccessfully to hide.

As Simon pulled the bell knob they heard the muffled reaction of the clanger inside the building. The die was cast – there was no going back now.

The footsteps of someone walking down the stone foyer to the door could be heard, and then the door opened, and a valet stood there, pale of face but with a half-smile which suggested a cautious welcome.

"Bonjour, Madame," he said, in a tone which embodied the question, without stating it: "May I know the purpose of your call?

"Bonjour, Monsieur," Charlotte replied, with a hint of a tremor in her voice. "I apologise for calling without a prior appointment, but if the Ambassador is in, and is not too busy, would it be possible for us to have an audience with him?"

"May I ask who it is who would like to see him?"

"My name is Lady Sutton," Charlotte replied, slightly more boldly.

The valet ushered them into the foyer and into a room to the left.

"Please wait in here. I will inform Vicomte Chateaubriand that you are here."

At the sound of his name Charlotte felt her heart quicken and her cheeks flush. Even at that stage, she was not sure that Francois would agree to see them – he might remember her if he saw her, but the name Lady Sutton would mean nothing to him.

After a short interval, they heard the steps of the valet returning down the stairs. To Charlotte they seemed slow and ponderous, almost as if they were making that short journey to convey bad news which the valet was reluctant to convey. After more drawn out moments he appeared at the door of the room in which they waited. He paused.

"He has declined to see us!" The though flashed through Charlotte's mind, masked by the wide-eyed, inquiring expression on her face, as she held her breath.

"The Ambassador will see you now. Please follow me."

Relief and apprehension mingled inside her, battling with her efforts to retain outward control, but she did so, and ushered the boys to follow the valet out of the room and up the stairs. They seemed so steep at that point, like a mountain, and fighting to control the shaking of her body made the ascent even harder. She felt a tinge of nausea.

Eventually they were on a wide landing, and the valet led them to a stout door of dark English oak. Deliberately, he put his hand on the handle to open it...

Those final few seconds before the moment Charlotte had been longing for seemed interminable. A quarter of a century of expectation, of ebbing and flowing emotions, of trying to forget but wanting to remember, of knowing she should let go completely of that adolescent love but always clinging on defiantly, steadfastly, to its last unbreakable fibres, of wanting to see him but fearing he would not want to see her: all those feelings were encapsulated in that fleeting instant in time.

Now that state of mind was about to end. In the next instant, she would know whether she was doing the right thing.

"Lady Sutton, Your Excellency."

19

Then she was in the room, Samuel and William on either side of her. It was a high ceilinged room, heavily panelled in oak, with light streaming in through the large sash window behind an expansive desk, on which stood a single oil lamp, an ink-holder, a number of pens, a small pile of papers neatly organised; and, centrally in front of the figure seated at the armchair behind the desk, pen in hand, another single sheet of paper on which he had been writing beside it.

Charlotte was still shaking as she entered, but was aware of the figure looking up from his work at that moment, an expression of concentration on his long face, with its prominent nose and dark brown eyes beneath hair which had once been full and black, but which now was receding and generously flecked with grey.

Francois got up and came round the desk towards them. But his businesslike smile evolved quickly into an expression of puzzlement – and then, as he moved forward to greet her, it opened out as his mind delved back over the years to find recognition, and remembrance of days long ago, when he was not burdened with public office, in a country far from his own land's troubles, where there was relaxation and few responsibilities.

So overcome was Charlotte that she was still trembling, and at first was unable to speak. For what seemed an age the two people stood there, facing each other, familiarising themselves with the person they had known and loved, long ago, in a different time, before destinies had intervened. Charlotte saw someone who seemed to her largely unchanged from the man she had nursed, and grown to love, in Bungay, seeing him as he was then, with that intense far away look on his face – the one she had known as he stood silently by the piano at the Parsonage, listening to her playing the piano. Francois, for his part, saw the girl he had come to love, whose interests in music and literature and history were in harmony with his. She was in mourning dress, but he saw her not in black, but in the blues, greens and crimsons of the dresses she had worn then, accentuating her figure, highlighting the youthful bloom on her cheeks – a woman in the springtime of her life. The years that had passed since then had left only the aura of springtime around this lady who now stood before him.

For those moments, no words were necessary. The time that had elapsed and the uncluttered memories were the balm that now caressed them both, were the scents that pervaded that panelled room, were the billions of specks caught in the shafts of sunlight streaming through the window, illuminating them both in an aurora that can sometimes be seen outlining the full moon, enhancing its natural beauty with holiness. An aura pregnant with the love they had known, each of the other, but had never confessed in words. For those moments, both of them were alone in a room where nothing else could be defined – no desk, no furniture, no walls, no portraits, no national emblems.

At last, almost reluctantly, hesitantly, her voice trembling with emotion, Charlotte spoke:

"My Lord, do you remember me?"

So overcome was Francois that he could not reply; instead, he went to her, fell on his knees, and took her hand, his tears dampening her soft skin as he kissed it – tears from the same source that had dampened her mother's hand a few minutes after the last time he had set eyes on Charlotte, his English rose, before he had fled from Bungay in shame and embarrassment.

Tears released Charlotte, too, from the emotion she had been controlling with such effort for so long, as Francois led her to a chair to sit down, and sat beside her, his hands still enfolding her's.

He studied her still, through his tears. And eventually he was able to bring himself to reply to her question with his own.

"And you, Charlotte, Madame, do you remember me?"

She raised her head, slowly, and met his eyes again. There was a sadness, a wistfulness, in the smile that lit her face as she did so – a smile which spoke of a yearning for what might have been; a smile of a reproach, now mellowed, for the nature of their parting. And there was love in it, also. Still their hands touched.

Eventually, Charlotte withdrew her hand, and moved her body, as if shaking herself out of a reverie to focus on reality again.

"My Lord, forgive me – these are two of my sons, Samuel, and William, the sons of Rear-Admiral Sutton, to whom I was married in 1806. We are in mourning for the loss of my mother, who you will remember. I am still grieving deeply for her, having lost Papa ten years ago. I must tell you that shortly before he died he asked me to pass you his best regards, if I ever saw you. Perhaps that is the main reason I am here. But today I – I am not myself, I am too overcome at meeting you after such a long passage of time. Perhaps...could we meet again, my Lord? I am in London for a few days more."

"Of course, Madame. If you leave your address with me I will come to you tomorrow."

Samuel and William had stood with their heads bowed, self-consciously, not knowing what to make of the effect the meeting had had on both the adults. And there was an expression of relief on both their faces when the Ambassador offered Charlotte his arm and walked her down the stairs and outside to the waiting carriage he had asked his valet to summon. The boys climbed in. Before Charlotte followed, she exchanged a lingering glance with Francois, who pressed her hand to his heart.

"Till tomorrow," he whispered.

The following day Francois, having told his valet to make no appointments, walked the short distance to the address in Mayfair that Charlotte had given him. He had been ambassador for only a short while, but he remembered the geography of London well from his time there as an émigré, and it had not changed greatly from those days, though the streets were somewhat busier but no less dirty. The day was bright, though the sun was largely obscured by high cloud as he made his way briskly and purposely to his appointment, eager to see Charlotte again.

He found her alone in the large, first floor withdrawing room of her apartment, which was sumptuously furnished and decorated with the accoutrements of the day, with curtained windows looking out towards Grosvenor Square. She seemed more relaxed than the previous day, and greeted him with a smile as she invited him to sit beside her on the cushioned sofa.

"My Lord, seeing you again is like stepping back in time to the days of my youth. I must have changed and grown old over the years, but you have not – I see you now as you were then, at Bungay, when you came suddenly and unexpectedly into my life; I see you standing at the piano as I play, sitting and applauding as I sing; I see your earnest face as you read to me from Plato and teach me about the Italian writers..."

"...And I, Charlotte, see you tending so gently and skilfully to my wounds, see you concentrating on your playing." Francois interrupted to take up the theme. "I see the sun streaming in from the garden and lighting the features of your beautiful face, see you among the grasses and the flowers on the Common where we walked so often, see you laugh so gaily at the humour of conversations at the dinner table. If you could know how greatly those memories have sustained me, encouraged me, comforted me in my low moments in the years that have passed between those times and now, inspire me in my writing..."

Then Charlotte again: "And likewise the memories have sustained me, my Lord – and I have had knowledge of your rise to prominence in France through the newspapers. For the first years after...after you left...after that I could only wonder where you were, what had become of you, what you were doing, whether you were lonely, or happy, or fulfilled, or depressed, as you sometimes became. It was a comfort after you returned to France and took your place in trying to solve her troubles. And...I read that you were re-united with, your wife."

She studied Francois's face as she said that, but then moved on quickly, without giving him the chance to speak.

"I married a good man, Samuel, who is devoted to me and cherishes me, even though I cannot give him my whole heart. You see, part of my heart has always remained with you, my Lord and master."

Charlotte's face was solemn now. "It was as if...as if it put us on equal terms in life. Knowing the feelings there were between us, feelings that would always be there. But you were married, and I realised I could best suffer that sadness, selfish though it was of me, by marrying a man who was able to give me his whole, heart, in return for a part of mine."

"My dearest Charlotte." Francois, who had been leaning back, sat upright as he spoke. "I could never tell you that I loved you. How could I? But you must have known, just as I was aware that you were falling in love with me. And yet..." He left his seat, and turned his back on Charlotte, pacing the room. "...and yet, Mon Deiu, I was not free to love you, I should not let myself love you. But I did, and in loving you and saying nothing, I deceived you. I told myself a hundred times that that deception was not intentional, and in so doing I deluded myself also, because I had it in myself, I had the time and opportunity, to tell you of my whole life – things of which I was proud, things of which I was ashamed.

"Miserable man that I am, I took the way of the coward. Well I remember, my dear Charlotte, that evening – it has come like a ghost to me often to torment me, adding to the daemons I already had, encouraging them to torment me more deeply..."

"My Lord, please..."

"No, no – do not try to excuse my actions – or lack of them! Look at me now, where I am now. I have achieved great status in the country of my birth, my writings are well received, even revered, throughout Europe, I have played my part in trying to lift my country from the ravages of the Revolution to her present state which, though not perfect, sees her along the road to stability. I have met with kings, and princes, with tyrants and revolutionaries, with writers of great note, and have filled illustrious appointments, as I am now in your country. How have I achieved these things, dead Charlotte? I have achieved them through being honest in all my dealings, saying what I felt in my heart and my mind. Oui, certainment, it has got me into trouble, but I have faced the consequences of that and at least I have been able to tell myself that the words I have spoken, always, have been my true feelings."

Francois returned to his seat beside Charlotte, who had been listening and watching him with great concentration, and clasped her hands in his.

"And yet the person who deserved my honesty above all other, I deceived. I did not lie to you, Charlotte, but in saying nothing of my marriage I deceived you as surely as if I had uttered an untruth. That was my sin, though I cursed my unsatisfactory marriage many times in the years that followed.

"That evening, back in Bungay, where I had been so lovingly cared for by your unassuming family, when it came to the moment I could deceive you and your parents no more, I fled. Like a miserable felon caught in the act of thieving I fled, without looking back, like a coward – wanting to get away from the scene of my crime as fast as I could, having not the courage to face those I had wronged. Cowardice is my only excuse, my dear Charlotte. Yes, I fled my country when the revolution was mounted – perhaps there was an element of cowardice in that. But I believe also that it was a matter of self-preservation, and I was not alone. Many of the aristocracy took the same decision, to flee, and were encouraged to do so – the alternative would have been arrest. We would almost certainly have been arrested, and after an unfair trial, if we had had a trial at all, died on the gallows. As providence allowed, eventually we were able to return to France and help our country to survive.

"But perhaps, for you, it would have been better if I had died at the guillotine, the cur that I am, and saved you all the sadness, and grief and tears that my actions bestowed upon you."

"No, my lord, no! Please don't say that! It would not have been better! Despite everything, I have had the joy of knowing you, of spending those precious months with you, learning from you, walking with you, enjoying being in your presence – touching you, feeling your love for me. Those things, those memories, have helped to sustain me in the years since you left. But..."

She clasped his hands tighter as she spoke, and gazed steadfastly into his eyes. There was gentle reproach in her tone, but one conveying love, and not anger.

"...But, why could you not tell me that you were married?"

Francois' reply was equally gentle, equally born of deep affection.

"You ask why? Because I loved you, and did not want to lose the love I knew you had for me, did no want to hurt you. I knew I should tell you. But the longer I delayed the harder it became. Love is selfish, sometimes, Charlotte, when it should be selfless. I have no excuse.

Only that I loved you."

The two held each other in their gaze. Twenty-five years that has passed since they last sat together, vanished. Charlotte was 15 again, Francois 26, and the feelings that had grown between them were of that moment. They drew together, naturally, the desire each to be held by the other not to be resisted, as they had resisted, all those years ago. Francois drew his English rose to him, enfolded her tightly in his arms, and she responded, her arms around him, whimpering as he kissed her neck, and did not resist, enjoying his strength, his warmth. This was beyond the gentle, tentative, prompted touching of lips Charlotte remembered from one of their walks on the common, more the release of inhibitions born of her upbringing then, and his honour as a visitor in her home.

Encouraged by that release their lips now met more passionately, as they kissed with an urgency born of lost time to be made up, or time too short until they had to part.

Finally in that apartment lost in the heart of London, the parson's daughter and the French Ambassador relaxed into holding each other close, as they sat on the sofa.

"Now – now we are both married," Charlotte reflected quietly, at last, tacitly comparing their situation now to that of days 25 years ago.

"Yes – we must try not to mourn for what might have been. And you have been honest with me, about your marriage. But I notice that you call me my Lord – it seems such a harsh title?"

There was no hesitation in Charlotte's reply.

"When I spoke of you to Papa and Mama, I always called you my Lord. It was a title that seemed right and natural – in my mind I saw you as my husband. That is how you were, in so many ways - my Lord and master. In those days, in my youthful way, when we were so close and did so many things together, for each other, I imagined that you were my husband."

Again the wistful expression gave Charlotte the appearance of a divine being in Francois' eyes as he gazed at her – it was as if, he thought, she was not born of a woman, but was created as the embodiment of all beauty. The emotion built up inside him again as he remembered how much he had loved her, how much he had wanted her – and how deeply saddened he was that that could never be.

But he said: "And you were my English rose – the most beautiful flower of all that Nature created. Do you remember, dear Charlotte, when I was feeling much stronger following my injury and we walked in the meadows at Bungay, and I picked a wild rose for you? I have thought of that often, over the years."

"I do my Lord – and do you remember when I picked a buttercup, and put it close to your chin, to see if you liked butter? That was a very old English belief."

Suddenly a smile lit up her face and she giggled in a girlish way as she added: "And do you remember that day in the garden, when we walked too close to the river's edge, and the bank was soft and you slipped into the water; and when your head came back above the surface, the leaf of a water lily had caught in your hair! That and the startled expression on your face, with your eyes wide and your mouth open, made me think of a frog *under* a water lily!"

And Charlotte's giggle turned to uncontrolled laughter as the picture of comedy came into her mind.

The incident triggered between them a prolonged series of memories of their days in Bungay, both on their own and with her parents, which caused the years between to vanish as they laughed, or smiled wryly, or paused quietly for sadness, at each memory unearthed and polished by its renewed light before being laid aside in favour of the next.

Sometimes they would clasp hands again as they laughed, sometimes they would sit back for a moment reflectively; always they would search each other's face for signs of what those memories meant to the other, heightened by the distance they had travelled through the years.

Eventually, Francois asked the question that had troubled his mind for all of that time:

"Tell me, Charlotte, on that night, after your mother had made her proposal, and I had...departed...how did she tell you of my re-action?"

He was not certain what response he had hoped for: confirmation of her mother's great shock and embarrassment, her anger at him for causing her daughter such humiliation; or a gentle, compassionate recounting of his confession and his tears.

But he got none of those. Charlotte seemed to stiffen slightly as he awaited a reply, appearing uncomfortable, ill at ease, and blushing. The bright mood of their rememberings had suddenly gone. She ignored the question. Instead she said:

"The reason I have come to see you in London is to make a request on behalf of Rear-Admiral Sutton's eldest son, Samuel, whom you met yesterday at the Embassy."

She explained that Samuel would like to go Bombay, and that Mr George Canning, a member of the English government, and a friend of Francois, had recently accepted an appointment as Governor-General of India.

"Frnncois, I would be so grateful if you would speak to Mr Canning, and encourage him to take Samuel out to India with him. I perceive that you have close association with him in your position as Ambassador, and it would make me exceedingly happy if I were able to owe to you the happiness of my first child."

First child. Francois noted that she put emphasis on those two words. He could not be sure what affect that stress was meant to have on him, but through his mind flitted a thought he could not control: the wish that he had been his first child too, he who had no children of his own. And he felt an irrational animosity, a jealousy, towards Rear-Admiral Sutton, the father of Charlotte's children.

"Ah, madame – what cruel turn of fate is this, this request from one who cared for me at your hospitable home, who dreamt perhaps of making him your husband and leading your whole life with him. Now you ask this favour of me in your own country, on behalf of your son. But I will see Canning immediately and put the request in front of him."

"Thank you, my lord. I will await news of your meeting."

Charlotte and Francois embraced tenderly once more, before he took his leave, reluctantly, and with a backward glance as his carriage moved off...

"Yes, I realise this is an unusual request, Mr Canning, but it is a favour I ask on behalf of Rear-Admiral Sutton, of His Majesty's Navy, who has great influence in all military matters. I urge you to find room for his son in your entourage when you take up your appointment in India – I can vouch for his commitment and his intelligence, and I have every confidence that he could fill his role well if you could take him. It is my belief, too, that granting this request would do much to enhance the relationship between my country and Britain."

Francois was at the Foreign Office in London, having been granted an audience with Mr Canning and the Foreign Secretary Lord Londonderry. The latter's response was cool.

"An unusual request indeed, your Excellency. Mr Canning's staff is already in place for the most part. To make changes or additions at this stage would be most irregular and there would need to be special circumstances. It would be difficult to see how a case could be made for young Sutton."

"With the greatest respect, Minister, I believe that the son of a man who has served his country so nobly in its Navy, risen to such seniority, and become a man of some influence at the Admiralty, is worthy of special consideration. There is every reason to hope that he can have a career to match that of his worthy father, if given the correct grounding. I ask you to consider that making him part of the staff in Bombay would be an excellent start for him."

He glanced at Canning for support.

"I am certain your judgement of the young man is sound, your Excellency," Canning said. "I have knowledge that Lord Nelson, before his untimely death at the moment of victory, was an admirer of Rear-Admiral Sutton's capability, and that would stand his son in very good stead in seeking any appointment. But making the appointment is not as straightforward as that – it would present a number of practical problems and difficulties, and time is not on our side."

"I understand that. But with the right will problems and difficulties can be overcome, and granting this request would do a great favour to me as well as Sutton. And the time may come when you seek a favour of France which you would ask me to support."

Canning and Lord Londonderry exchanged glances.

"We will give it serious consideration. Let us inquire about other appointments to the staff to see where Sutton might be included. We can make no promises, but we will do all we can to accede to your request, your Excellency."

Francois visited Charlotte at her apartment the next day to recount what steps he had taken on behalf of Samuel. Again she was alone, again they sat together on the sofa as they talked, he taking her hand, sometimes holding it against his heart; again they embraced passionately and held each other for awhile, reluctant to release their touch; again their conversations were of days gone by.

Things one remembered the other had not, and each brought new warmth, new smiles from long ago. At last Charlotte learned of what Francois had felt after he had fled – of his agonies, his self-recrimination, his urge, on many occasions, to return to Bungay in the hope of seeing her, his weeks, even months, of doing little but think of her, writing to her letters he destroyed before sending, his battle with his daemons which came in their swarms to attack and demoralise him further, till he thought he was going mad. And he told of his more rational feelings, his regrets, his triumphs, his disappointments.

Charlotte listened quietly at those times, her head leaning on his shoulder, content simply at hearing his voice, feeling him close, feeling relaxed, taking succour from being with the man she had loved, and lost, and found again.

For three more days Francois called on her. Each was precious to them both, until finally she told him she was returning to Bungay.

"The house where we live looks out over the Common where you and I walked so often," she said." Sometimes I see a young couple walking there, by the river, beside the flag irises, through the long grass, and I imagine it is you and I there, still, hand in hand, talking lazily, as the birds sing and the buds swell. But I know we can never be there again, like that, just the two of us, close, believing as I did, then, that one day it would always be; believing there would be a day when our children would walk there beside us, and play among the grass and fall in the dyke, and pick the flowers of spring and summer. And at home I would still play the piano and sing for you, and you would continue to teach me more and more of the world, and of its literature. I would encourage your writing and be proud when it made you famous, and I would feel so proud to go with you to the grand social occasions in Bungay and nearby towns; and people would say, 'That is the famous writer, Vicomte Chateaubriand, and his wife.'

"Such dreams, my Lord. I continued to dream them for many years, after I was married, and prayed to God for forgiveness for the unfaithfulness of my mind to Samuel. What would he say now, if he knew I was here, with my head on your shoulder? It should not be; it must not be, any longer. And yet I am glad that I have come to you, and spent these days with you. They have not been days of now, but distant days of long ago when, unknown to myself, or to Celeste, she loaned to me her husband for awhile, to comfort during his loneliness in a far off land, and to care for when he was injured, and to learn from him in return.

"Now I must leave that time again, my dear Francois, my Lord, and travel back to the present, and to Bungay, with my husband and my family."

She hesitated, before adding: "When you left Bungay so suddenly, one of the things that distressed me most was that you did not even say goodbye to me. Just as I was hoping for a message of happiness, you were suddenly gone. Now, this is goodbye, my Lord – we must say goodbye, face to face, softly, sadly, reluctantly, but...goodbye, adieu. I will not see you again."

Francois had been listening, his eyes closed, as Charlotte spoke. But at those words he opened them and sat up.

"You will see me again! You will – I will come to Bungay to bring your son's commission! This is not the end of our meeting."

He clasped both of her hands in his once more as he spoke. Charlotte's face had taken on its wistful look, and her eyes glistened with tears as she shook her head, almost imperceptibly.

"You will not come. Your life will take you elsewhere."

She withdrew her hands gently from his, went over to the dresser, and took a packet from the drawer. She pressed it into his hand, and held it there with hers, as if reluctant to release it, a long-established link she did not want to break, but knew she must.. She was sobbing as she spoke again:

"Take this. It contains items from our past life. Please don't be offended if I retain nothing of yours – nothing that is linked to our past lives, nothing that holds us back from the paths we must now follow. Take it, so that I can offer my whole heart to Samuel, as you must offer yours to Celeste. Thank you for seeing me again. Thank you for our memories. Farewell, my lord and master. Farewell!"

Charlotte kissed him quickly on the cheek, leaving some of her tears there, and withdrew.

"I will bring Samuel's commission to you! I will. I..."
But she was gone, gone from his sight.

With a heavy heart, Francois left the apartment and returned to the Embassy, hurried up to his room, closed the door and eagerly opened the package, keen to discover its contents. Surely it would include a letter to him from Charlotte?

There was no letter. He found only some unimportant notes he had written for her to help the progress of her studies, some comments he had written on poets they had studied together, some sheets of manuscript with, in the margins, notes, in Charlotte's youthful handwriting, in English, French and Latin.

In great disappointment, he shuffled the papers into order. As he did so, two which were more weighty, fell out on to the floor, and he bent to pick them up.

On to one was pressed a wild rose, now brittle and faded, but still intact. Beneath it, in the same handwriting, was written: "Picked for me this day by Francois, who called me his English rose. May 1796."

On the other was pressed a primrose, the pale yellow of its petals remarkably well preserved, and beside it were the words: "My Lord's gift of springtime to me! My lord – my love."

He laid them side by side on his desk, and studied them for some time, many thoughts going through his head, more memories, more regrets – some thoughts of days to come. Eventually, with a long, thoughtful sigh, he took up his pen, drew paper from a drawer, and resumed his memoirs...

Admiral Sutton's business at the Admiralty was finished. It was time to return to Bungay, and a carriage took him to his family's apartment, where they were waiting, with bags packed and boys eager to go home. They had enjoyed London, the places they had seen which, until then, they had only heard of: St Paul's Cathedral, the Palace of Westminster, the Tower of London, and they had walked along the banks of the mighty River Thames, and marvelled at is size compared with the River Waveney which flowed past their home. But they had concluded that there were too many people in London, too many unsavoury characters, too many unpleasant smells, too much dirt and too many carriages. They were ready to leave it behind.

On its way to meet the mail coach for Yarmouth, their carriage took them past the French Embassy. Charlotte tried to peer out to see the first floor windows, wondering whether Francois might be standing there. But she saw no one, and it was quickly out of sight.

The mail coach jerked and bumped through the streets of London, drawn at a brisk trot by two powerful nut-brown horses, fresh and eager, and having to be expertly controlled by the driver. Gradually they left the heart of the city behind, buildings became sparse, the dirt an noise lessening with each mile, until suddenly they were out in open country, making their way beside the fields of Essex, with only occasional farms to be seen. As the scenery changed from the turmoil of the capital to the more peaceful rural landscape, so Charlotte's mood changed, her mind cleared, she felt relaxed and content.

And suddenly she knew she had done the right thing in visiting Francois, talking to him, holding him, listening to his thoughts and feelings, remembering times with him, sharing joys and sorrows. It was like opening the doors of a cluttered cupboard, full of things not seen or used for a long time which tumbled out, and had to be sorted and tidied, and saved or discarded, each prompting a memory, and the ones to be retained returned to the cupboard in an orderly way, and the cupboard doors closed, finally.

On one side of the carriage the boys were animated and playful, as Charlotte and Samuel sat side by side opposite them.

"You are quiet, my dear. Did your meeting with Francois go well? I imagine you had much to talk about."

"Yes, it went well – very well. We talked about many things, many times, his fame and his responsibilities. I am glad I took courage and made the visit. It has taught me much."

"Then I am pleased. I trust a week in London was not too much for you? Perhaps the change of air and scenery was not a remedy after all."

"No, dearest Samuel, quite the reverse – I have learned much during my stay, and I am content. The old cobwebs, and the regrets, are behind me. Perhaps that is why I am quiet and relaxed."

She paused, and then added: "Samuel, thank you for being so understanding, so patient with me. You are so supportive, you care for me so well. I feel cherished and needed – as I need you."

She linked her arm in his and lent against him.

"Samuel," she whispered, not wanting the boys to hear.

"Yes, dearest?"

"I want to tell you that, I love you – that I love you with *all* of my heart."

THE END

Epilogue

I n his autobiography, *Memoires D'Outre-Tombe,* now recognised as one of the great works of European literature, Chateaubriand dwells emotionally on his relationship with Charlotte, his love for her shining through clearly. As well as the main chapter about her, he refers to her from time to time elsewhere, speaking of how the vision of her guided his thinking.

At the end of the passage on their meeting at the Embassy, and at her apartment in London, he wrote:

"That is the story of Miss Ives and I. As I bring it to an end, it seems to me I am losing Charlotte for a second time, in the same island where I lost her at first. But between what I feel for her at this moment, and what I may have felt in those moments whose tenderness I recall, lies all the extent of innocence: passions have intervened in those years between Miss Ives and Lady Sutton. I would no longer be offering an artless girl innocent longing; the sweet ingenuousness of love lies on the borders of dream. I wrote then on a wave of melancholy; I am no longer adrift on life's waves. Ah well, if I have held in my arms a wife and mother, she who was destined for me as a virgin bride, it has been with a kind of rage, to wither, to fill with pain and

suffocate, those twenty-five years which were given to another, after having been offered to me!

"I should have regard for the love I have just recalled, as the first of its kind to enter my heart; yet it was not in tune with my stormy nature, which would have corrupted it, and would have rendered me incapable of savouring those holy joys for long. It was then that, embittered by misfortune, already a pilgrim overseas, having begun my solitary voyage, it was then that the wild ideas evoked in that mysterious tale of Rene*, obsessed me and made of me the most tormented of beings on this earth.

"Be that as it may, the chaste image of Charlotte, in allowing a few rays of true light to penetrate the depths of my heart, first dissipated there a cloud of phantoms: my daemon, like an evil genie, plunged once more into the abyss; she waited for the effects of time before making a fresh appearance."

And in a later chapter, having left his role as French Ambassador and returned to France in September, 1822, after rueing the changes in England, with the valleys now filled with the fumes of factories and forges, obscuring the charming and formidable England he had known as an émigré, with her ships, and herds, and religion, and the "cradles of science" at Oxford and Cambridge, he writes:

"Besides those moments, around which a void is beginning to form, I left the rediscovered days of my springtime; I separated from my youth a second time, on the same shore where I had abandoned it once before. Charlotte had suddenly re-appeared like that light, the joy of the darkness, which, retarded in its monthly course, will rise at midnight. If you are not too weary, go and seek in Book X of these memoirs the effect that sudden sight of that woman had on me in 1822. When she knew me previously I had not met those other Englishwomen, a crowd of whom surrounded me in my days of power and fame: their homage brought a kind of mildness to my fate. Now, when sixteen long years have vanished since my London Embassy, and when so much else has been destroyed, my gaze returns towards that daughter of the land of Desdemona and Juliet**: she is no less important to my thoughts than that day when her unexpected presence relit the torch of my memories.

Chateaubriand's meeting with Charlotte in 1822 was not, in fact, the last time they met. The following year, after he had become France's Minister for Foreign Affairs, she travelled to Paris with some of her family, and John Barber Scott, a wealthy Bungay gentleman, and attended one of his official soirees. Of that occasion, writing towards the end of his life, he wrote, again emotionally, perhaps irrationally:

"By one of those inexplicable human misfortunes, pre-occupied as I was with a war on which the fate of the French monarchy depended, something was doubtless lacking in my response, since Charlotte, on returning to England, sent me a letter in which she appeared wounded by the coldness of my reception of her. I dared neither to write to her, nor return the literary fragments she had sent me, which I had promised to add to, and forward to her. If it were true that she had real cause for complaint, I would throw what I have written of my first journey abroad into the fire.

"It has often occurred to me to seek clarification of my doubts; but how can I return to England, I who am too weak even to dare to visit the native rock where I have marked out my tomb? I am afraid of sensation now: time, in stealing my youth, has left me like those soldiers whose limbs remain on the field of battle; my blood, having a smaller path in which to circulate, reaches my heart with so rapid a flow that this old organ of my joys and sorrows beats as though ready to burst. The desire to burn what appertains to Charlotte, even though she may have been treated there with religious respect, mingles in me with the wish to destroy these Memoirs; if they still belonged to me, or if I could buy them back, I might succumb to the temptation. I have such a disgust with everything, such a contempt for the present and immediate future, so firm a persuasion that men, from now on, taken together as "the

public" (and for several centuries ahead), will be pitiful, that I blush to employ my last moments in telling of things past, in depicting a lost world whose language and names are no longer known."

Because of financial difficulties, Chateaubriand sold his memoirs before they were completed – "a mortgage on his tomb," is what he called it. He died in Paris, where he had a ground floor apartment, on July 4th, 1848, aged 83. He was buried at his birthplace, St Malo, where there is a monument to him. At the house in Bridge Street, Bungay, which was the home of the Ives family, there is a simple plaque noting that he stayed there in 1796.

Rear-Admiral Samuel Sutton died in 1832, aged 72, at Woodbridge, to where he and Charlotte moved in 1831.

Samuel Ives Sutton rose to the rank of Captain in the Army. It is not clear whether he did go with Canning to India, though it seems unlikely, as later, with the help of the wealth his father accrued through his share of the bounty from the captured Spanish vessels, Rear-Admiral Sutton bought each of his sons a commission in the Army. He died at Kenilworth of dysentery in 1850, aged 43.

Lady Charlotte Sutton outlived her first son, dying at Aldeburgh in Suffolk, about 25 miles from Bungay, in 1852, aged 72. Both she and her husband were buried in St Mary's Church, Woodbridge – their tomb is in the north porch though, sadly, the church organ was built over it in 1875, just 23 years after Charlotte's death, and it can no